the Archie® DIGEST LIBRARY

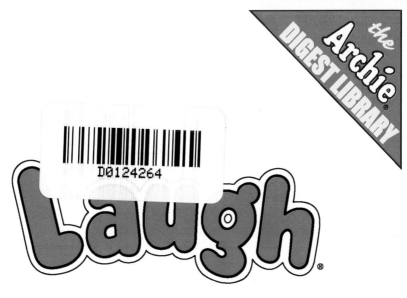

Laugh®

– with –

Lucky Day

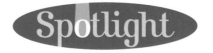

Spotlight

visit us at
www.abdopublishing.com

Exclusive Spotlight library bound edition published in 2007 by Spotlight, a division of ABDO Publishing Group, Edina, Minnesota. Spotlight produces high-quality reinforced library bound editions for schools and libraries. Published by agreement with Archie Comic Publications, Inc.

Library of Congress Cataloging-in-Publication Data

Laugh with lucky day / edited by Nelson Ribeiro & Victor Gorelick. -- Library bound ed.
   p. cm. -- (The Archie digest library)
  Revision of issue no. 169 (Nov. 2001) of Laugh digest magazine.
  ISBN-13: 978-1-59961-280-5
  ISBN-10: 1-59961-280-1
   1. Comic books, strips, etc. I. Ribeiro, Nelson. II. Gorelick, Victor. III. Laugh digest magazine. 169. IV. Title: Lucky day.

PN6728.A72L39 2007
741.5'973--dc22

2006049145

07-1228

All Spotlight books are reinforced library binding and manufactured in the United States of America.

Contents

Laugh®

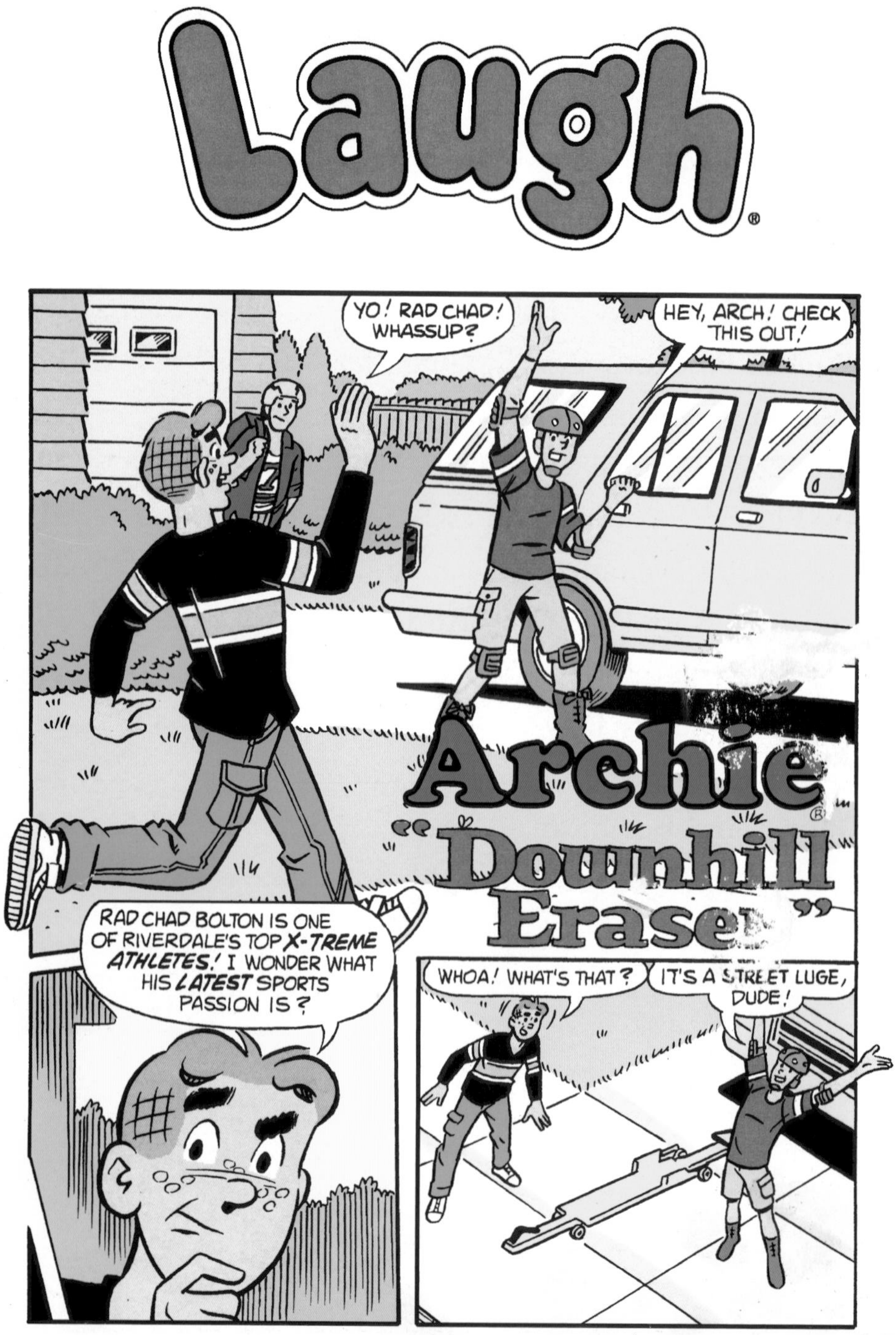

YO! RAD CHAD! WHASSUP?
HEY, ARCH! CHECK THIS OUT!
Archie®
"Downhill Erase"
RAD CHAD BOLTON IS ONE OF RIVERDALE'S TOP X-TREME ATHLETES! I WONDER WHAT HIS LATEST SPORTS PASSION IS?
WHOA! WHAT'S THAT?
IT'S A STREET LUGE, DUDE!

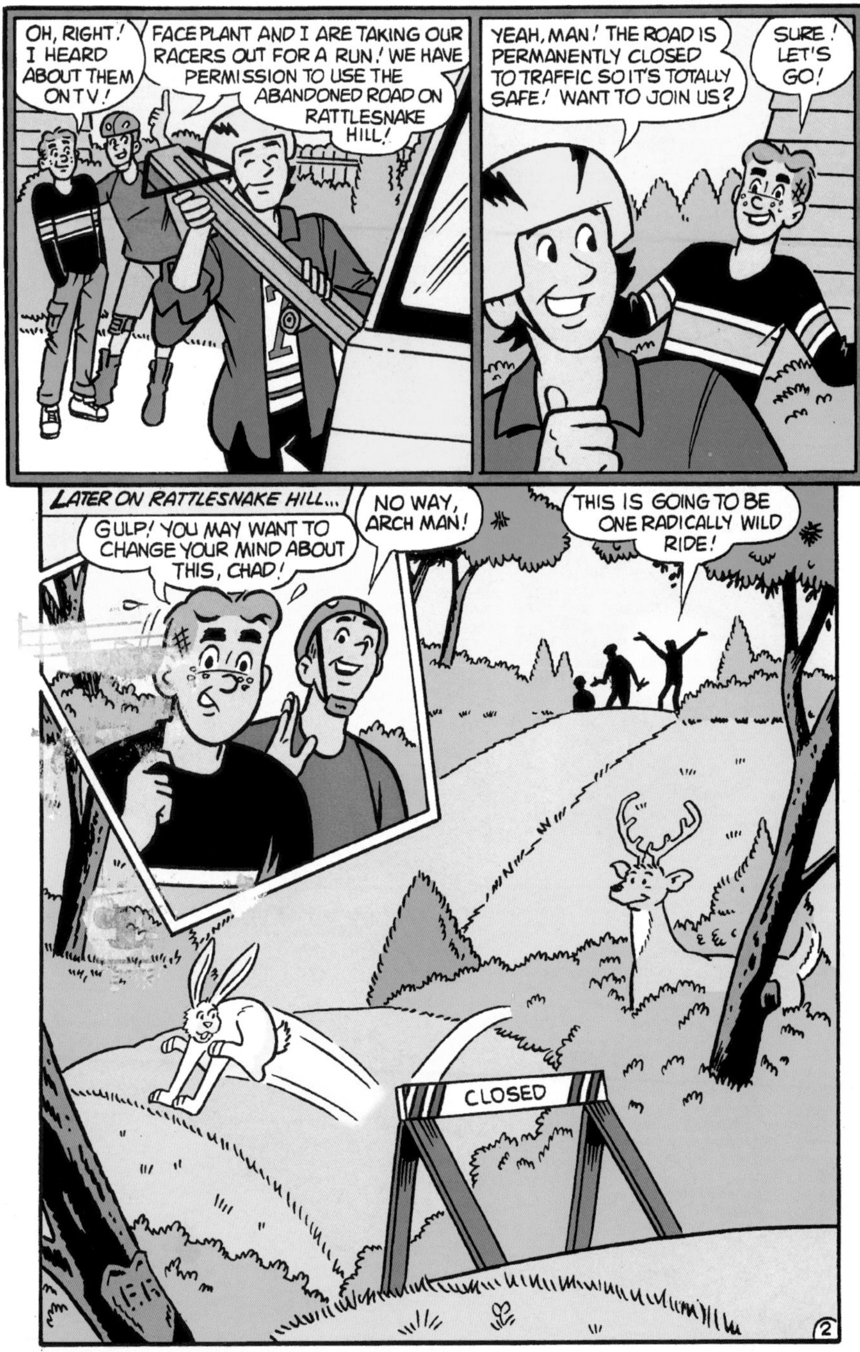
OH, RIGHT! I HEARD ABOUT THEM ON TV!
FACE PLANT AND I ARE TAKING OUR RACERS OUT FOR A RUN! WE HAVE PERMISSION TO USE THE ABANDONED ROAD ON RATTLESNAKE HILL!
YEAH, MAN! THE ROAD IS PERMANENTLY CLOSED TO TRAFFIC SO IT'S TOTALLY SAFE! WANT TO JOIN US?
SURE! LET'S GO!
LATER ON RATTLESNAKE HILL...
GULP! YOU MAY WANT TO CHANGE YOUR MIND ABOUT THIS, CHAD!
NO WAY, ARCH MAN!
THIS IS GOING TO BE ONE RADICALLY WILD RIDE!
CLOSED
2

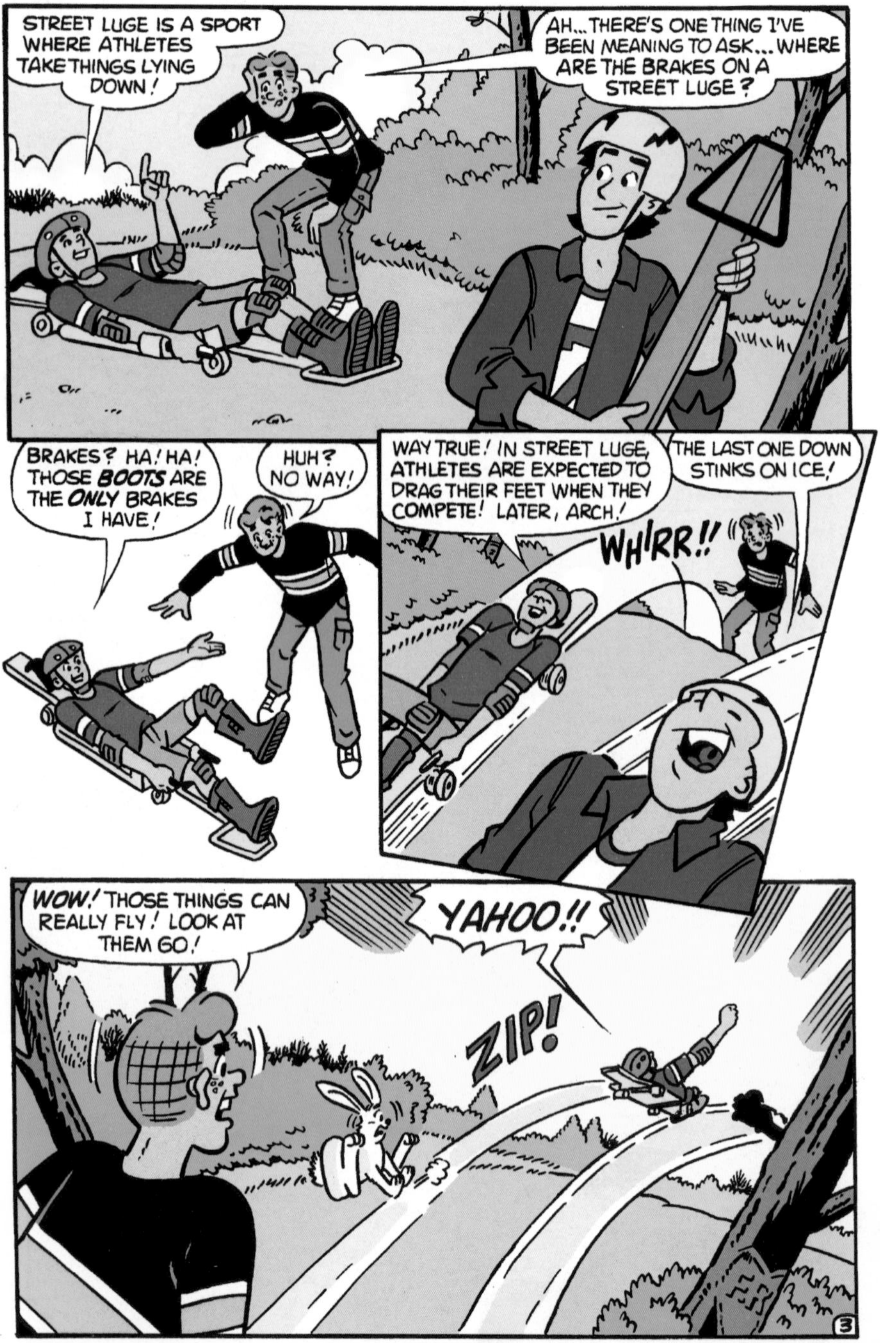
STREET LUGE IS A SPORT WHERE ATHLETES TAKE THINGS LYING DOWN!
AH... THERE'S ONE THING I'VE BEEN MEANING TO ASK... WHERE ARE THE BRAKES ON A STREET LUGE?
BRAKES? HA! HA! THOSE BOOTS ARE THE ONLY BRAKES I HAVE!
HUH? NO WAY!
WAY TRUE! IN STREET LUGE, ATHLETES ARE EXPECTED TO DRAG THEIR FEET WHEN THEY COMPETE! LATER, ARCH!
THE LAST ONE DOWN STINKS ON ICE!
WHIRR!!
WOW! THOSE THINGS CAN REALLY FLY! LOOK AT THEM GO!
YAHOO!!
ZIP!
3

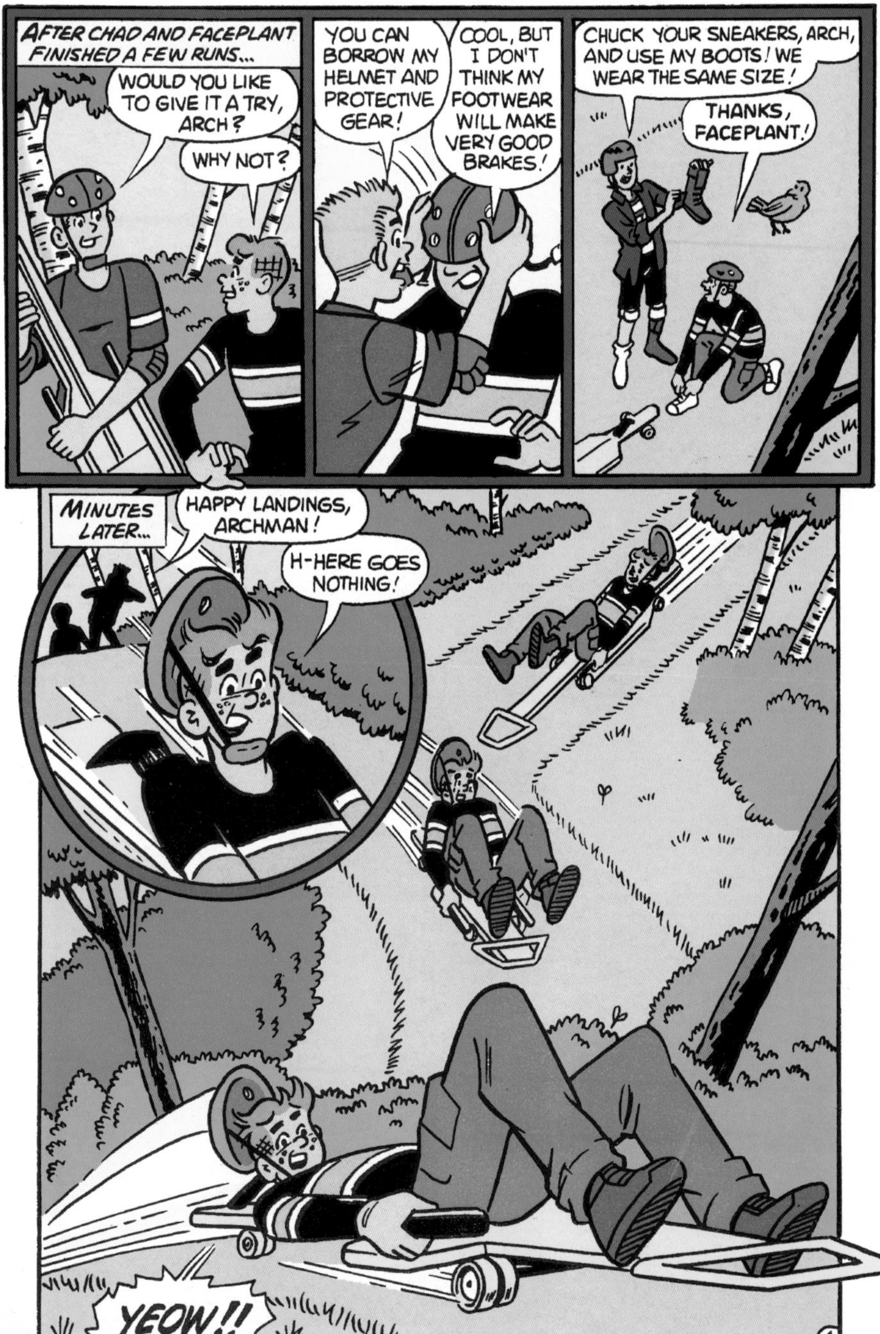
AFTER CHAD AND FACEPLANT FINISHED A FEW RUNS...
WOULD YOU LIKE TO GIVE IT A TRY, ARCH?
WHY NOT?
YOU CAN BORROW MY HELMET AND PROTECTIVE GEAR!
COOL, BUT I DON'T THINK MY FOOTWEAR WILL MAKE VERY GOOD BRAKES!
CHUCK YOUR SNEAKERS, ARCH, AND USE MY BOOTS! WE WEAR THE SAME SIZE!
THANKS, FACEPLANT!
MINUTES LATER...
HAPPY LANDINGS, ARCHMAN!
H-HERE GOES NOTHING!
YEOW!!
4

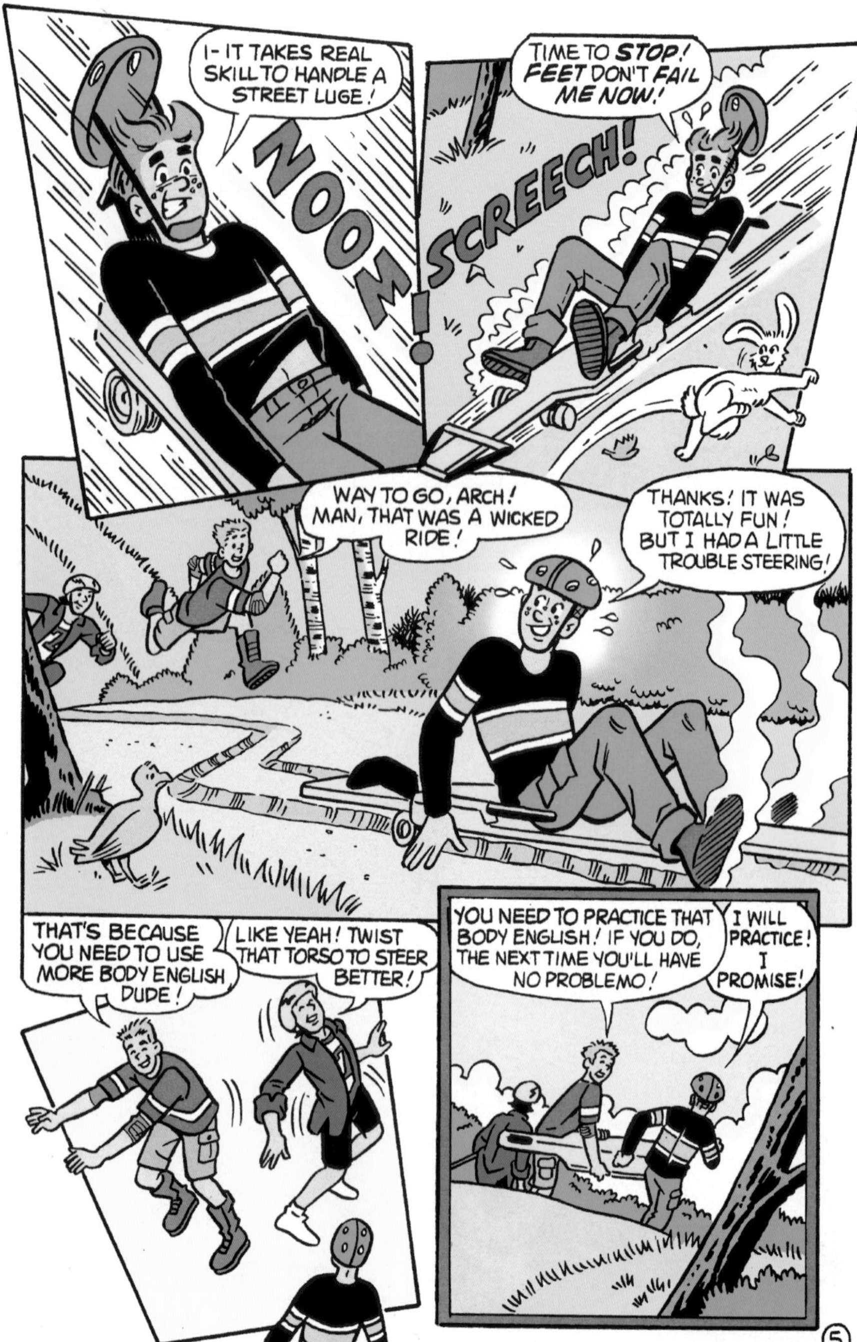
I- IT TAKES REAL SKILL TO HANDLE A STREET LUGE!
NOOOM!
TIME TO STOP! FEET DON'T FAIL ME NOW!
SCREECH!
WAY TO GO, ARCH! MAN, THAT WAS A WICKED RIDE!
THANKS! IT WAS TOTALLY FUN! BUT I HAD A LITTLE TROUBLE STEERING!
THAT'S BECAUSE YOU NEED TO USE MORE BODY ENGLISH DUDE!
LIKE YEAH! TWIST THAT TORSO TO STEER BETTER!
YOU NEED TO PRACTICE THAT BODY ENGLISH! IF YOU DO, THE NEXT TIME YOU'LL HAVE NO PROBLEMO!
I WILL PRACTICE! I PROMISE!
5

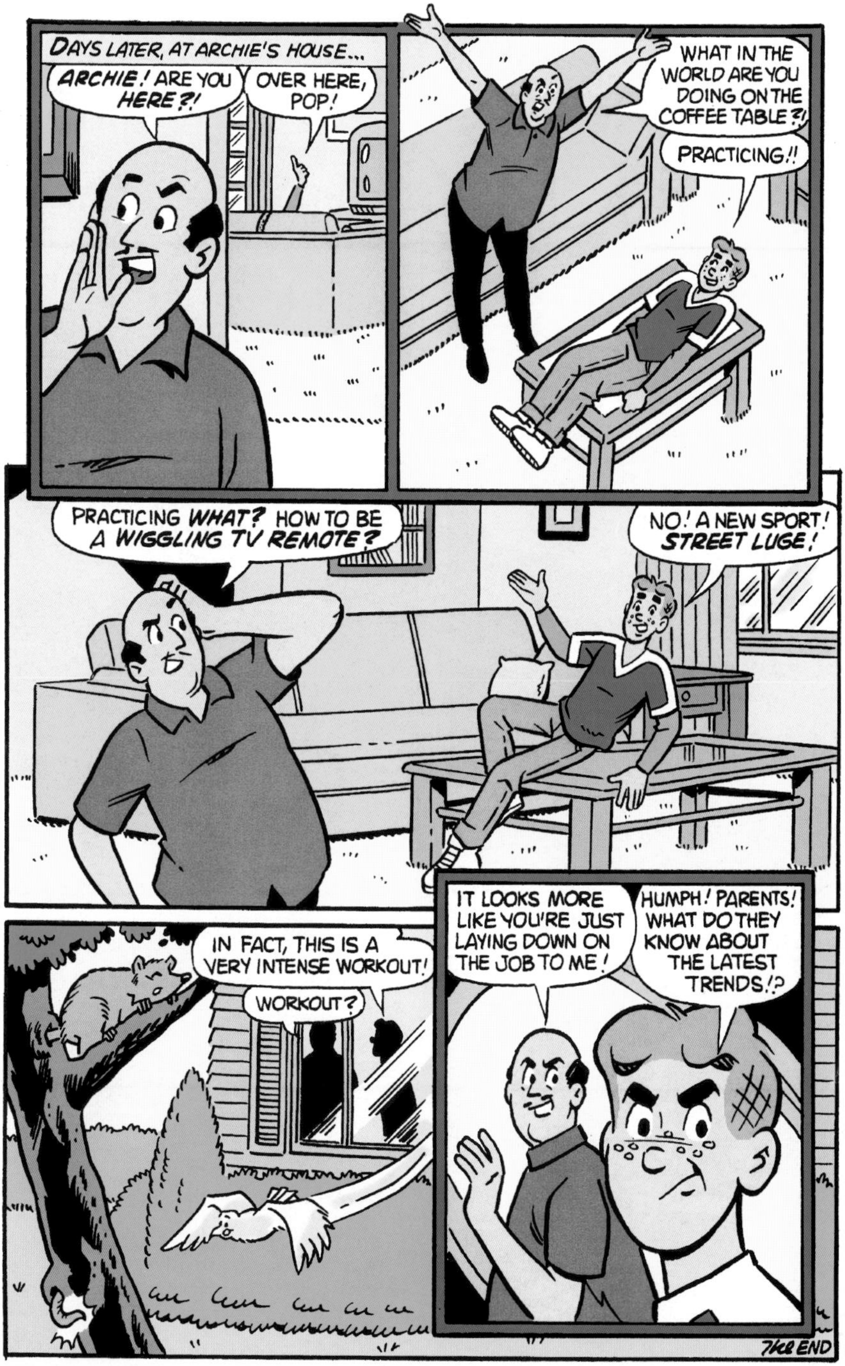
DAYS LATER, AT ARCHIE'S HOUSE...
ARCHIE! ARE YOU HERE?!
OVER HERE, POP!
WHAT IN THE WORLD ARE YOU DOING ON THE COFFEE TABLE?!
PRACTICING!!
PRACTICING WHAT? HOW TO BE A WIGGLING TV REMOTE?
NO! A NEW SPORT! STREET LUGE!
IN FACT, THIS IS A VERY INTENSE WORKOUT!
WORKOUT?
IT LOOKS MORE LIKE YOU'RE JUST LAYING DOWN ON THE JOB TO ME!
HUMPH! PARENTS! WHAT DO THEY KNOW ABOUT THE LATEST TRENDS!?
THE END

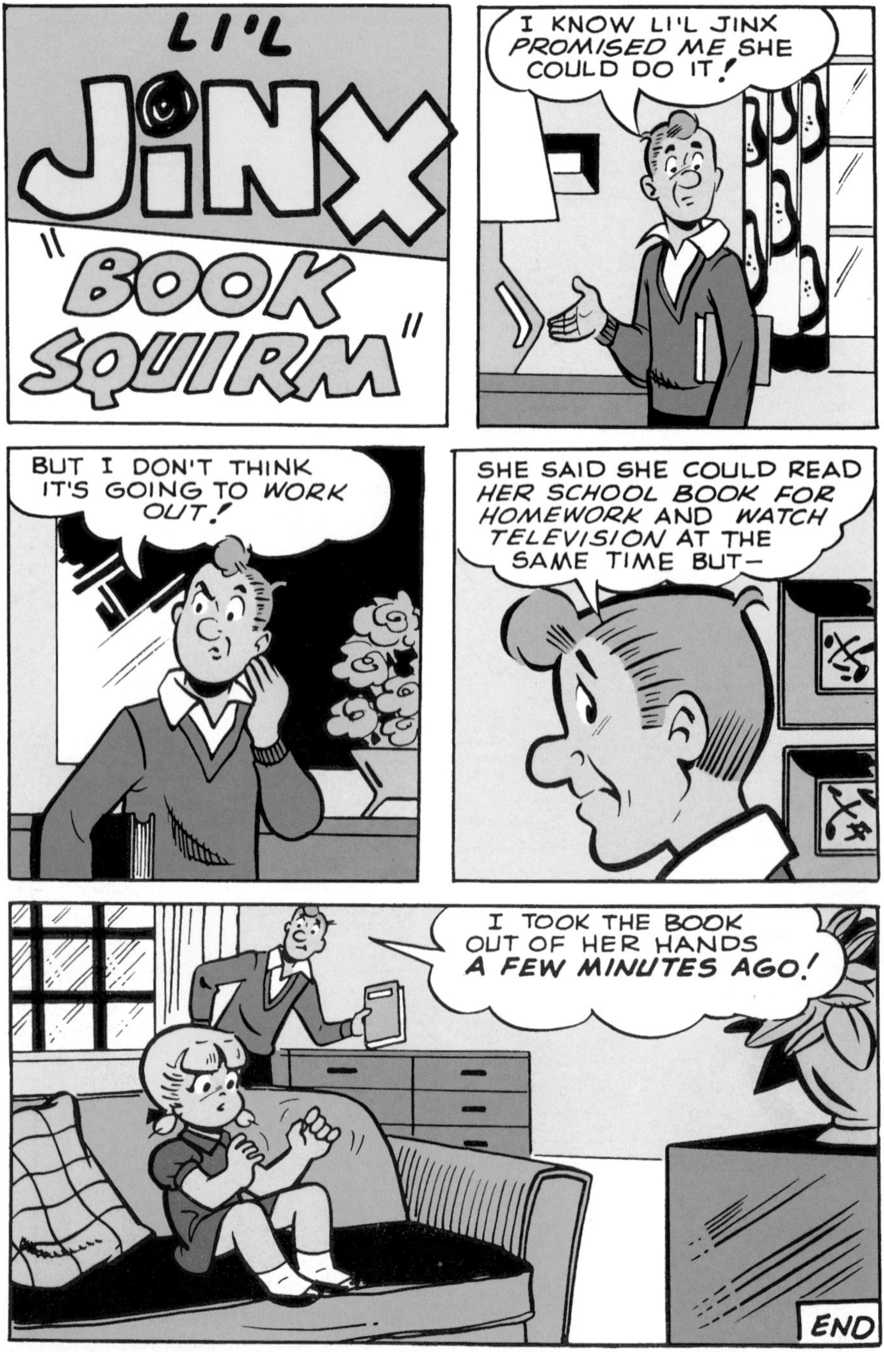
LI'L JINX
"BOOK SQUIRM"
I KNOW LI'L JINX PROMISED ME SHE COULD DO IT!
BUT I DON'T THINK IT'S GOING TO WORK OUT!
SHE SAID SHE COULD READ HER SCHOOL BOOK FOR HOMEWORK AND WATCH TELEVISION AT THE SAME TIME BUT—
I TOOK THE BOOK OUT OF HER HANDS A FEW MINUTES AGO!
END

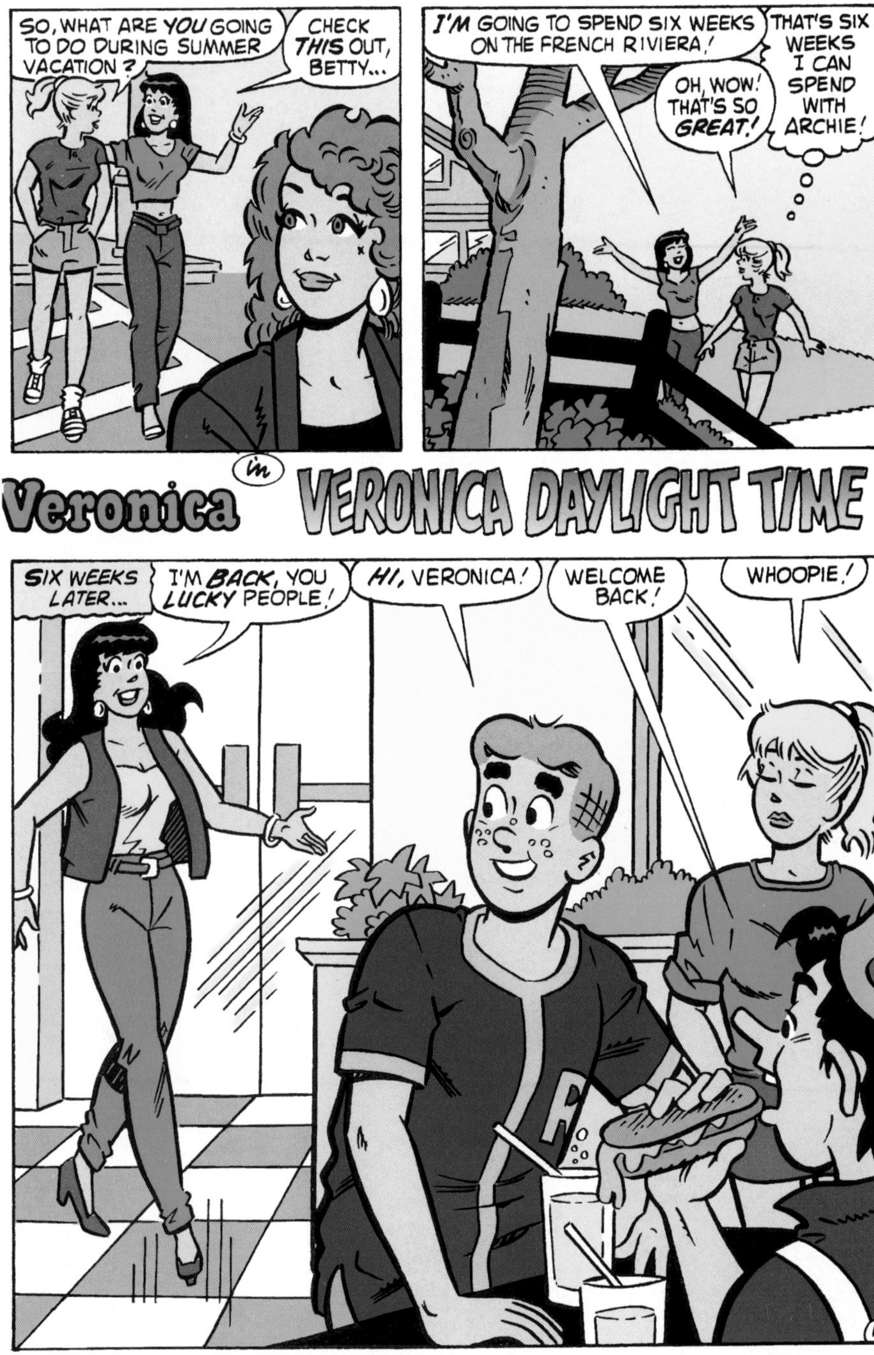
SO, WHAT ARE YOU GOING TO DO DURING SUMMER VACATION ?
CHECK THIS OUT, BETTY...
I'M GOING TO SPEND SIX WEEKS ON THE FRENCH RIVIERA!
OH, WOW! THAT'S SO GREAT!
THAT'S SIX WEEKS I CAN SPEND WITH ARCHIE!
Veronica in VERONICA DAYLIGHT TIME
SIX WEEKS LATER...
I'M BACK, YOU LUCKY PEOPLE!
HI, VERONICA!
WELCOME BACK!
WHOOPIE!
1

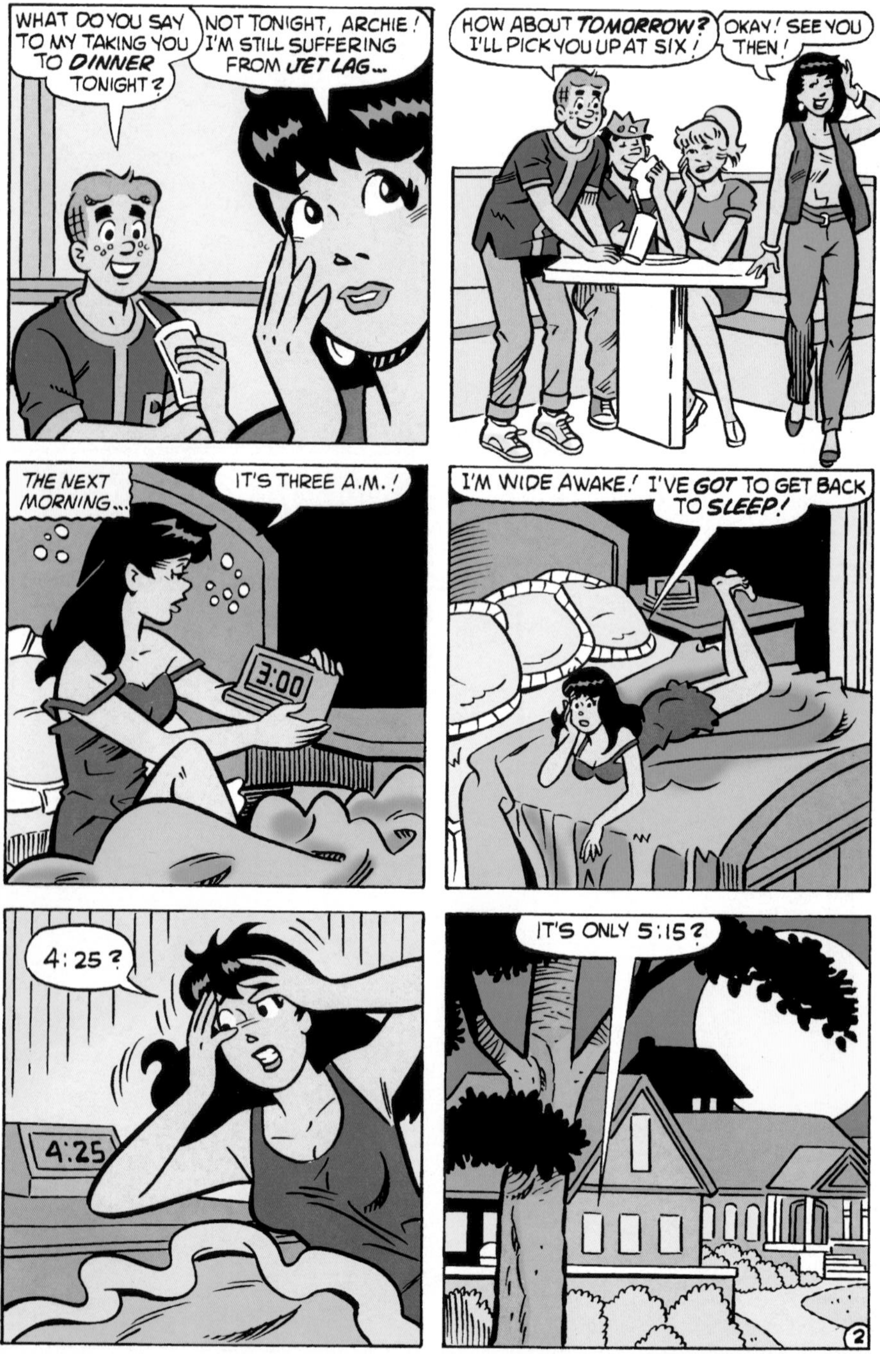
WHAT DO YOU SAY TO MY TAKING YOU TO DINNER TONIGHT?
NOT TONIGHT, ARCHIE! I'M STILL SUFFERING FROM JET LAG...
HOW ABOUT TOMORROW? I'LL PICK YOU UP AT SIX!
OKAY! SEE YOU THEN!
THE NEXT MORNING...
IT'S THREE A.M.!
3:00
I'M WIDE AWAKE! I'VE GOT TO GET BACK TO SLEEP!
4:25?
4:25
IT'S ONLY 5:15?
2

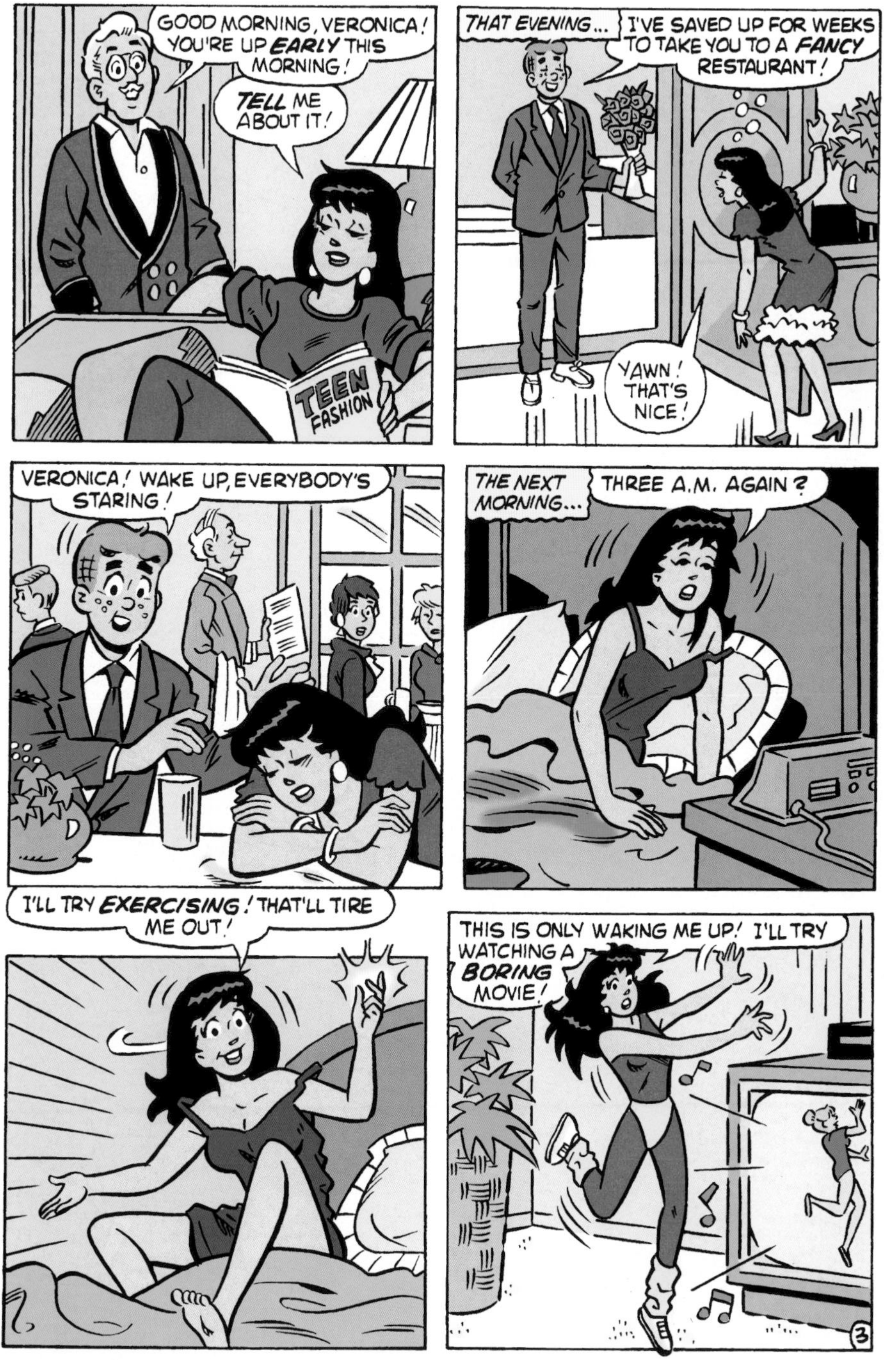
GOOD MORNING, VERONICA! YOU'RE UP EARLY THIS MORNING!
TELL ME ABOUT IT!
THAT EVENING...
I'VE SAVED UP FOR WEEKS TO TAKE YOU TO A FANCY RESTAURANT!
YAWN! THAT'S NICE!
VERONICA! WAKE UP, EVERYBODY'S STARING!
THE NEXT MORNING...
THREE A.M. AGAIN?
I'LL TRY EXERCISING! THAT'LL TIRE ME OUT!
THIS IS ONLY WAKING ME UP! I'LL TRY WATCHING A BORING MOVIE!
3

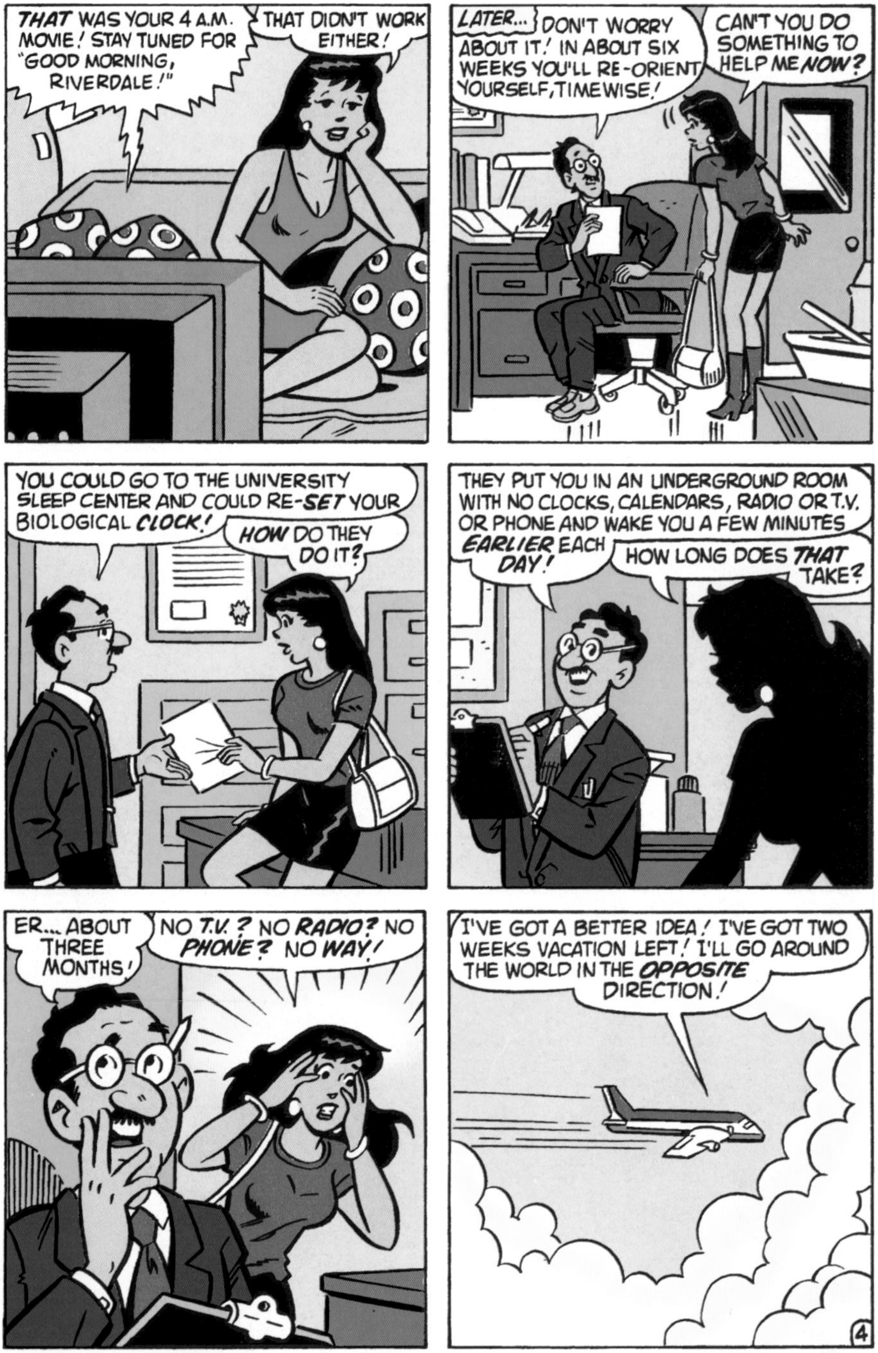
THAT WAS YOUR 4 A.M. MOVIE! STAY TUNED FOR "GOOD MORNING, RIVERDALE!"
THAT DIDN'T WORK EITHER!
LATER...
DON'T WORRY ABOUT IT! IN ABOUT SIX WEEKS YOU'LL RE-ORIENT YOURSELF, TIMEWISE!
CAN'T YOU DO SOMETHING TO HELP ME NOW?
YOU COULD GO TO THE UNIVERSITY SLEEP CENTER AND COULD RE-SET YOUR BIOLOGICAL CLOCK!
HOW DO THEY DO IT?
THEY PUT YOU IN AN UNDERGROUND ROOM WITH NO CLOCKS, CALENDARS, RADIO OR T.V. OR PHONE AND WAKE YOU A FEW MINUTES EARLIER EACH DAY!
HOW LONG DOES THAT TAKE?
ER... ABOUT THREE MONTHS!
NO T.V.? NO RADIO? NO PHONE? NO WAY!
I'VE GOT A BETTER IDEA! I'VE GOT TWO WEEKS VACATION LEFT! I'LL GO AROUND THE WORLD IN THE OPPOSITE DIRECTION!
4

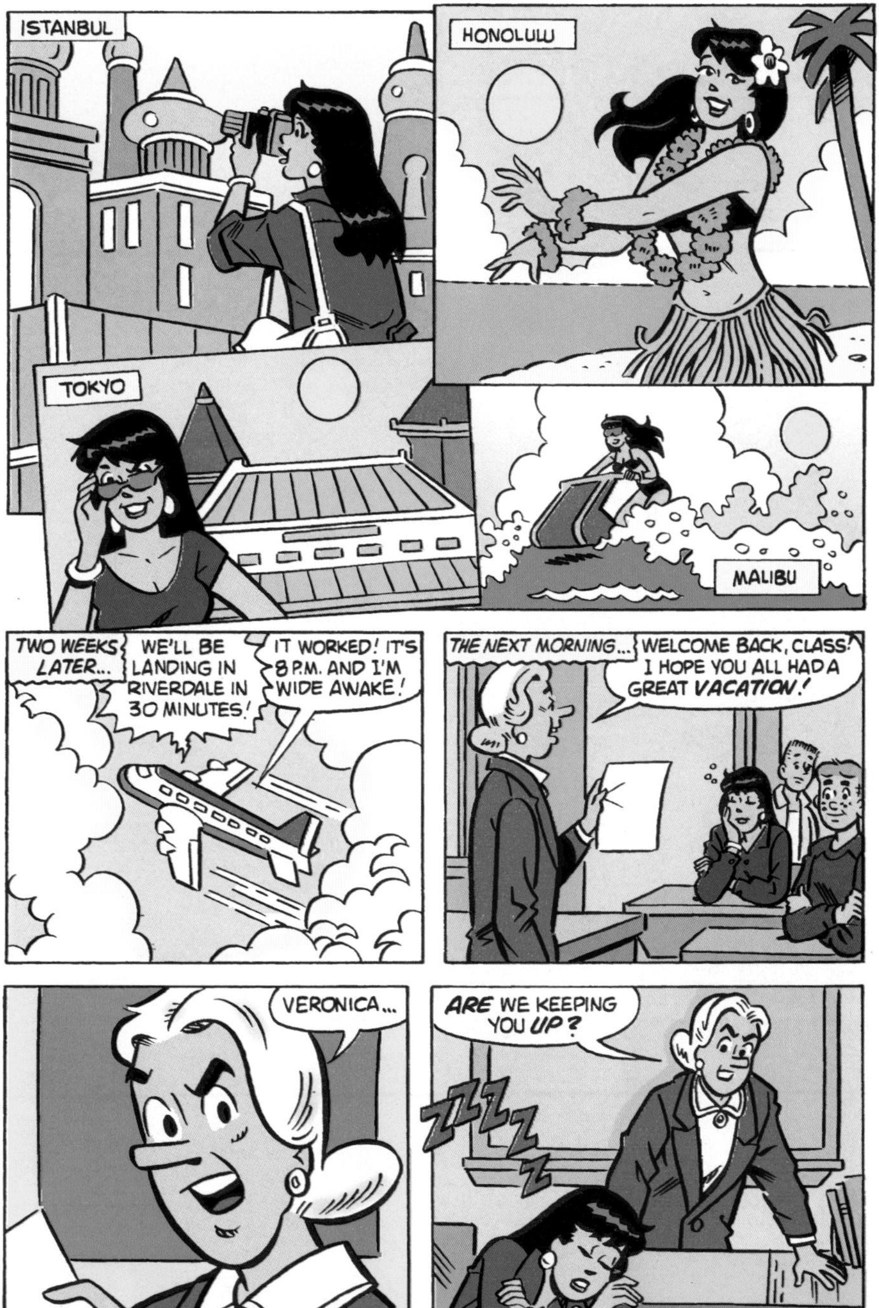
ISTANBUL
HONOLULU
TOKYO
MALIBU
TWO WEEKS LATER...
WE'LL BE LANDING IN RIVERDALE IN 30 MINUTES!
IT WORKED! IT'S 8 P.M. AND I'M WIDE AWAKE!
THE NEXT MORNING...
WELCOME BACK, CLASS! I HOPE YOU ALL HAD A GREAT VACATION!
VERONICA...
ARE WE KEEPING YOU UP?
ZZZZZ
END

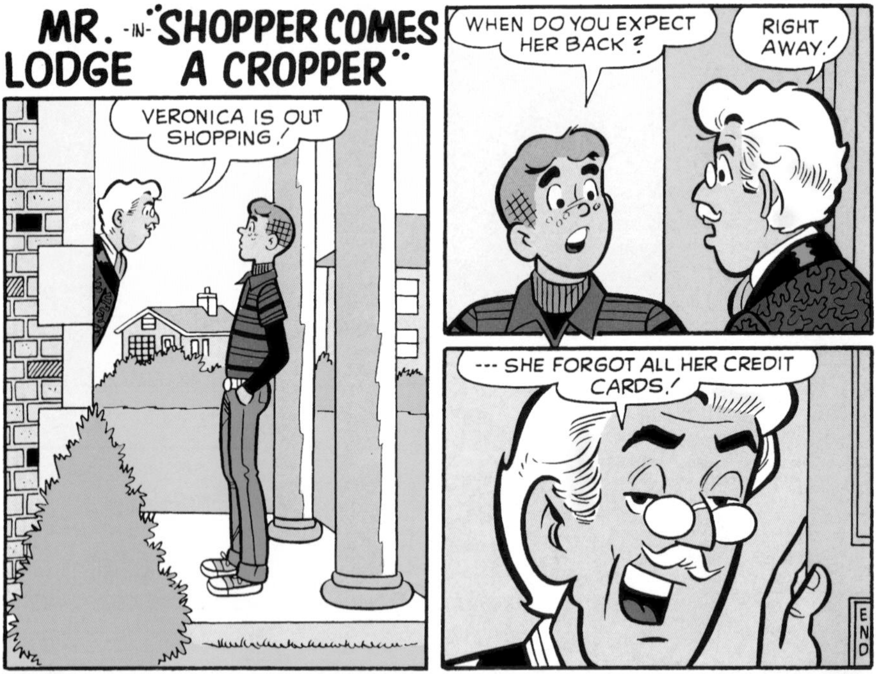
MR. LODGE -IN- "SHOPPER COMES A CROPPER"
VERONICA IS OUT SHOPPING!
WHEN DO YOU EXPECT HER BACK?
RIGHT AWAY!
--- SHE FORGOT ALL HER CREDIT CARDS!
END

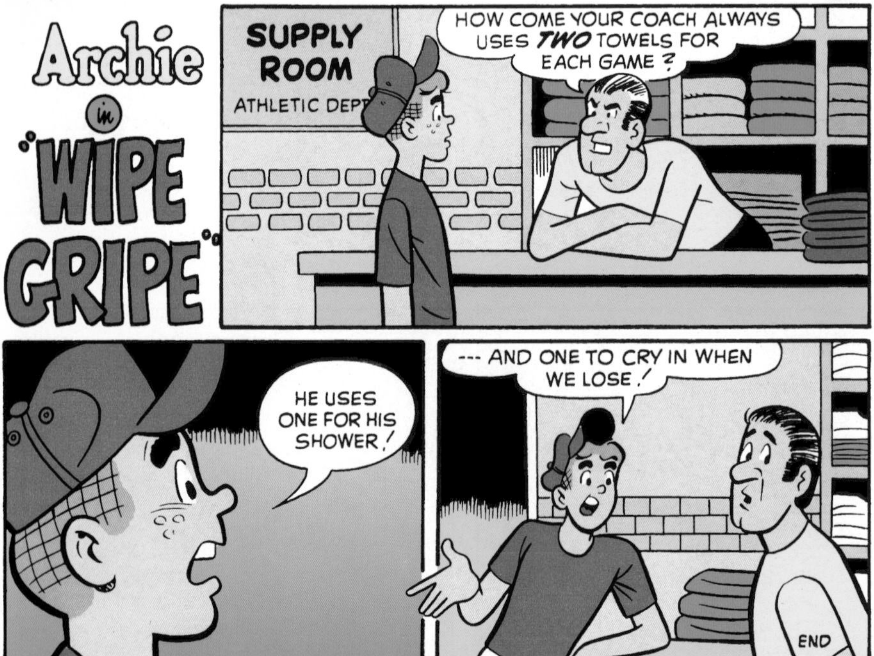
Archie in "WIPE GRIPE"
SUPPLY ROOM
ATHLETIC DEPT
HOW COME YOUR COACH ALWAYS USES TWO TOWELS FOR EACH GAME?
HE USES ONE FOR HIS SHOWER!
--- AND ONE TO CRY IN WHEN WE LOSE!
END

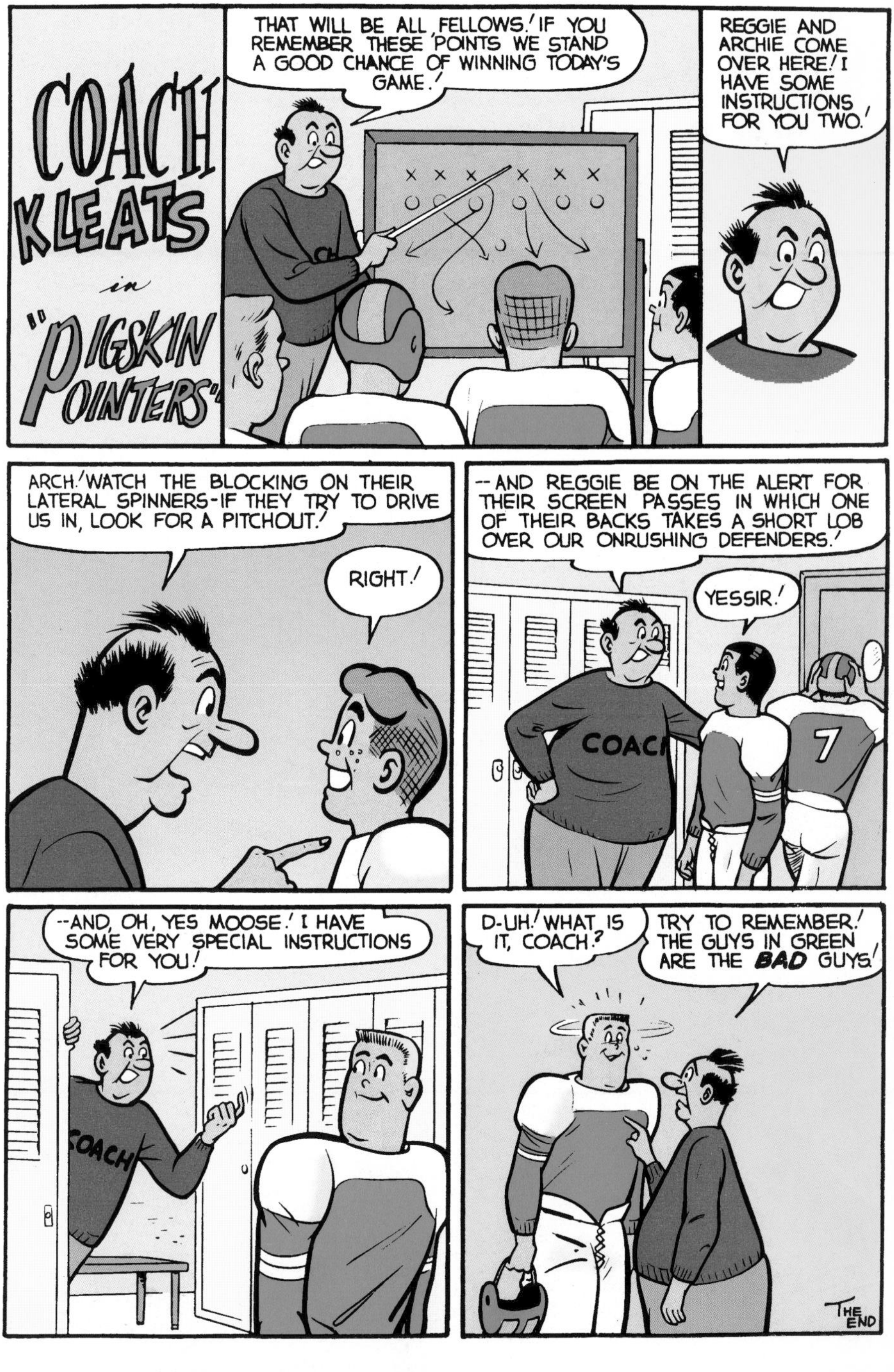
COACH KLEATS in "PIGSKIN POINTERS"
THAT WILL BE ALL, FELLOWS! IF YOU REMEMBER THESE POINTS WE STAND A GOOD CHANCE OF WINNING TODAY'S GAME!
REGGIE AND ARCHIE COME OVER HERE! I HAVE SOME INSTRUCTIONS FOR YOU TWO!
ARCH! WATCH THE BLOCKING ON THEIR LATERAL SPINNERS-IF THEY TRY TO DRIVE US IN, LOOK FOR A PITCHOUT!
RIGHT!
--AND REGGIE BE ON THE ALERT FOR THEIR SCREEN PASSES IN WHICH ONE OF THEIR BACKS TAKES A SHORT LOB OVER OUR ONRUSHING DEFENDERS!
YESSIR!
COACH
7
--AND, OH, YES MOOSE! I HAVE SOME VERY SPECIAL INSTRUCTIONS FOR YOU!
COACH
D-UH! WHAT IS IT, COACH?
TRY TO REMEMBER! THE GUYS IN GREEN ARE THE BAD GUYS!
THE END

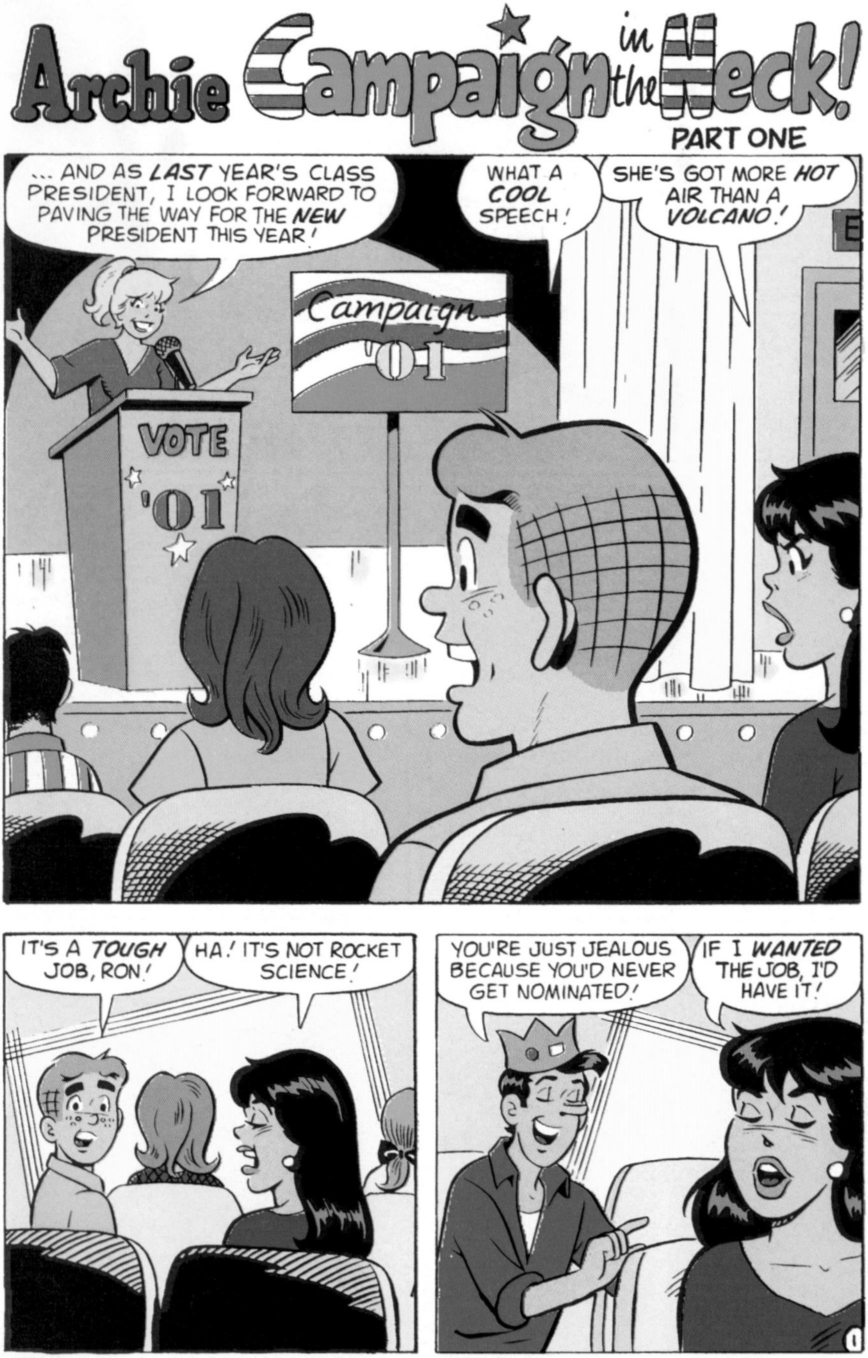
Archie
Campaign in the Neck!
PART ONE
... AND AS LAST YEAR'S CLASS PRESIDENT, I LOOK FORWARD TO PAVING THE WAY FOR THE NEW PRESIDENT THIS YEAR!
WHAT A COOL SPEECH!
SHE'S GOT MORE HOT AIR THAN A VOLCANO!
Campaign '01
VOTE '01
IT'S A TOUGH JOB, RON!
HA! IT'S NOT ROCKET SCIENCE!
YOU'RE JUST JEALOUS BECAUSE YOU'D NEVER GET NOMINATED!
IF I WANTED THE JOB, I'D HAVE IT!
1

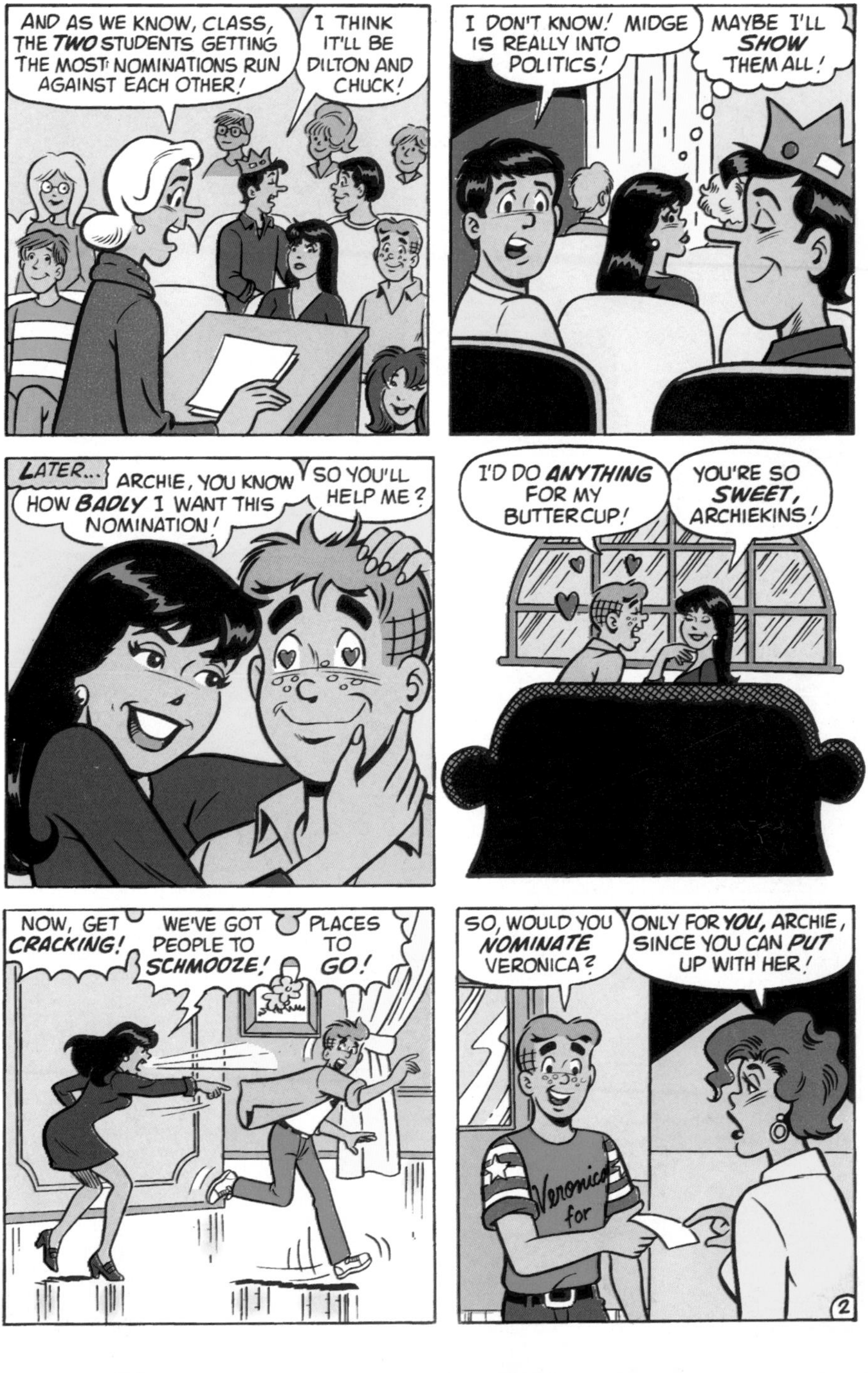
AND AS WE KNOW, CLASS, THE TWO STUDENTS GETTING THE MOST NOMINATIONS RUN AGAINST EACH OTHER!
I THINK IT'LL BE DILTON AND CHUCK!
I DON'T KNOW! MIDGE IS REALLY INTO POLITICS!
MAYBE I'LL SHOW THEM ALL!
LATER...
ARCHIE, YOU KNOW HOW BADLY I WANT THIS NOMINATION!
SO YOU'LL HELP ME?
I'D DO ANYTHING FOR MY BUTTERCUP!
YOU'RE SO SWEET, ARCHIEKINS!
NOW, GET CRACKING!
WE'VE GOT PEOPLE TO SCHMOOZE!
PLACES TO GO!
SO, WOULD YOU NOMINATE VERONICA?
ONLY FOR YOU, ARCHIE, SINCE YOU CAN PUT UP WITH HER!
Veronica for
2

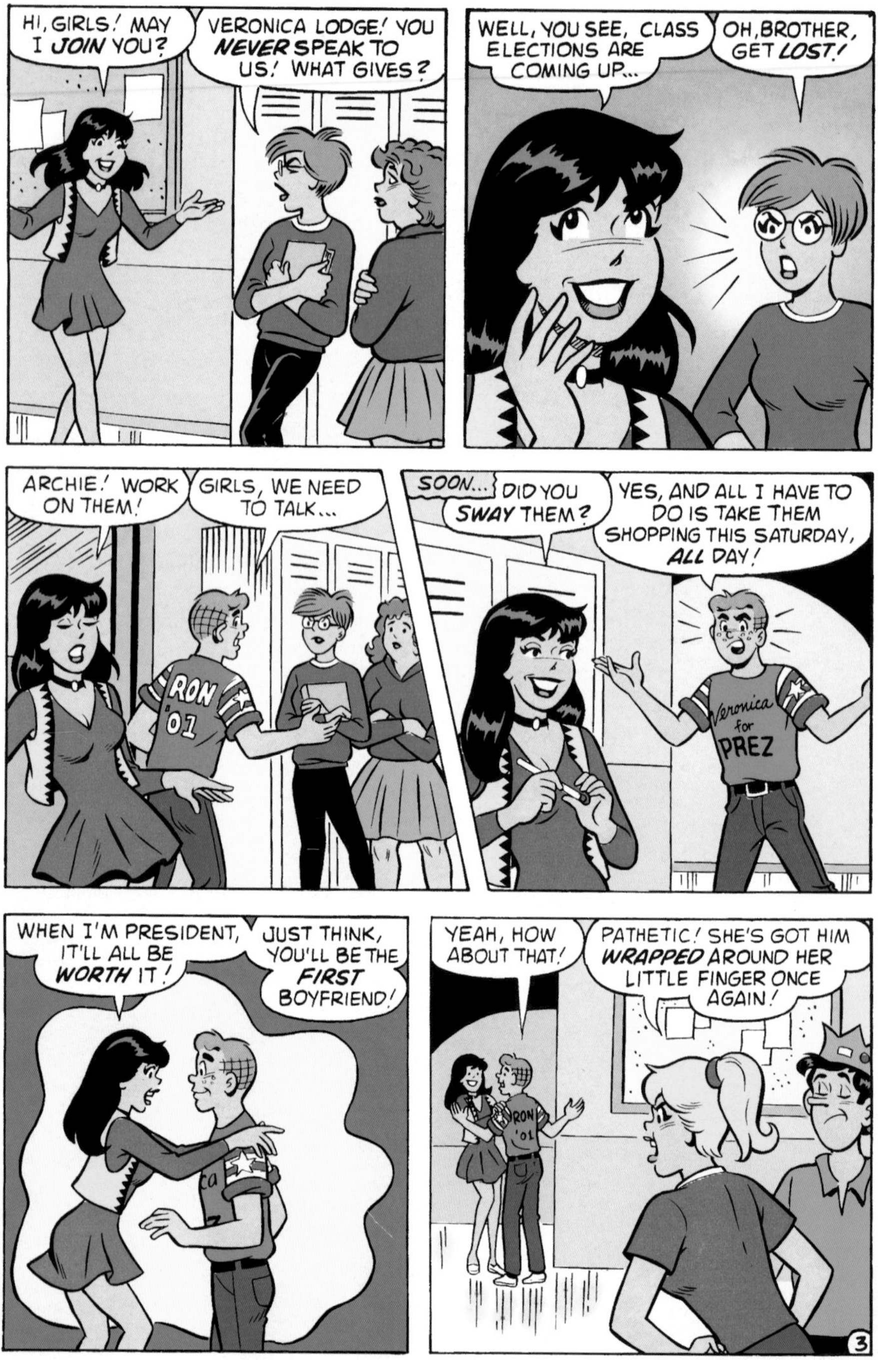
HI, GIRLS! MAY I JOIN YOU?
VERONICA LODGE! YOU NEVER SPEAK TO US! WHAT GIVES?
WELL, YOU SEE, CLASS ELECTIONS ARE COMING UP...
OH, BROTHER, GET LOST!
ARCHIE! WORK ON THEM!
GIRLS, WE NEED TO TALK...
RON '01
SOON...
DID YOU SWAY THEM?
YES, AND ALL I HAVE TO DO IS TAKE THEM SHOPPING THIS SATURDAY, ALL DAY!
Veronica for PREZ
WHEN I'M PRESIDENT, IT'LL ALL BE WORTH IT!
JUST THINK, YOU'LL BE THE FIRST BOYFRIEND!
YEAH, HOW ABOUT THAT!
PATHETIC! SHE'S GOT HIM WRAPPED AROUND HER LITTLE FINGER ONCE AGAIN!
RON '01
3

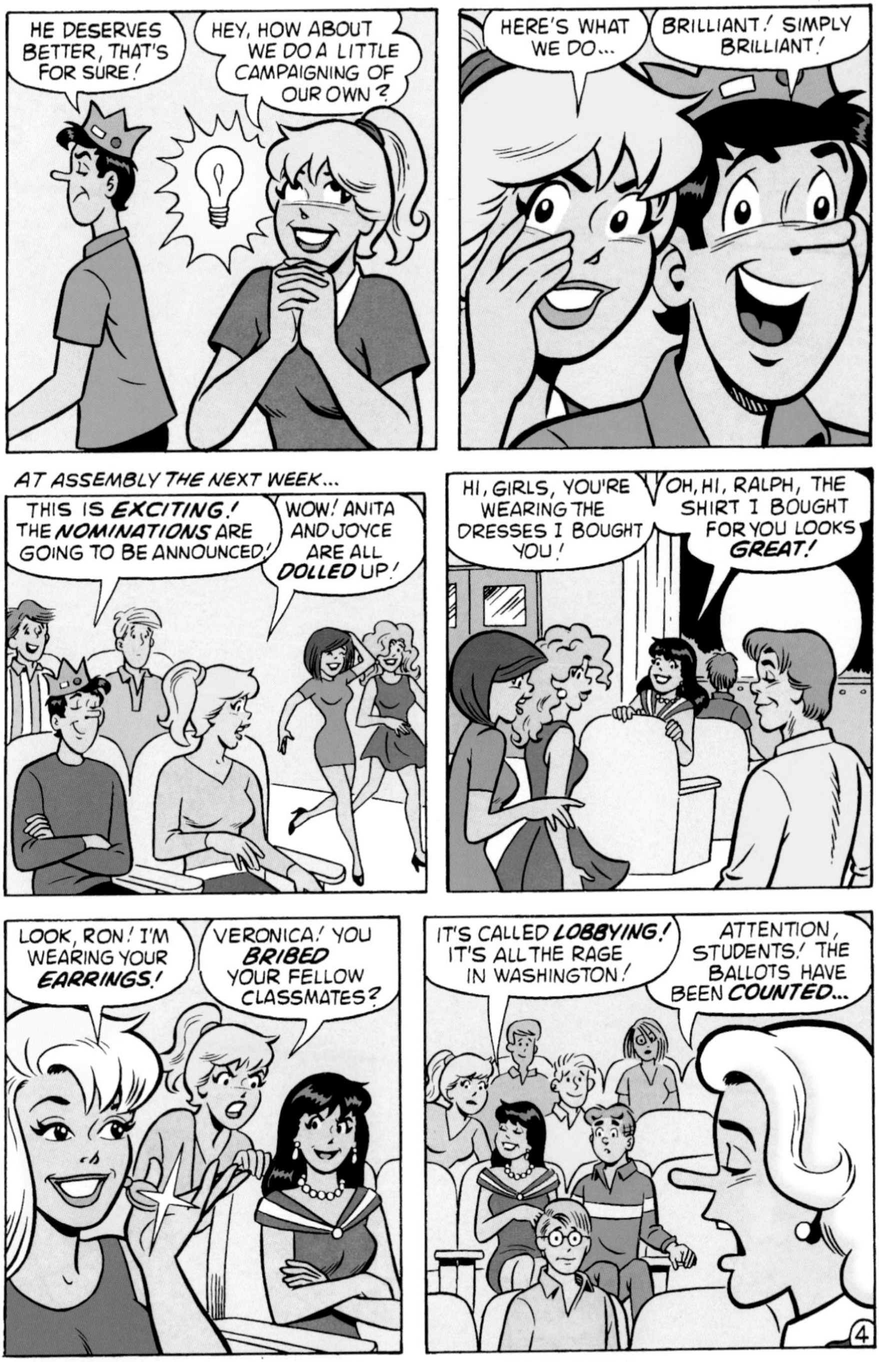
HE DESERVES BETTER, THAT'S FOR SURE!
HEY, HOW ABOUT WE DO A LITTLE CAMPAIGNING OF OUR OWN?
HERE'S WHAT WE DO...
BRILLIANT! SIMPLY BRILLIANT!
AT ASSEMBLY THE NEXT WEEK...
THIS IS EXCITING! THE NOMINATIONS ARE GOING TO BE ANNOUNCED!
WOW! ANITA AND JOYCE ARE ALL DOLLED UP!
HI, GIRLS, YOU'RE WEARING THE DRESSES I BOUGHT YOU!
OH, HI, RALPH, THE SHIRT I BOUGHT FOR YOU LOOKS GREAT!
LOOK, RON! I'M WEARING YOUR EARRINGS!
VERONICA! YOU BRIBED YOUR FELLOW CLASSMATES?
IT'S CALLED LOBBYING! IT'S ALL THE RAGE IN WASHINGTON!
ATTENTION, STUDENTS! THE BALLOTS HAVE BEEN COUNTED...
4

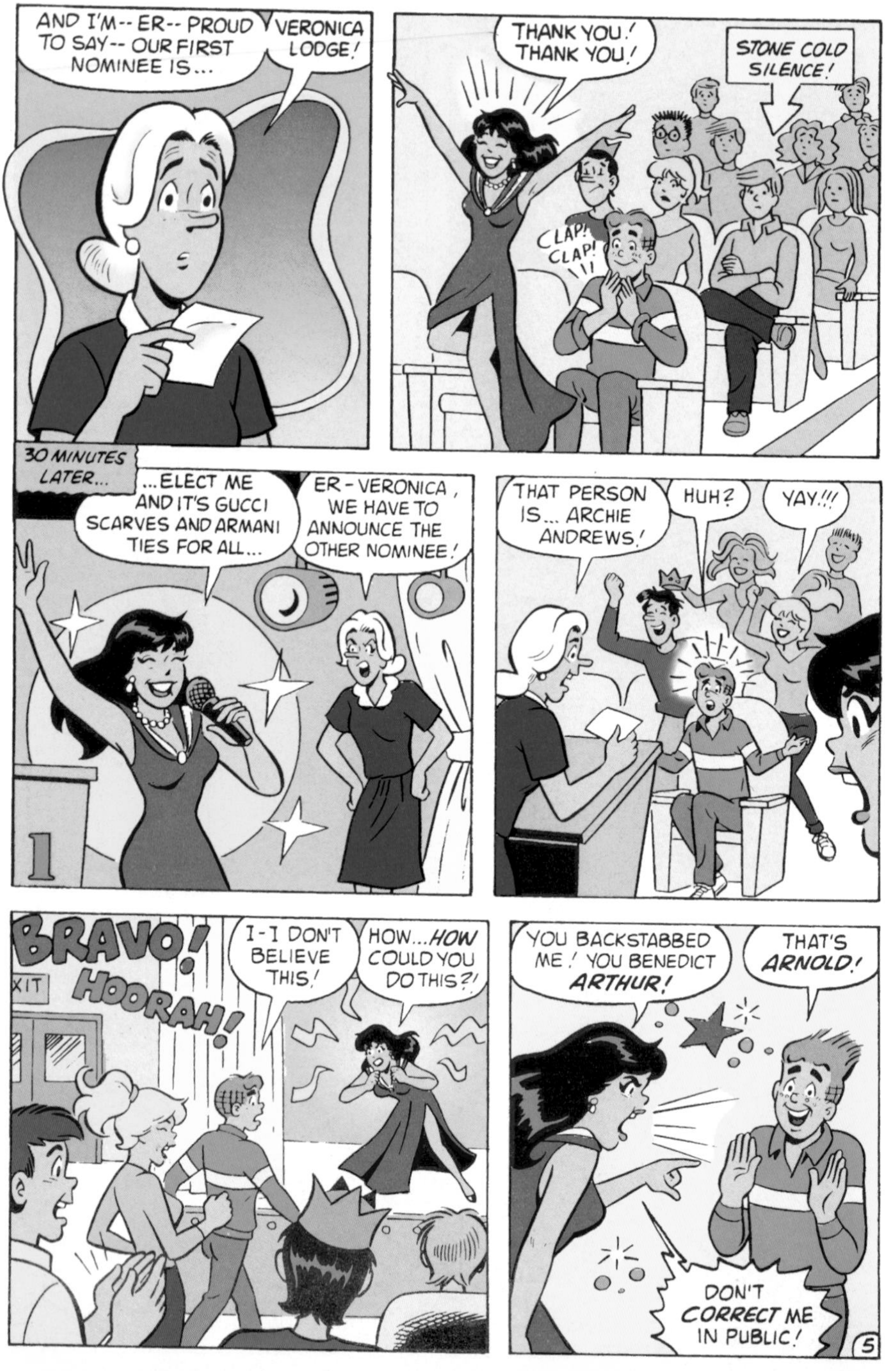
AND I'M-- ER-- PROUD TO SAY-- OUR FIRST NOMINEE IS...
VERONICA LODGE!
THANK YOU! THANK YOU!
STONE COLD SILENCE!
CLAP! CLAP!
30 MINUTES LATER...
...ELECT ME AND IT'S GUCCI SCARVES AND ARMANI TIES FOR ALL...
ER - VERONICA, WE HAVE TO ANNOUNCE THE OTHER NOMINEE!
THAT PERSON IS... ARCHIE ANDREWS!
HUH?
YAY!!!
BRAVO!
HOORAH!
XIT
I-I DON'T BELIEVE THIS!
HOW...HOW COULD YOU DO THIS?!
YOU BACKSTABBED ME! YOU BENEDICT ARTHUR!
THAT'S ARNOLD!
DON'T CORRECT ME IN PUBLIC!
5

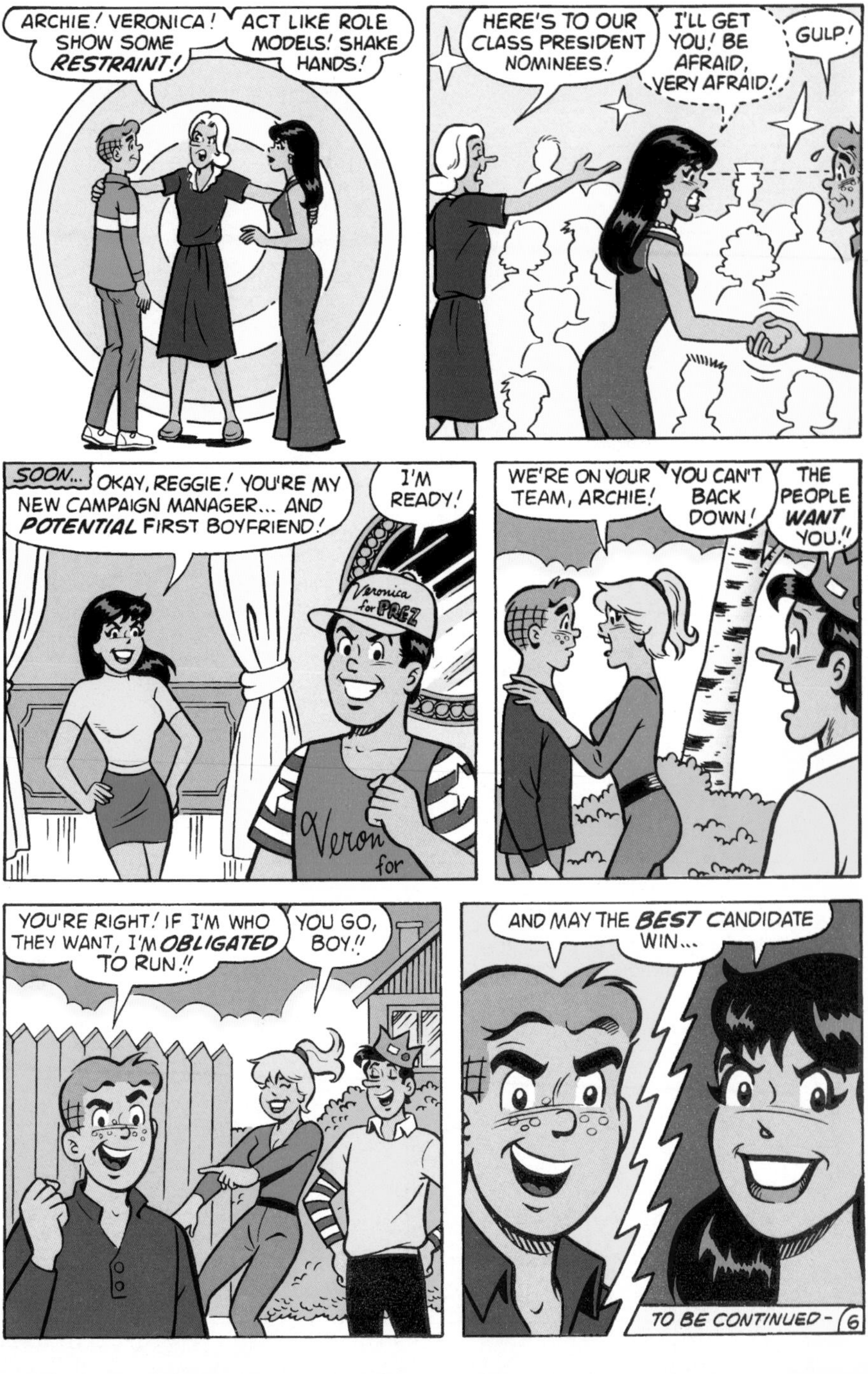
ARCHIE! VERONICA! SHOW SOME RESTRAINT!
ACT LIKE ROLE MODELS! SHAKE HANDS!
HERE'S TO OUR CLASS PRESIDENT NOMINEES!
I'LL GET YOU! BE AFRAID, VERY AFRAID!
GULP!
SOON...
OKAY, REGGIE! YOU'RE MY NEW CAMPAIGN MANAGER... AND POTENTIAL FIRST BOYFRIEND!
I'M READY!
Veronica for PREZ
Veron for
WE'RE ON YOUR TEAM, ARCHIE!
YOU CAN'T BACK DOWN!
THE PEOPLE WANT YOU!!
YOU'RE RIGHT! IF I'M WHO THEY WANT, I'M OBLIGATED TO RUN!!
YOU GO, BOY!!
AND MAY THE BEST CANDIDATE WIN...
TO BE CONTINUED - 6

Archie Campaign in the Heck!

PART TWO

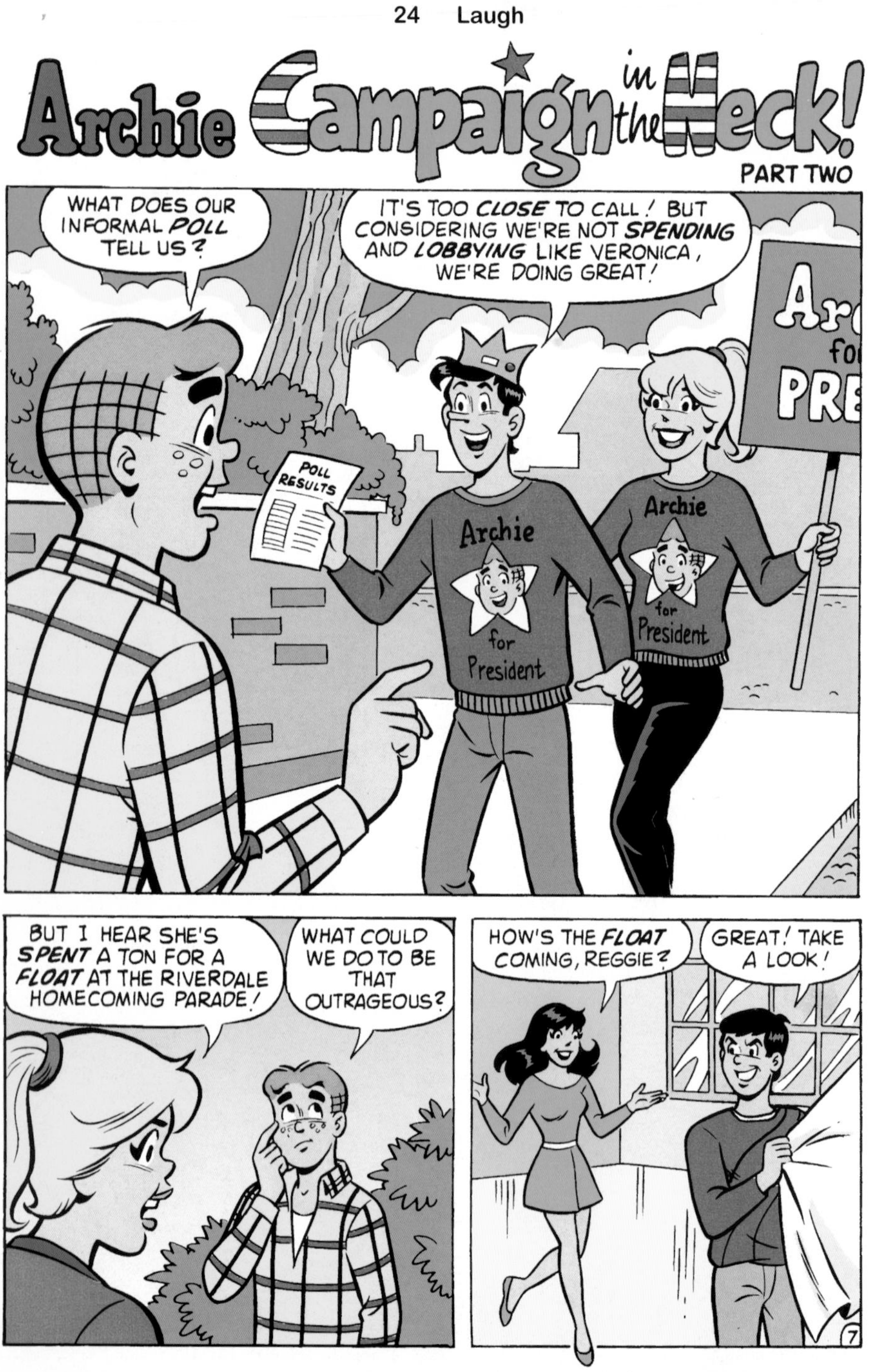
WHAT DOES OUR INFORMAL *POLL* TELL US?
IT'S TOO *CLOSE* TO CALL! BUT CONSIDERING WE'RE NOT *SPENDING* AND *LOBBYING* LIKE VERONICA, WE'RE DOING GREAT!
POLL RESULTS
Archie for President
Archie for President
BUT I HEAR SHE'S *SPENT* A TON FOR A *FLOAT* AT THE RIVERDALE HOMECOMING PARADE!
WHAT COULD WE DO TO BE THAT OUTRAGEOUS?
HOW'S THE *FLOAT* COMING, REGGIE?
GREAT! TAKE A LOOK!
7

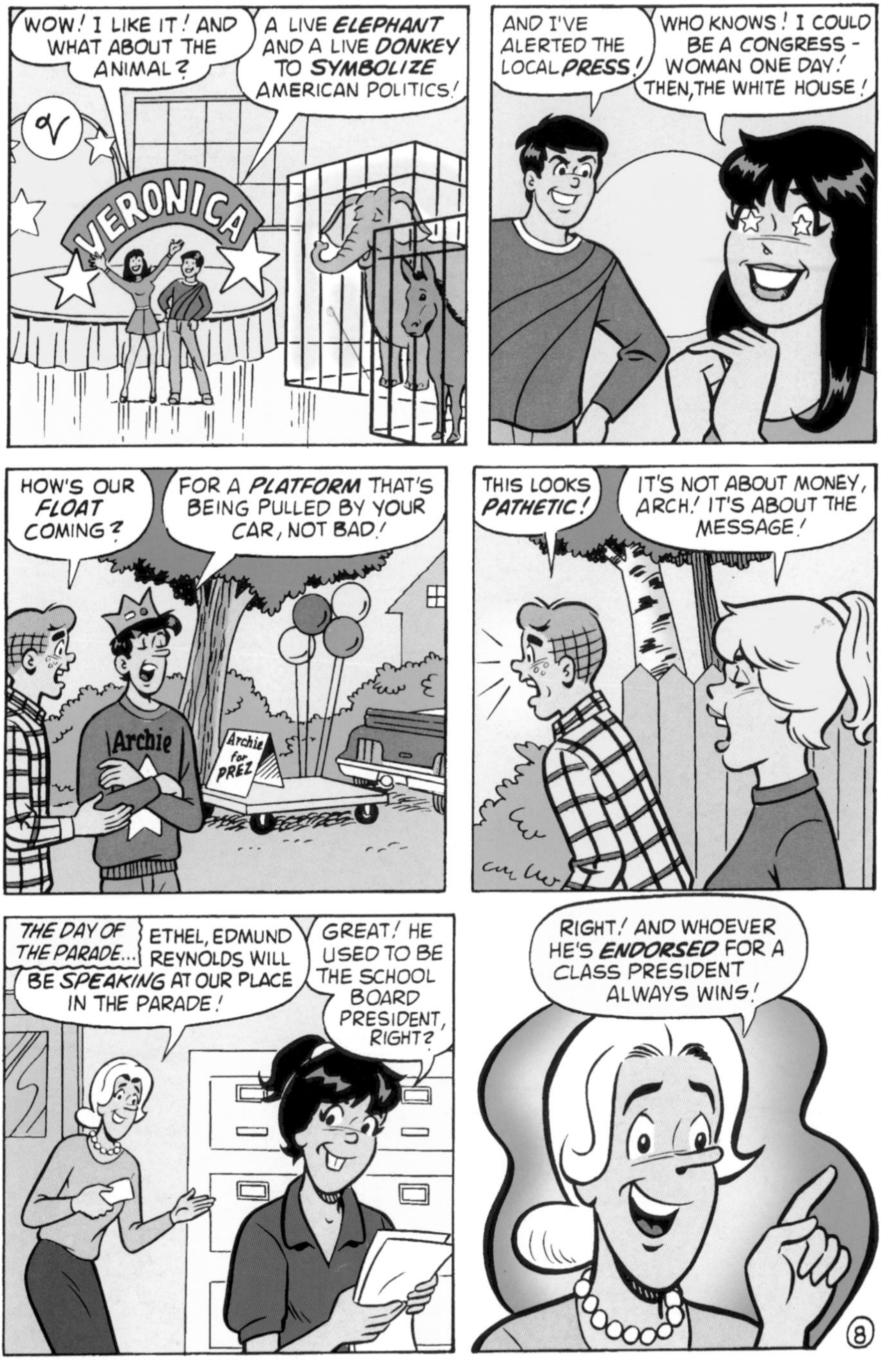
WOW! I LIKE IT! AND WHAT ABOUT THE ANIMAL?
A LIVE ELEPHANT AND A LIVE DONKEY TO SYMBOLIZE AMERICAN POLITICS!
VERONICA
AND I'VE ALERTED THE LOCAL PRESS!
WHO KNOWS! I COULD BE A CONGRESS - WOMAN ONE DAY! THEN, THE WHITE HOUSE!
HOW'S OUR FLOAT COMING?
FOR A PLATFORM THAT'S BEING PULLED BY YOUR CAR, NOT BAD!
Archie
Archie for PREZ
THIS LOOKS PATHETIC!
IT'S NOT ABOUT MONEY, ARCH! IT'S ABOUT THE MESSAGE!
THE DAY OF THE PARADE...
ETHEL, EDMUND REYNOLDS WILL BE SPEAKING AT OUR PLACE IN THE PARADE!
GREAT! HE USED TO BE THE SCHOOL BOARD PRESIDENT, RIGHT?
RIGHT! AND WHOEVER HE'S ENDORSED FOR A CLASS PRESIDENT ALWAYS WINS!
8

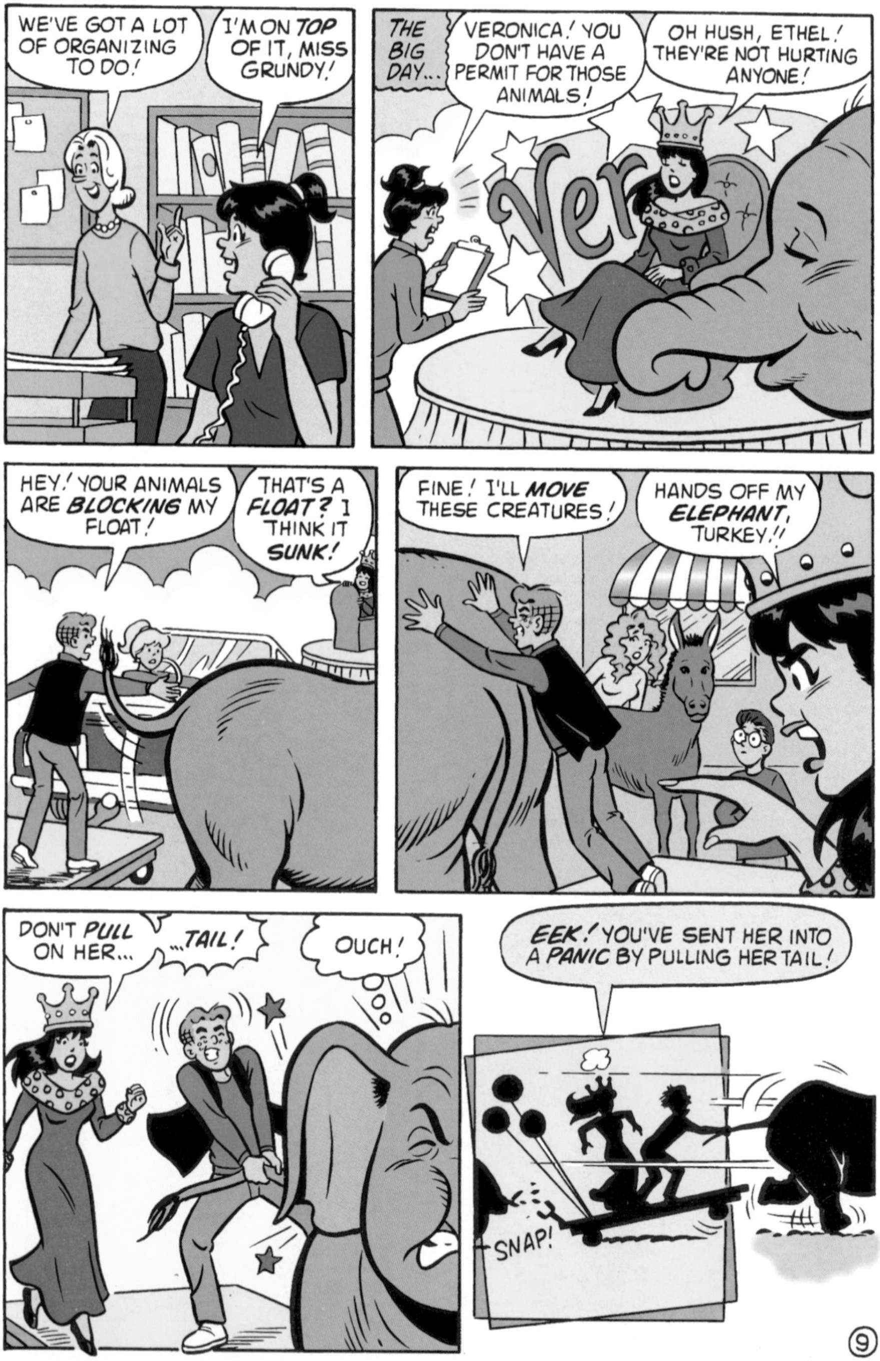
WE'VE GOT A LOT OF ORGANIZING TO DO!
I'M ON TOP OF IT, MISS GRUNDY!
THE BIG DAY...
VERONICA! YOU DON'T HAVE A PERMIT FOR THOSE ANIMALS!
OH HUSH, ETHEL! THEY'RE NOT HURTING ANYONE!
Ver
HEY! YOUR ANIMALS ARE BLOCKING MY FLOAT!
THAT'S A FLOAT? I THINK IT SUNK!
FINE! I'LL MOVE THESE CREATURES!
HANDS OFF MY ELEPHANT, TURKEY!!
DON'T PULL ON HER...
...TAIL!
OUCH!
EEK! YOU'VE SENT HER INTO A PANIC BY PULLING HER TAIL!
SNAP!

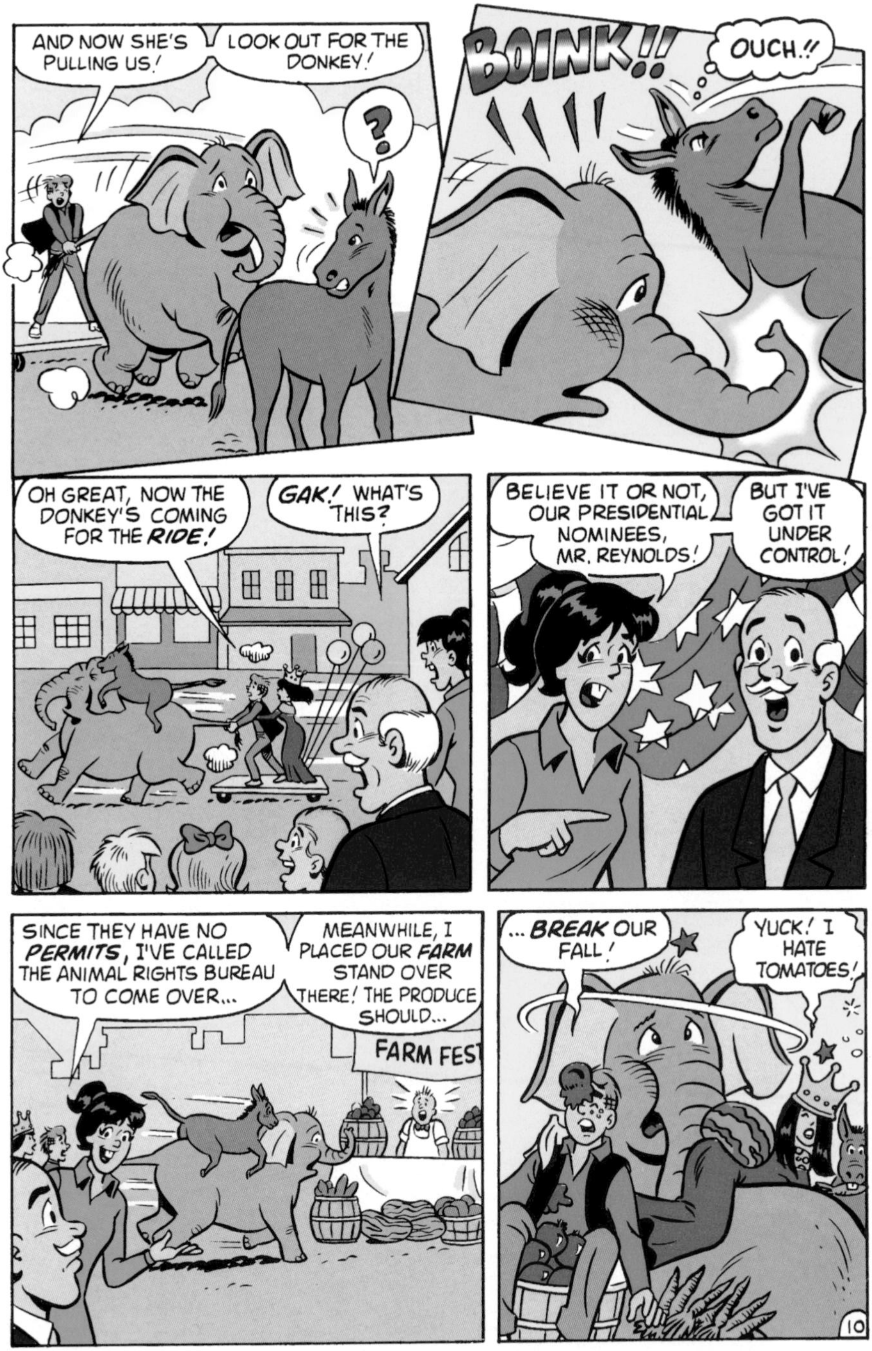
AND NOW SHE'S PULLING US!
LOOK OUT FOR THE DONKEY!
?
BOINK!!
OUCH!!
OH GREAT, NOW THE DONKEY'S COMING FOR THE *RIDE!*
GAK! WHAT'S THIS?
BELIEVE IT OR NOT, OUR PRESIDENTIAL NOMINEES, MR. REYNOLDS!
BUT I'VE GOT IT UNDER CONTROL!
SINCE THEY HAVE NO *PERMITS*, I'VE CALLED THE ANIMAL RIGHTS BUREAU TO COME OVER...
MEANWHILE, I PLACED OUR *FARM* STAND OVER THERE! THE PRODUCE SHOULD...
FARM FEST
... *BREAK* OUR FALL!
YUCK! I HATE TOMATOES!
10

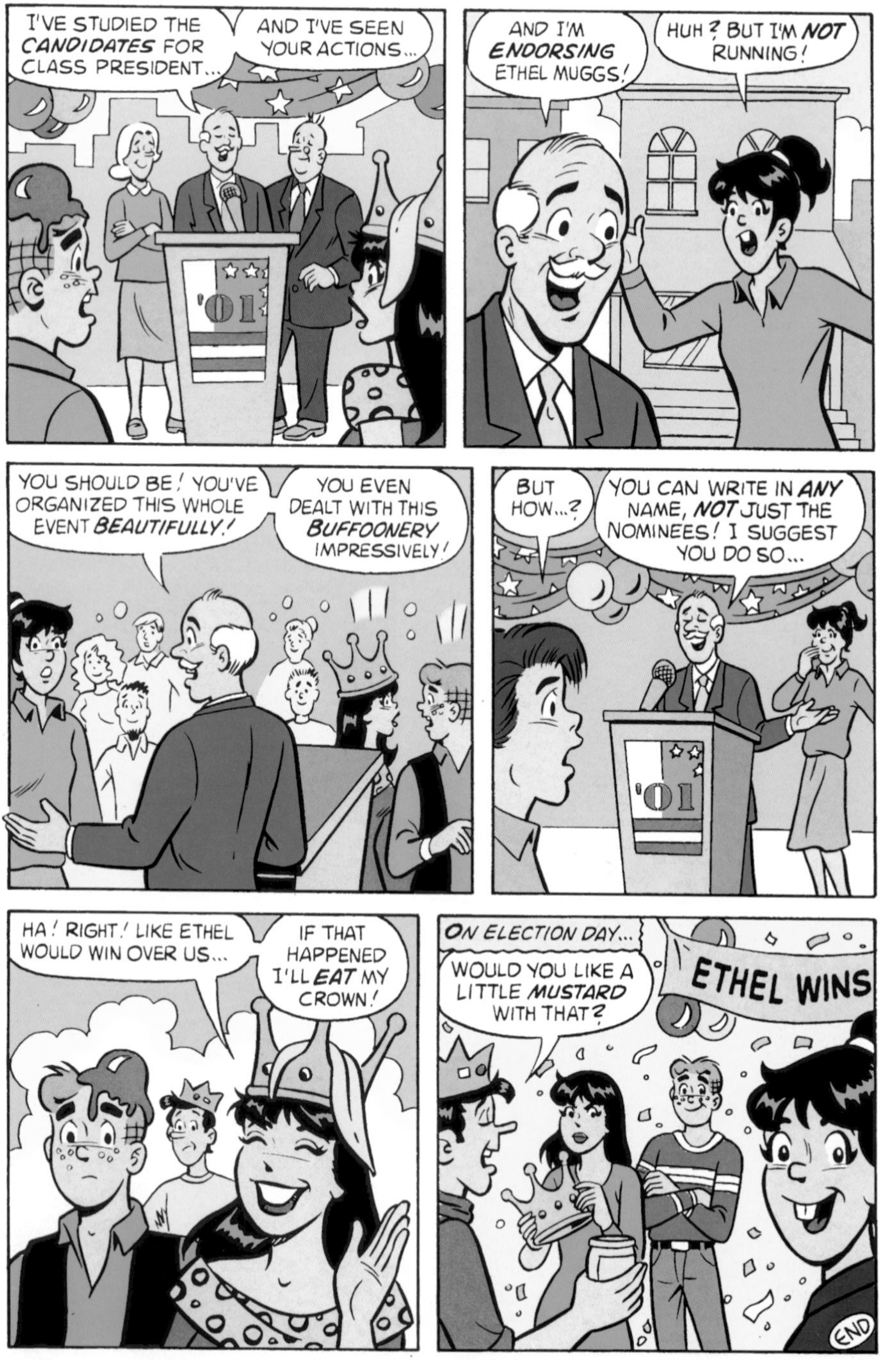
I'VE STUDIED THE CANDIDATES FOR CLASS PRESIDENT...
AND I'VE SEEN YOUR ACTIONS...
AND I'M ENDORSING ETHEL MUGGS!
HUH? BUT I'M NOT RUNNING!
YOU SHOULD BE! YOU'VE ORGANIZED THIS WHOLE EVENT BEAUTIFULLY!
YOU EVEN DEALT WITH THIS BUFFOONERY IMPRESSIVELY!
BUT HOW...?
YOU CAN WRITE IN ANY NAME, NOT JUST THE NOMINEES! I SUGGEST YOU DO SO...
HA! RIGHT! LIKE ETHEL WOULD WIN OVER US...
IF THAT HAPPENED I'LL EAT MY CROWN!
ON ELECTION DAY...
WOULD YOU LIKE A LITTLE MUSTARD WITH THAT?
ETHEL WINS
END

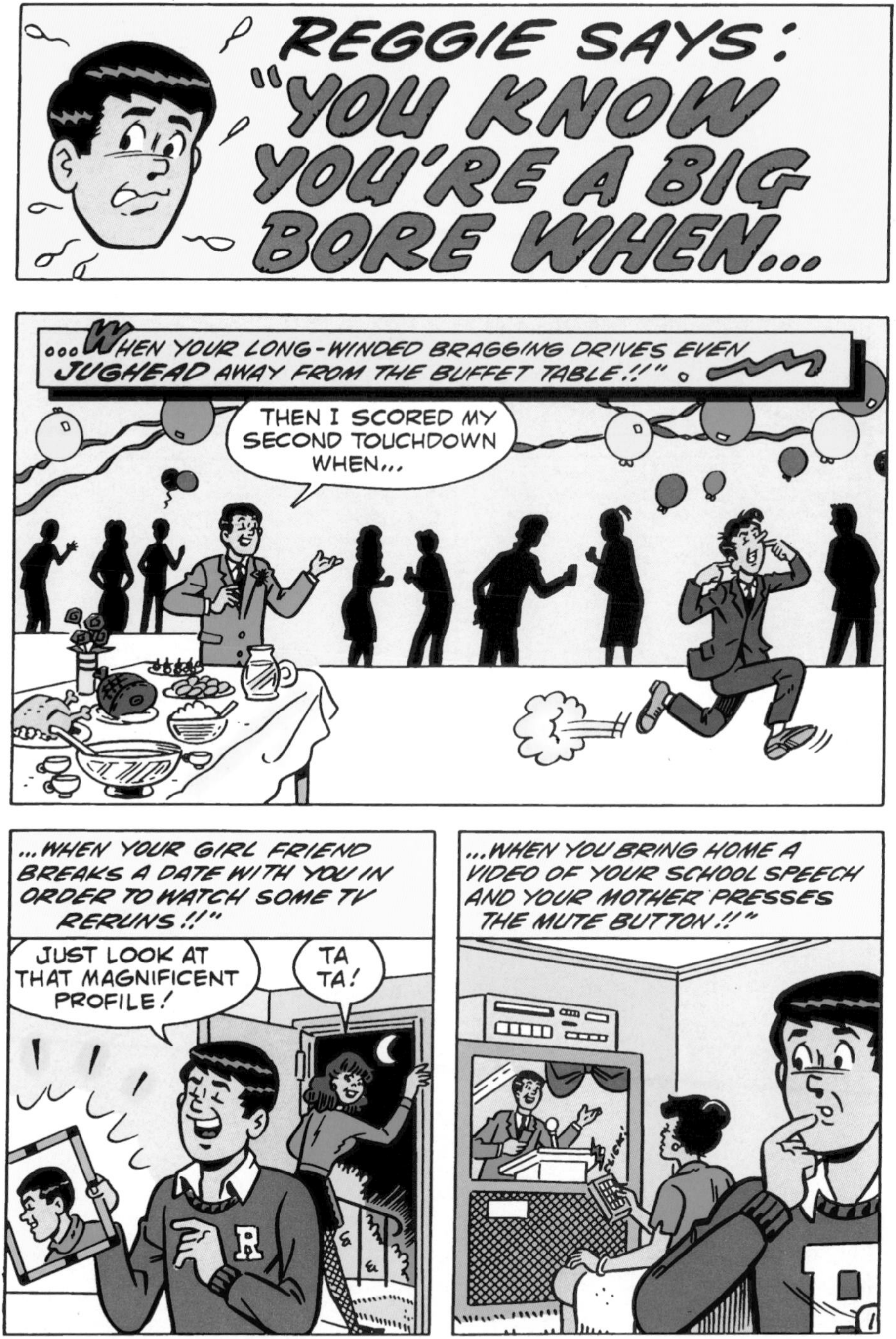
REGGIE SAYS:
"YOU KNOW YOU'RE A BIG BORE WHEN...
...WHEN YOUR LONG-WINDED BRAGGING DRIVES EVEN JUGHEAD AWAY FROM THE BUFFET TABLE!!"
THEN I SCORED MY SECOND TOUCHDOWN WHEN...
...WHEN YOUR GIRL FRIEND BREAKS A DATE WITH YOU IN ORDER TO WATCH SOME TV RERUNS!!"
JUST LOOK AT THAT MAGNIFICENT PROFILE!
TA TA!
...WHEN YOU BRING HOME A VIDEO OF YOUR SCHOOL SPEECH AND YOUR MOTHER PRESSES THE MUTE BUTTON!!"
CLICK!

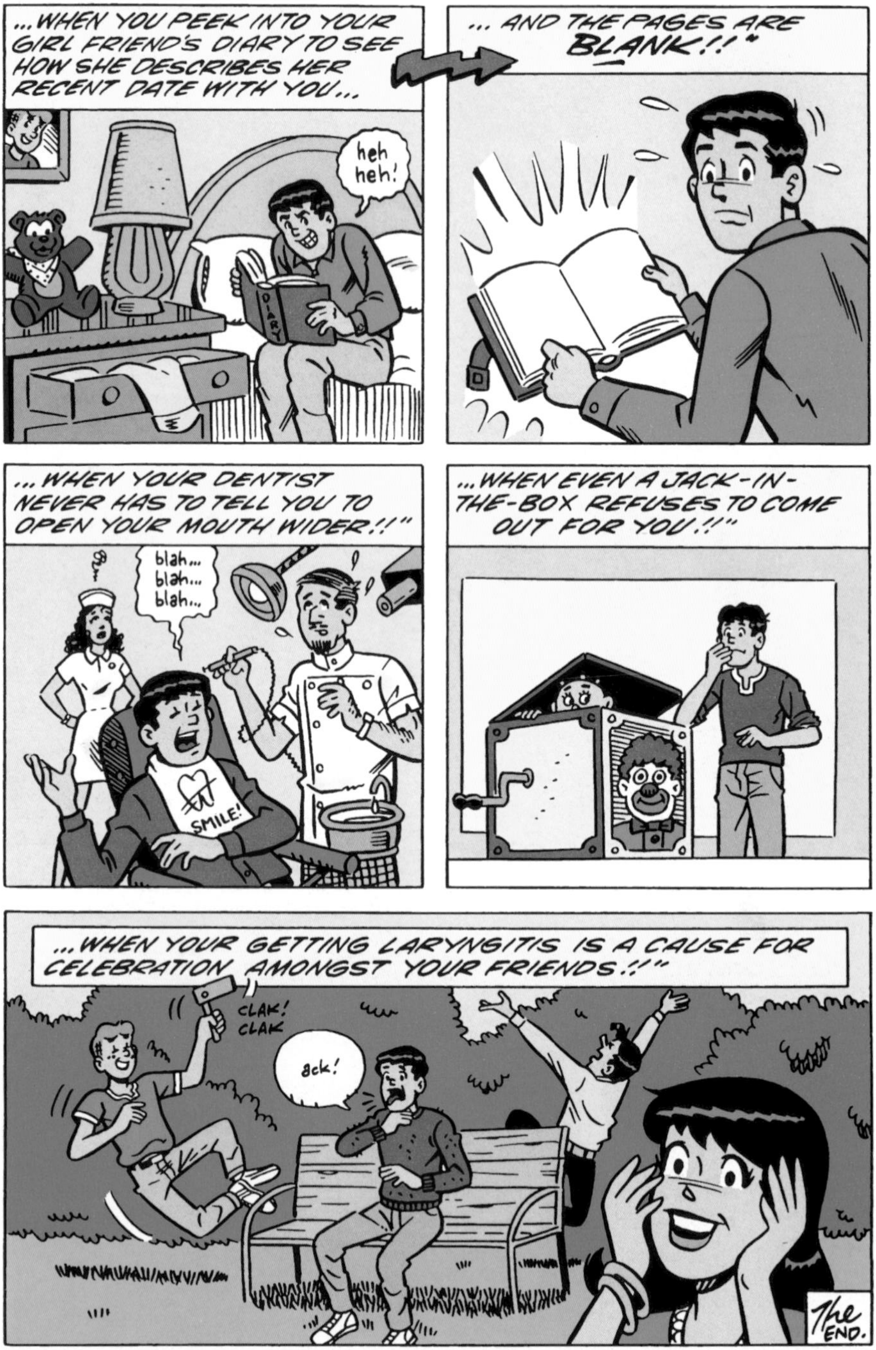
...WHEN YOU PEEK INTO YOUR GIRL FRIEND'S DIARY TO SEE HOW SHE DESCRIBES HER RECENT DATE WITH YOU...
heh heh!
DIARY
... AND THE PAGES ARE BLANK!!"
...WHEN YOUR DENTIST NEVER HAS TO TELL YOU TO OPEN YOUR MOUTH WIDER!!"
blah... blah... blah...
SMILE!
...WHEN EVEN A JACK-IN-THE-BOX REFUSES TO COME OUT FOR YOU!!"
...WHEN YOUR GETTING LARYNGITIS IS A CAUSE FOR CELEBRATION AMONGST YOUR FRIENDS!!"
CLAK! CLAK
ack!
The END.

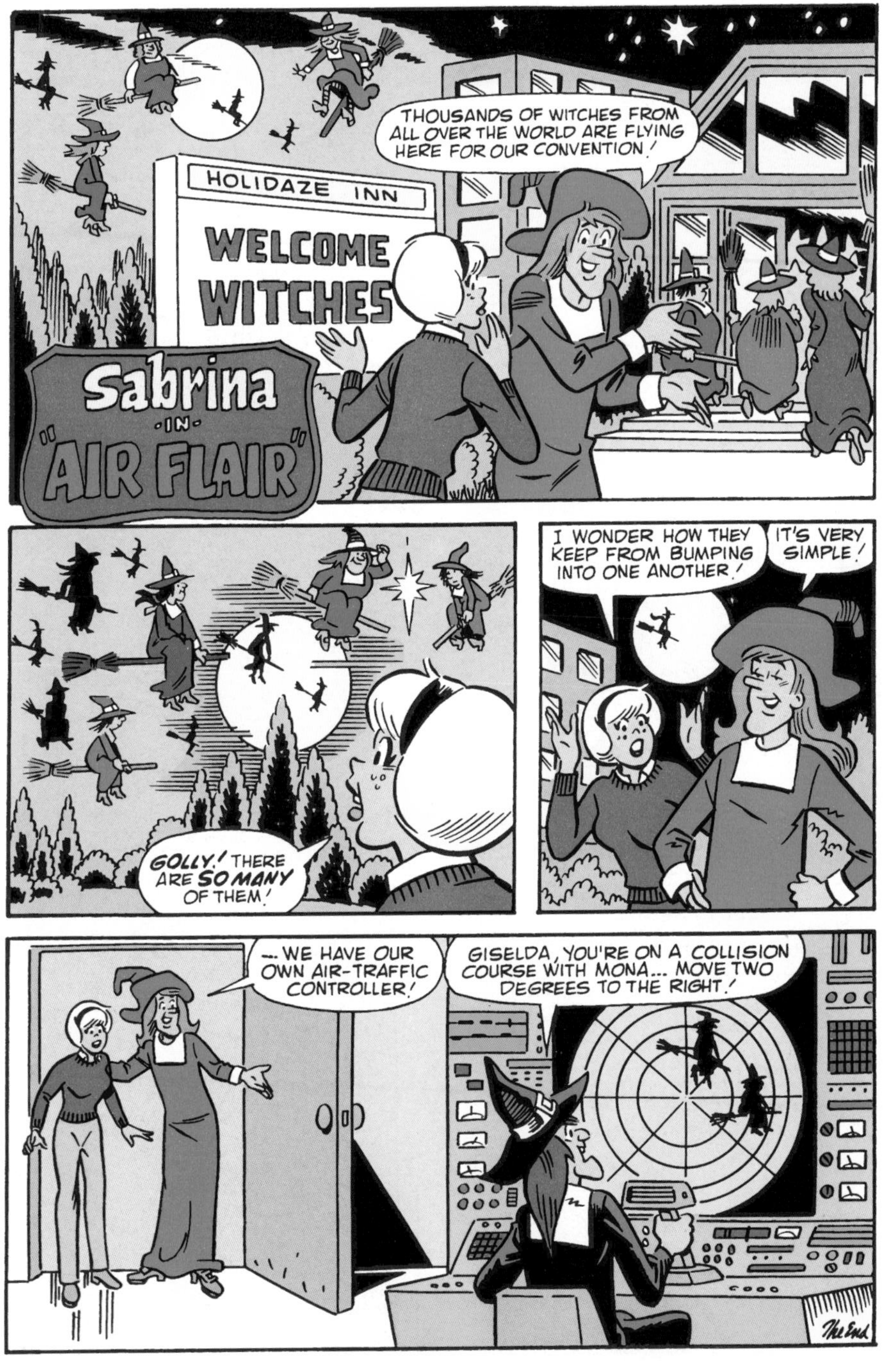
Sabrina
-IN-
"AIR FLAIR"
HOLIDAZE INN
WELCOME WITCHES
THOUSANDS OF WITCHES FROM ALL OVER THE WORLD ARE FLYING HERE FOR OUR CONVENTION!
GOLLY! THERE ARE SO MANY OF THEM!
I WONDER HOW THEY KEEP FROM BUMPING INTO ONE ANOTHER!
IT'S VERY SIMPLE!
...WE HAVE OUR OWN AIR-TRAFFIC CONTROLLER!
GISELDA, YOU'RE ON A COLLISION COURSE WITH MONA... MOVE TWO DEGREES TO THE RIGHT!
The End

Betty in "ONE GIRL'S TREASURE"

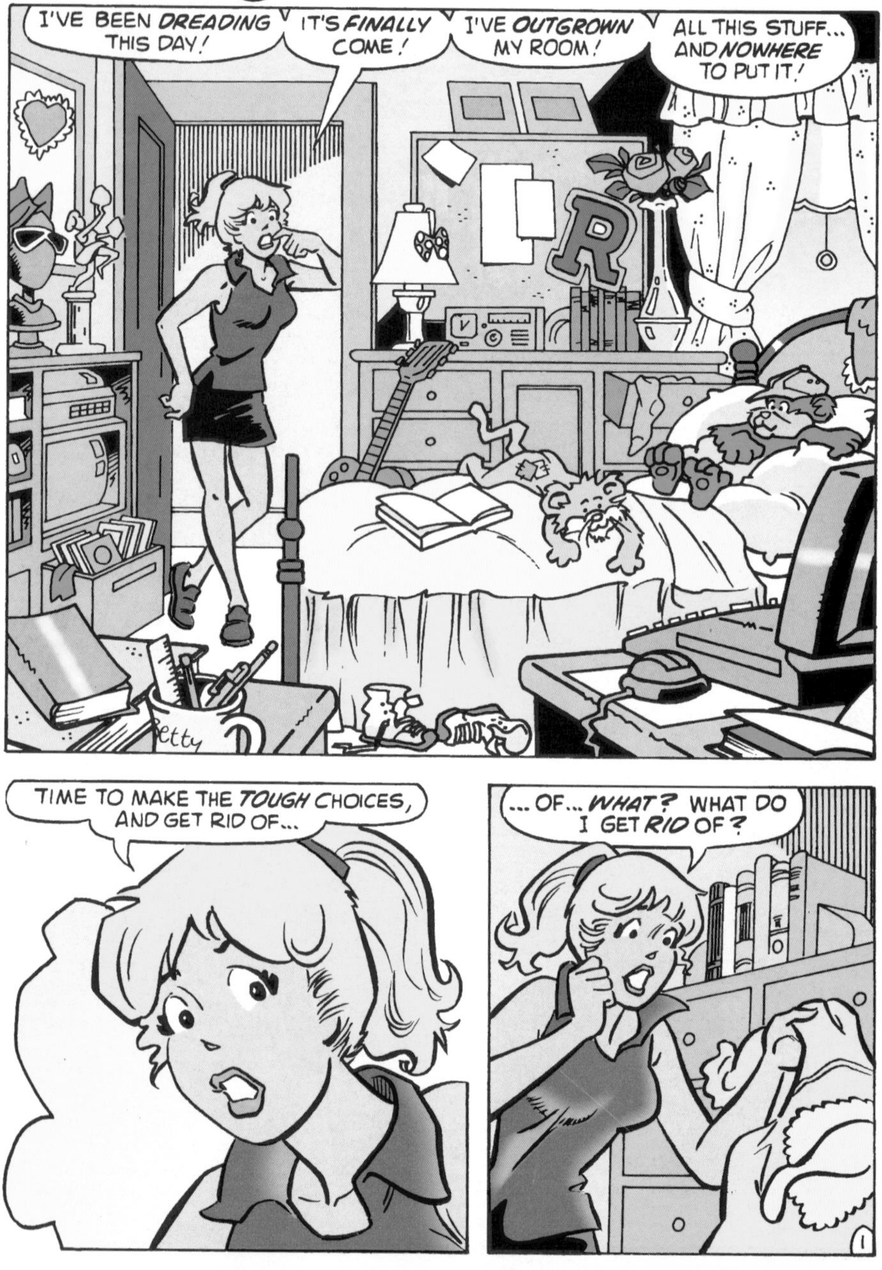
I'VE BEEN DREADING THIS DAY!
IT'S FINALLY COME!
I'VE OUTGROWN MY ROOM!
ALL THIS STUFF... AND NOWHERE TO PUT IT!
TIME TO MAKE THE TOUGH CHOICES, AND GET RID OF...
...OF... WHAT? WHAT DO I GET RID OF?

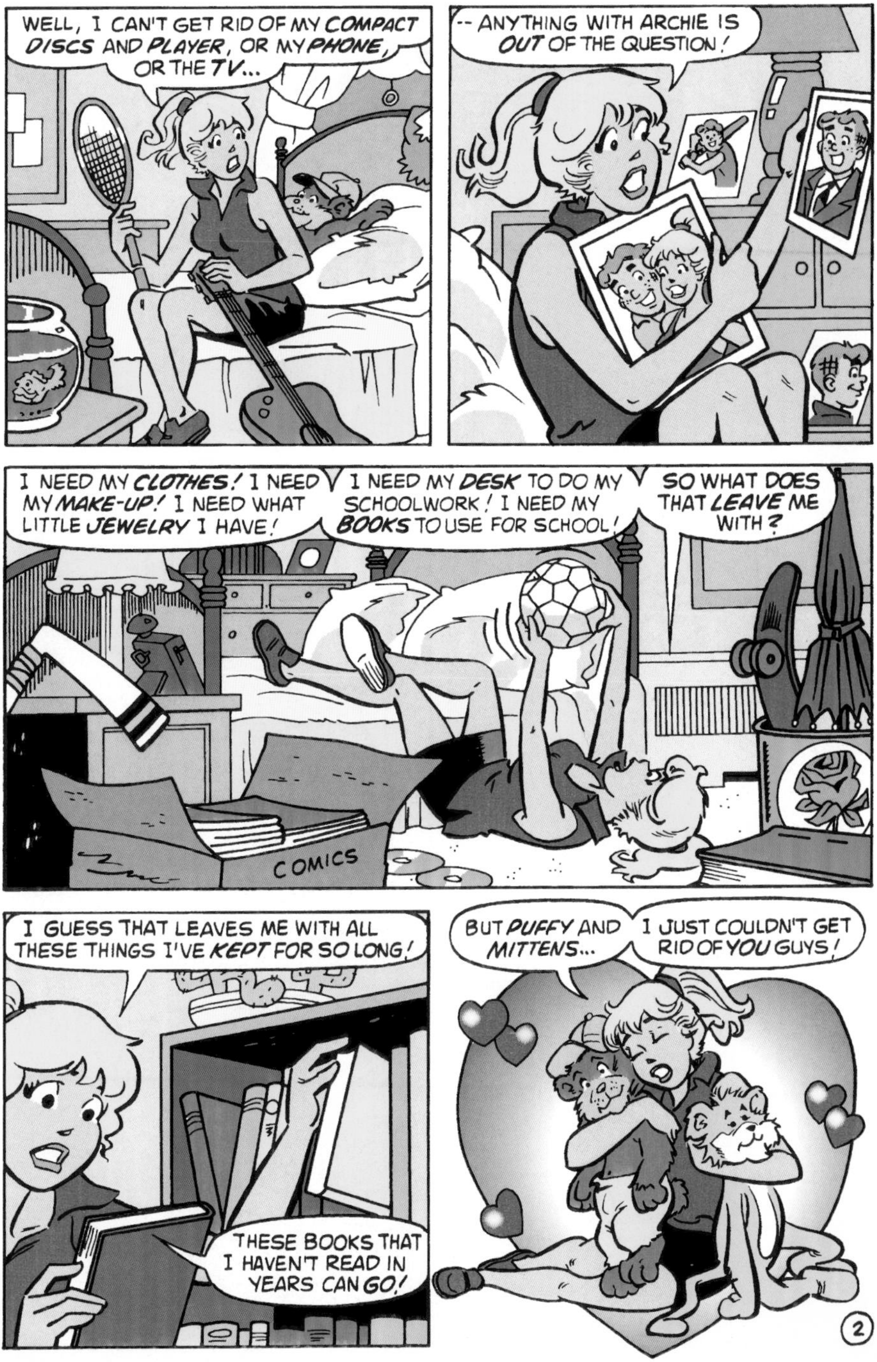
WELL, I CAN'T GET RID OF MY COMPACT DISCS AND PLAYER, OR MY PHONE, OR THE TV...
-- ANYTHING WITH ARCHIE IS OUT OF THE QUESTION!
I NEED MY CLOTHES! I NEED MY MAKE-UP! I NEED WHAT LITTLE JEWELRY I HAVE!
I NEED MY DESK TO DO MY SCHOOLWORK! I NEED MY BOOKS TO USE FOR SCHOOL!
SO WHAT DOES THAT LEAVE ME WITH?
COMICS
I GUESS THAT LEAVES ME WITH ALL THESE THINGS I'VE KEPT FOR SO LONG!
THESE BOOKS THAT I HAVEN'T READ IN YEARS CAN GO!
BUT PUFFY AND MITTENS...
I JUST COULDN'T GET RID OF YOU GUYS!
2

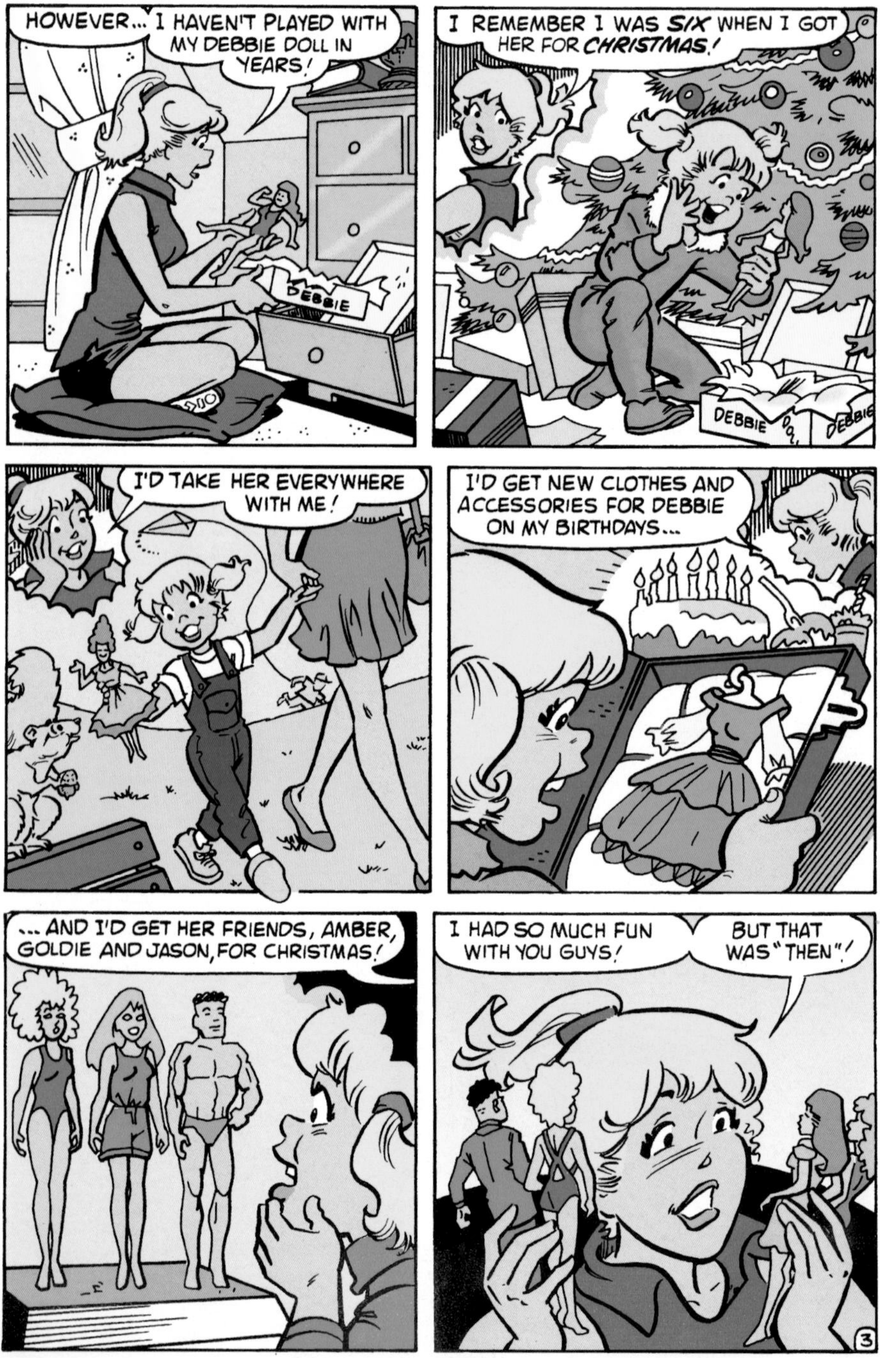
HOWEVER...
I HAVEN'T PLAYED WITH MY DEBBIE DOLL IN YEARS!
DEBBIE
I REMEMBER I WAS SIX WHEN I GOT HER FOR CHRISTMAS!
DEBBIE
I'D TAKE HER EVERYWHERE WITH ME!
I'D GET NEW CLOTHES AND ACCESSORIES FOR DEBBIE ON MY BIRTHDAYS...
... AND I'D GET HER FRIENDS, AMBER, GOLDIE AND JASON, FOR CHRISTMAS!
I HAD SO MUCH FUN WITH YOU GUYS!
BUT THAT WAS "THEN"!
3

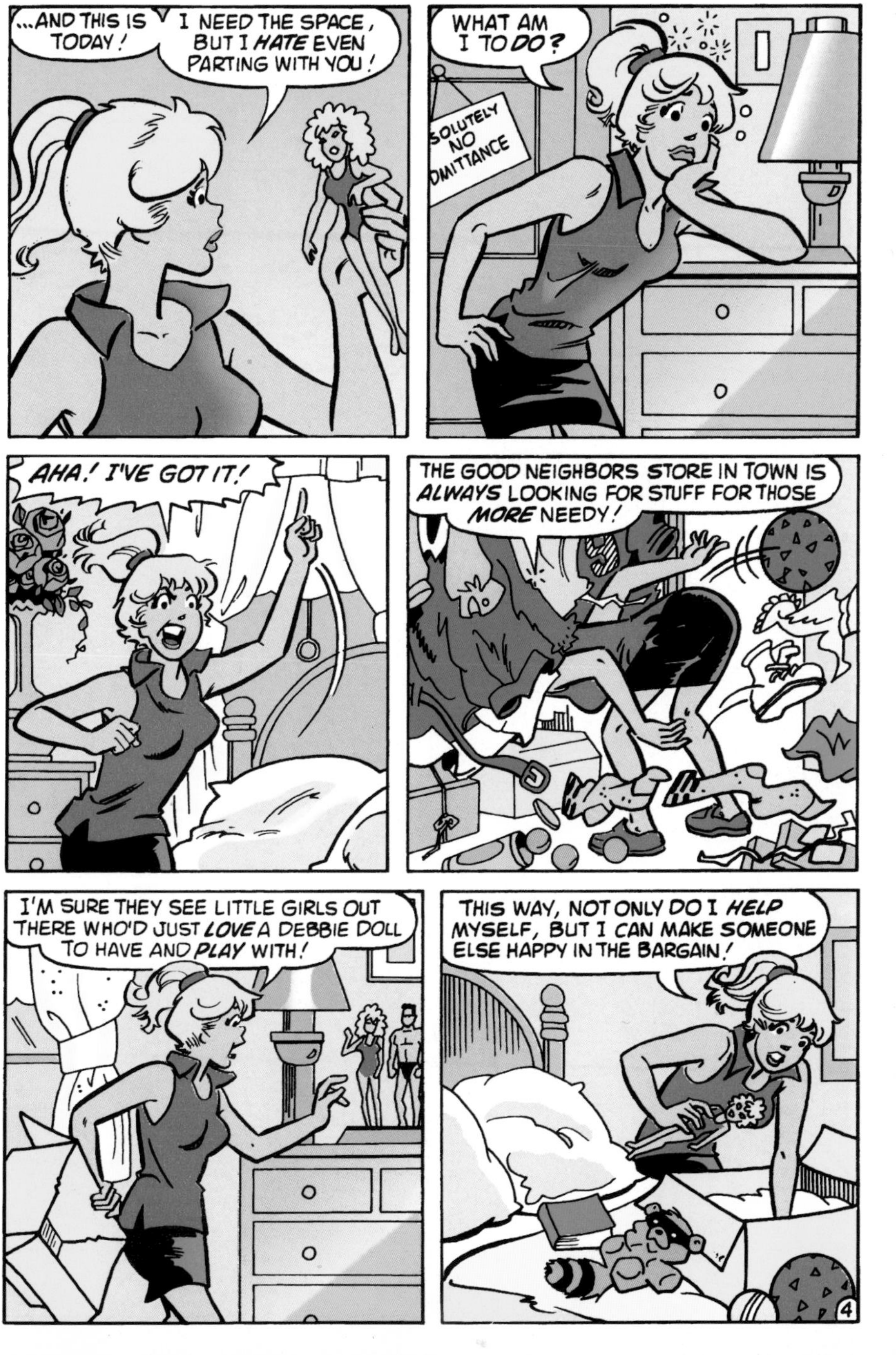
...AND THIS IS TODAY!
I NEED THE SPACE, BUT I HATE EVEN PARTING WITH YOU!
WHAT AM I TO DO?
SOLUTELY NO DMITTANCE
AHA! I'VE GOT IT!
THE GOOD NEIGHBORS STORE IN TOWN IS ALWAYS LOOKING FOR STUFF FOR THOSE MORE NEEDY!
I'M SURE THEY SEE LITTLE GIRLS OUT THERE WHO'D JUST LOVE A DEBBIE DOLL TO HAVE AND PLAY WITH!
THIS WAY, NOT ONLY DO I HELP MYSELF, BUT I CAN MAKE SOMEONE ELSE HAPPY IN THE BARGAIN!
4

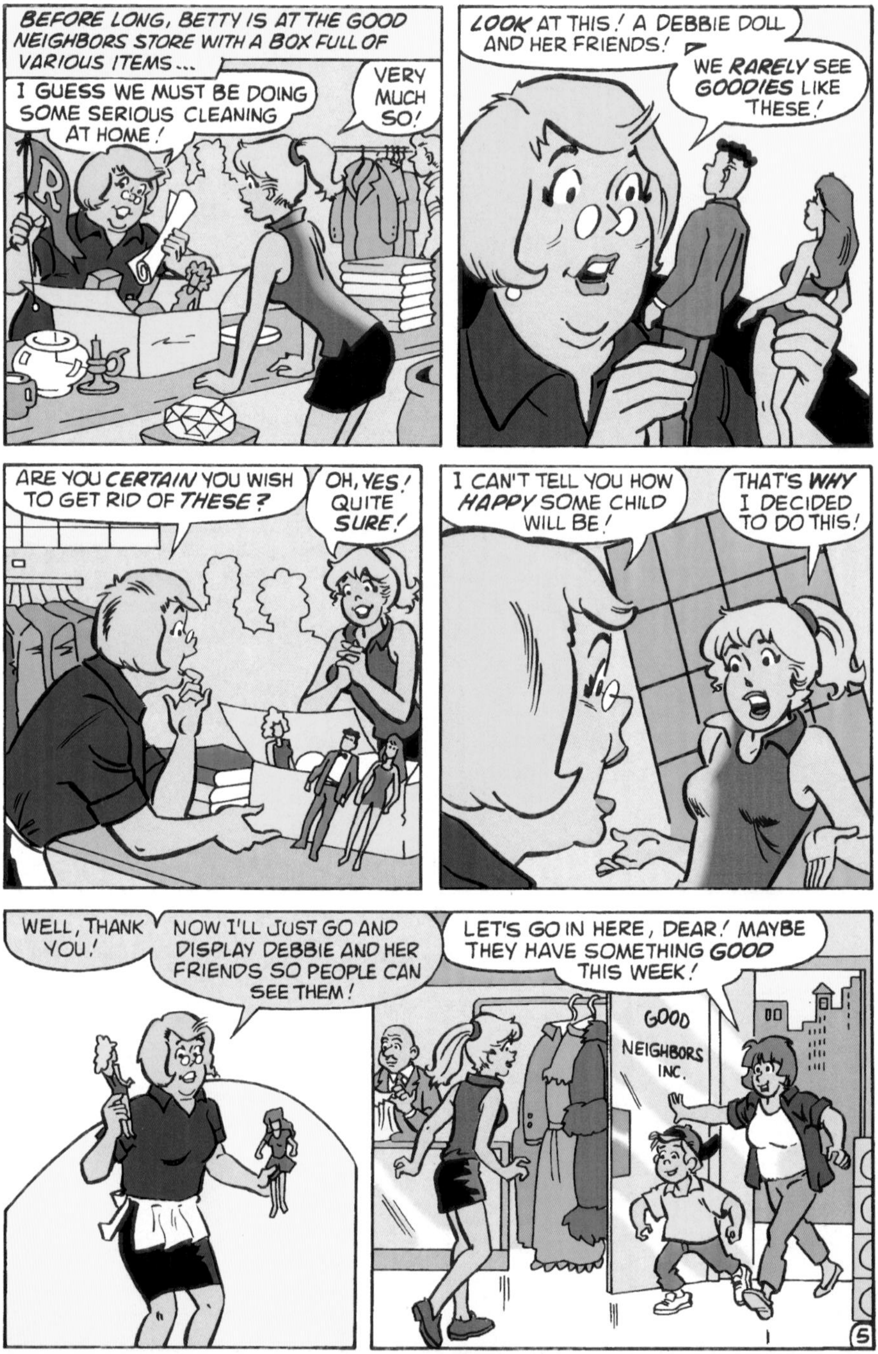
BEFORE LONG, BETTY IS AT THE GOOD NEIGHBORS STORE WITH A BOX FULL OF VARIOUS ITEMS ...
I GUESS WE MUST BE DOING SOME SERIOUS CLEANING AT HOME!
VERY MUCH SO!
LOOK AT THIS! A DEBBIE DOLL AND HER FRIENDS!
WE RARELY SEE GOODIES LIKE THESE!
ARE YOU CERTAIN YOU WISH TO GET RID OF THESE?
OH, YES! QUITE SURE!
I CAN'T TELL YOU HOW HAPPY SOME CHILD WILL BE!
THAT'S WHY I DECIDED TO DO THIS!
WELL, THANK YOU!
NOW I'LL JUST GO AND DISPLAY DEBBIE AND HER FRIENDS SO PEOPLE CAN SEE THEM!
LET'S GO IN HERE, DEAR! MAYBE THEY HAVE SOMETHING GOOD THIS WEEK!
GOOD NEIGHBORS INC.
5

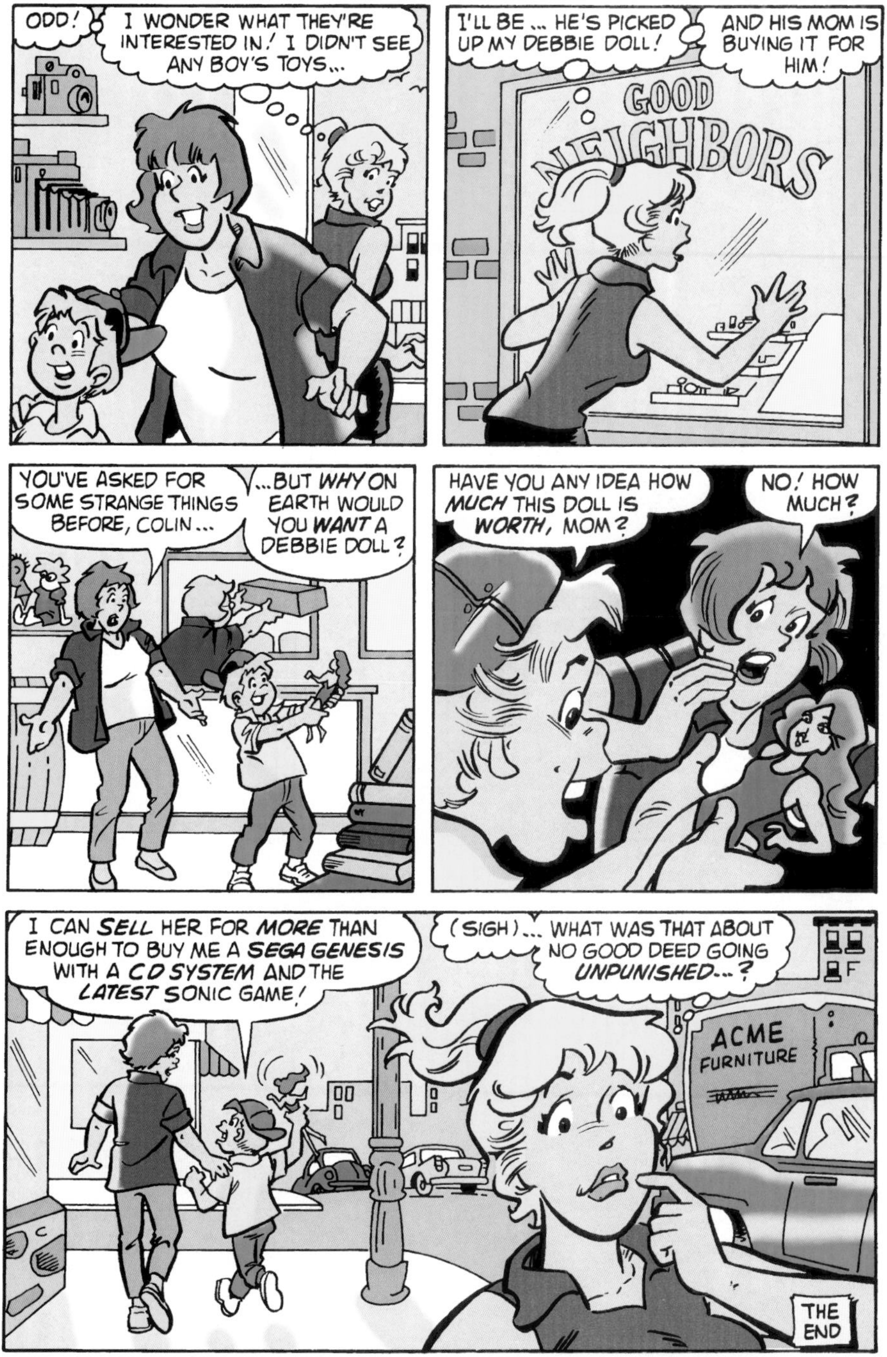
ODD!
I WONDER WHAT THEY'RE INTERESTED IN! I DIDN'T SEE ANY BOY'S TOYS...
I'LL BE ... HE'S PICKED UP MY DEBBIE DOLL!
AND HIS MOM IS BUYING IT FOR HIM!
GOOD NEIGHBORS
YOU'VE ASKED FOR SOME STRANGE THINGS BEFORE, COLIN ...
...BUT WHY ON EARTH WOULD YOU WANT A DEBBIE DOLL?
HAVE YOU ANY IDEA HOW MUCH THIS DOLL IS WORTH, MOM?
NO! HOW MUCH?
I CAN SELL HER FOR MORE THAN ENOUGH TO BUY ME A SEGA GENESIS WITH A CD SYSTEM AND THE LATEST SONIC GAME!
(SIGH)... WHAT WAS THAT ABOUT NO GOOD DEED GOING UNPUNISHED...?
ACME FURNITURE
THE END

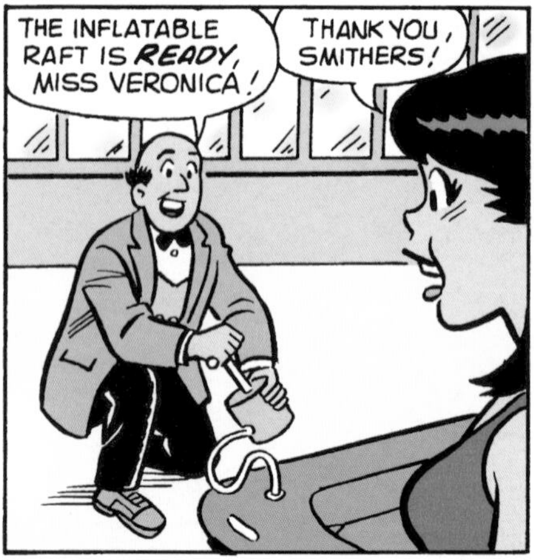
THE INFLATABLE RAFT IS *READY*, MISS VERONICA!
THANK YOU, SMITHERS!

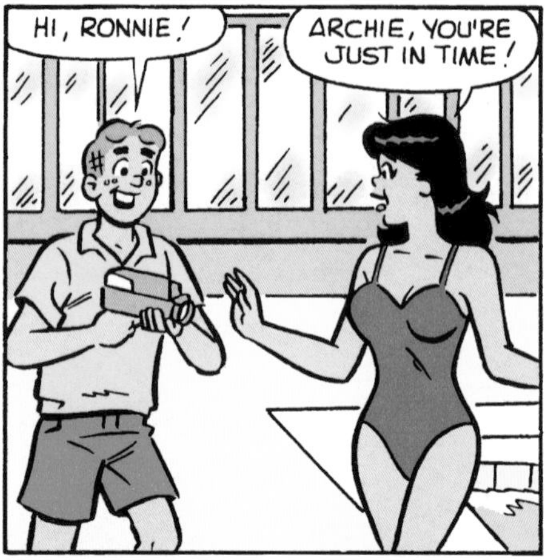
HI, RONNIE!
ARCHIE, YOU'RE JUST IN TIME!

Veronica in "RONNIE'S RAFT-WRESTLING RODEO"

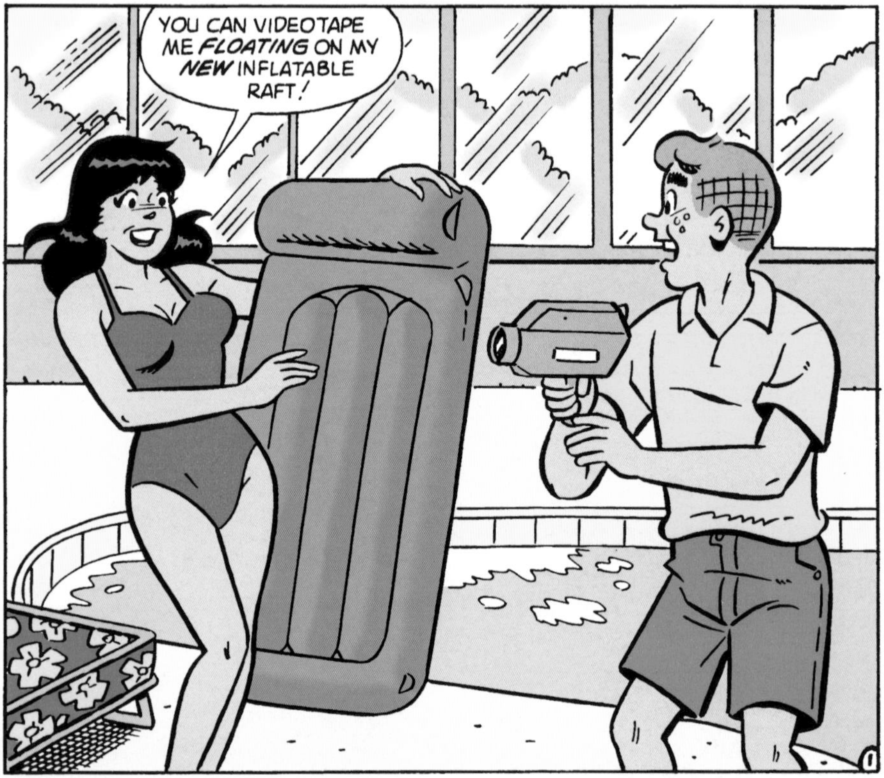
YOU CAN VIDEOTAPE ME *FLOATING* ON MY *NEW* INFLATABLE RAFT!

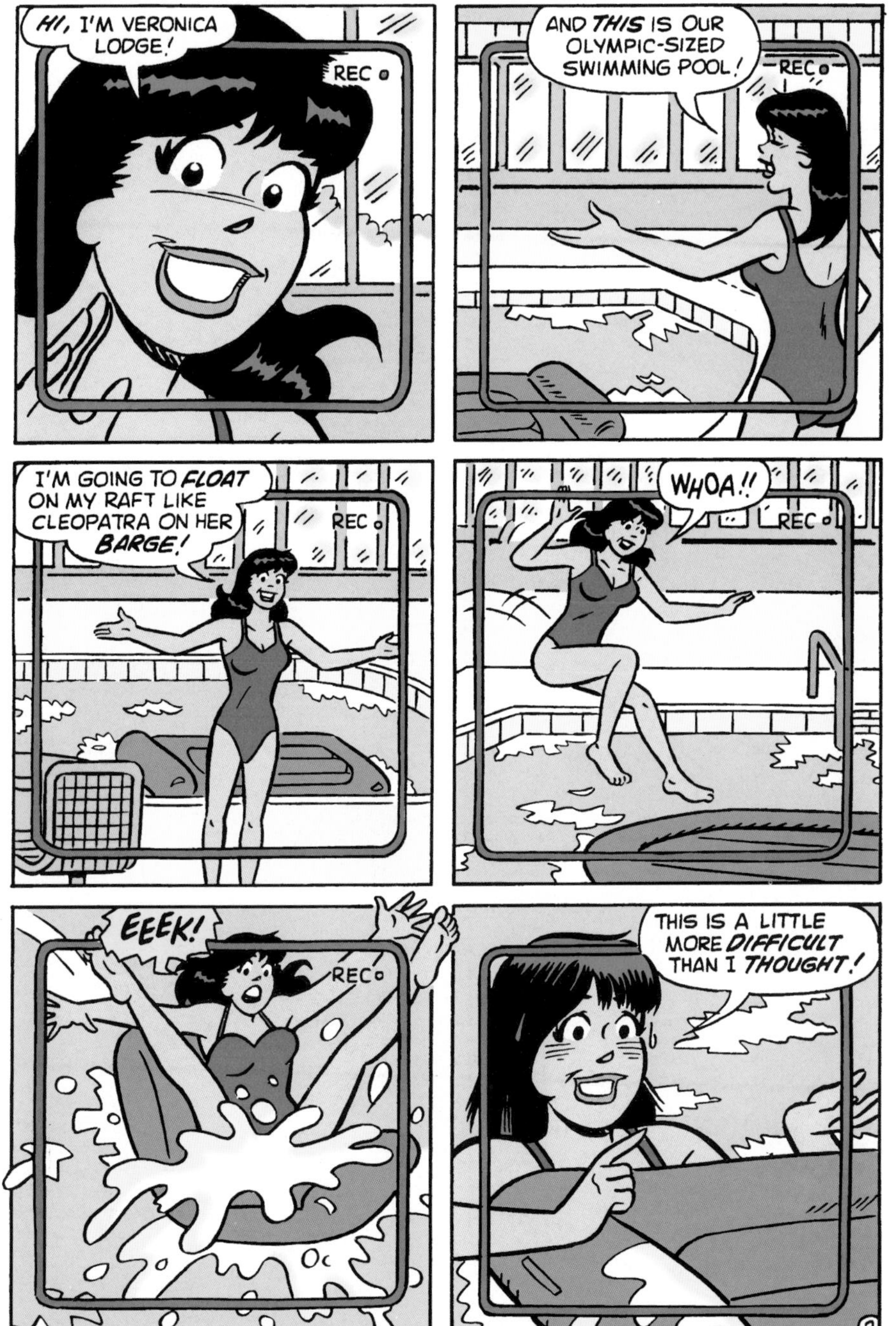
HI, I'M VERONICA LODGE!
REC
AND THIS IS OUR OLYMPIC-SIZED SWIMMING POOL!
REC
I'M GOING TO FLOAT ON MY RAFT LIKE CLEOPATRA ON HER BARGE!
REC
WHOA!!
REC
EEEK!
REC
THIS IS A LITTLE MORE DIFFICULT THAN I THOUGHT!
2

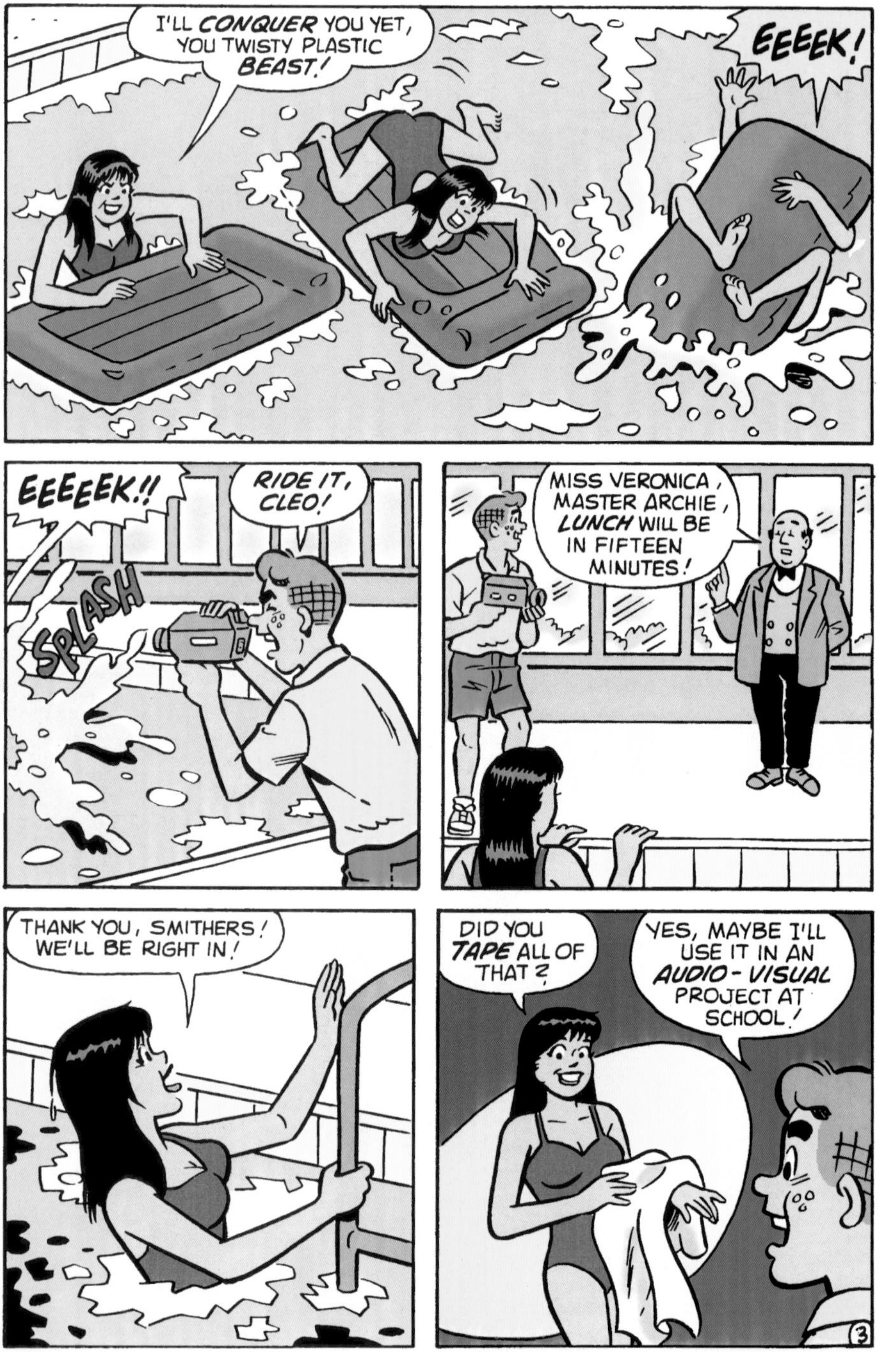
I'LL CONQUER YOU YET, YOU TWISTY PLASTIC BEAST!
EEEEK!
EEEEEK!!
RIDE IT, CLEO!
SPLASH
MISS VERONICA, MASTER ARCHIE, LUNCH WILL BE IN FIFTEEN MINUTES!
THANK YOU, SMITHERS! WE'LL BE RIGHT IN!
DID YOU TAPE ALL OF THAT?
YES, MAYBE I'LL USE IT IN AN AUDIO-VISUAL PROJECT AT SCHOOL!
3

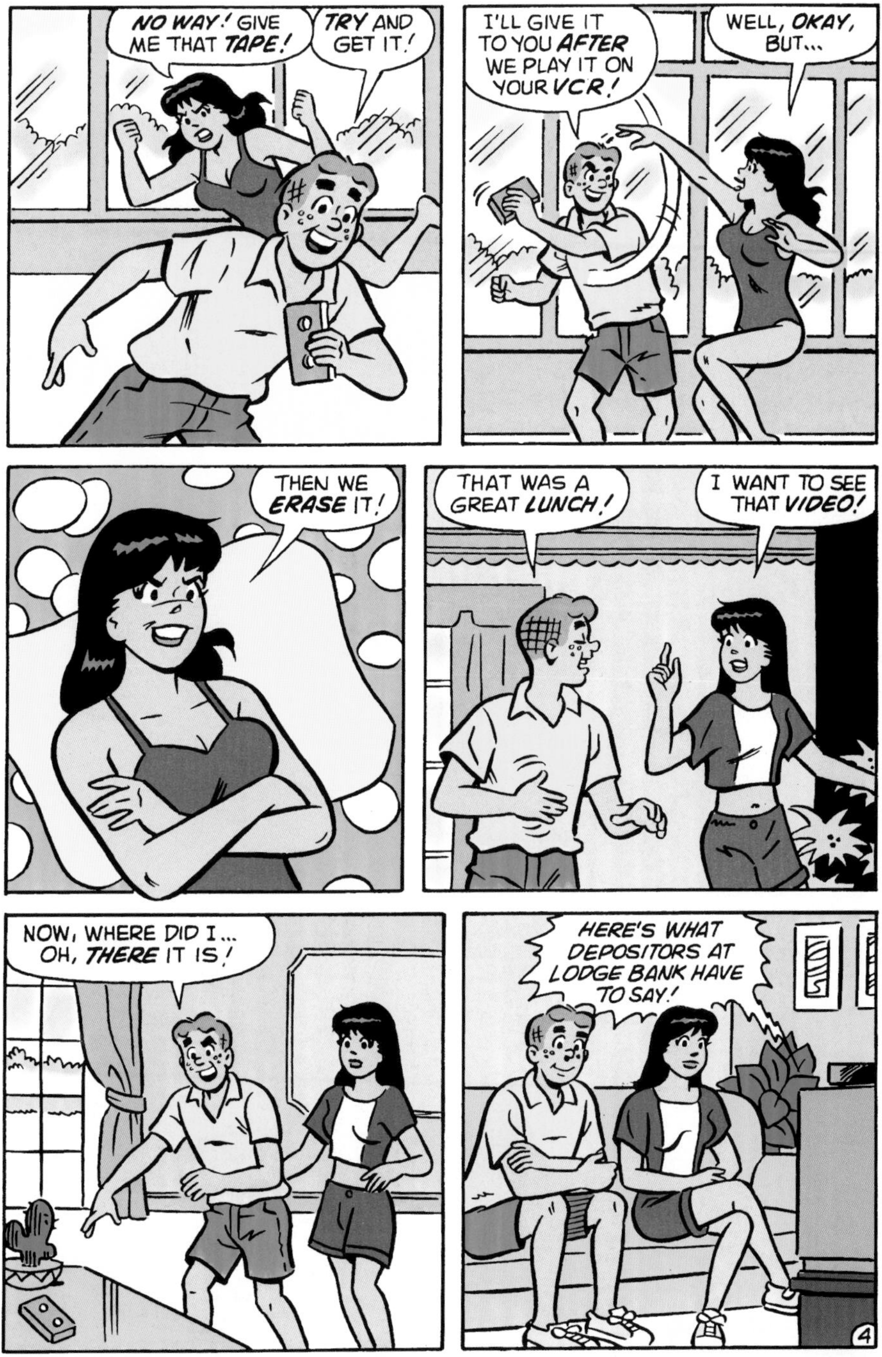
NO WAY! GIVE ME THAT TAPE!
TRY AND GET IT!
I'LL GIVE IT TO YOU AFTER WE PLAY IT ON YOUR VCR!
WELL, OKAY, BUT...
THEN WE ERASE IT!
THAT WAS A GREAT LUNCH!
I WANT TO SEE THAT VIDEO!
NOW, WHERE DID I... OH, THERE IT IS!
HERE'S WHAT DEPOSITORS AT LODGE BANK HAVE TO SAY!
4

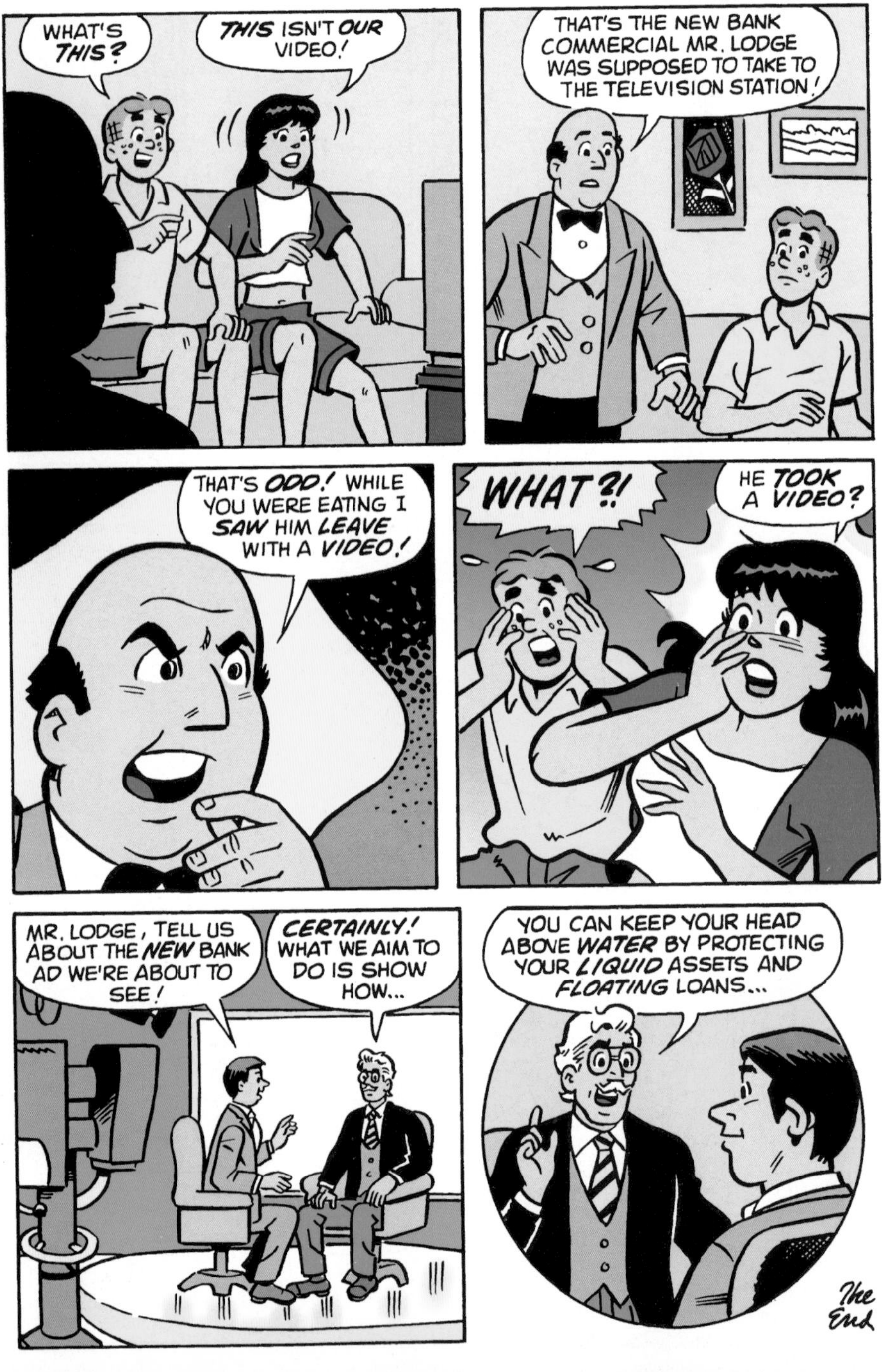
WHAT'S THIS?
THIS ISN'T OUR VIDEO!
THAT'S THE NEW BANK COMMERCIAL MR. LODGE WAS SUPPOSED TO TAKE TO THE TELEVISION STATION!
THAT'S ODD! WHILE YOU WERE EATING I SAW HIM LEAVE WITH A VIDEO!
WHAT?!
HE TOOK A VIDEO?
MR. LODGE, TELL US ABOUT THE NEW BANK AD WE'RE ABOUT TO SEE!
CERTAINLY! WHAT WE AIM TO DO IS SHOW HOW...
YOU CAN KEEP YOUR HEAD ABOVE WATER BY PROTECTING YOUR LIQUID ASSETS AND FLOATING LOANS...
The End

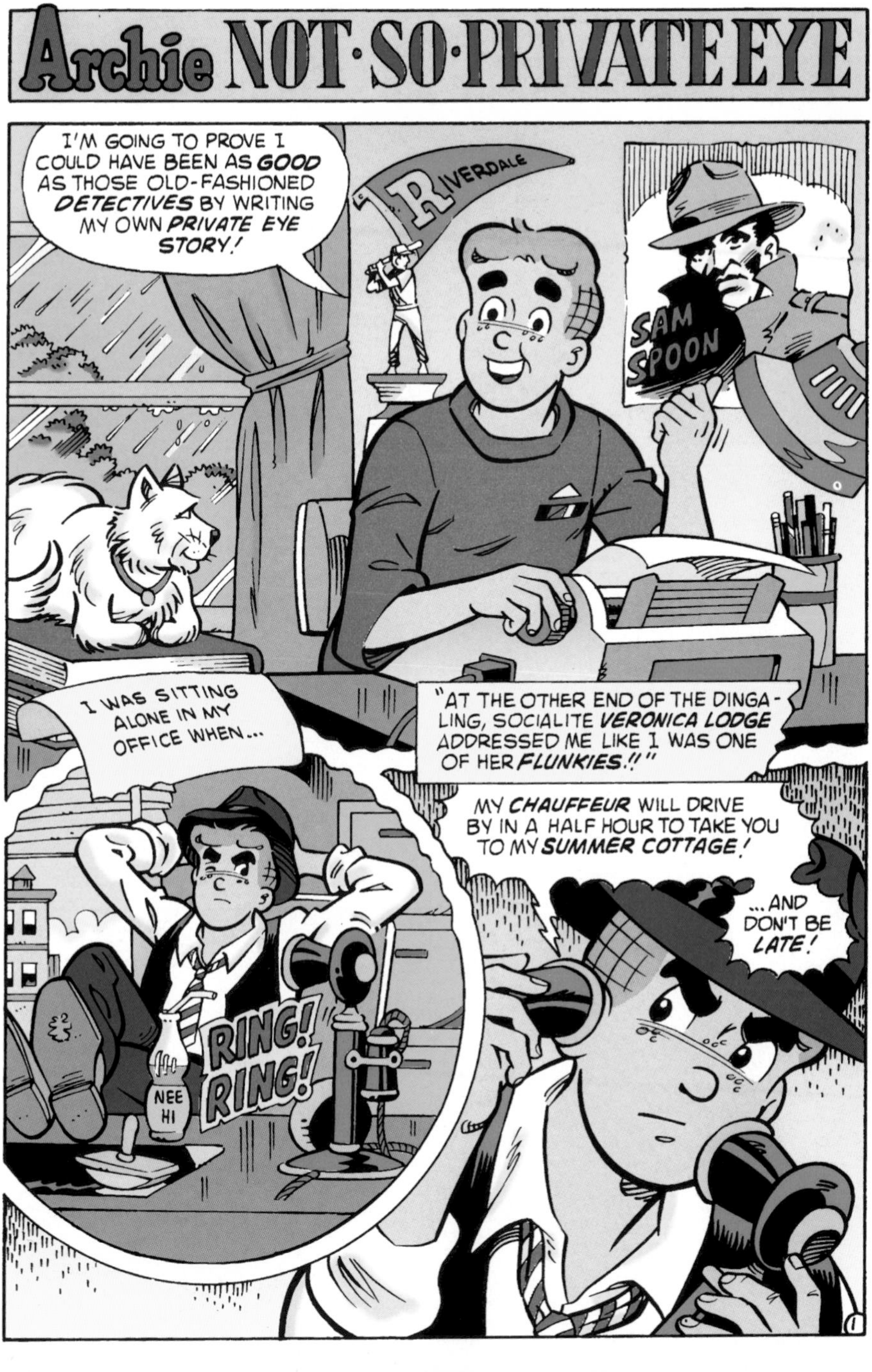
Archie NOT·SO·PRIVATE EYE
I'M GOING TO PROVE I COULD HAVE BEEN AS GOOD AS THOSE OLD-FASHIONED DETECTIVES BY WRITING MY OWN PRIVATE EYE STORY!
RIVERDALE
SAM SPOON
I WAS SITTING ALONE IN MY OFFICE WHEN...
"AT THE OTHER END OF THE DINGA-LING, SOCIALITE VERONICA LODGE ADDRESSED ME LIKE I WAS ONE OF HER FLUNKIES!!"
RING! RING!
NEE HI
MY CHAUFFEUR WILL DRIVE BY IN A HALF HOUR TO TAKE YOU TO MY SUMMER COTTAGE!
...AND DON'T BE LATE!

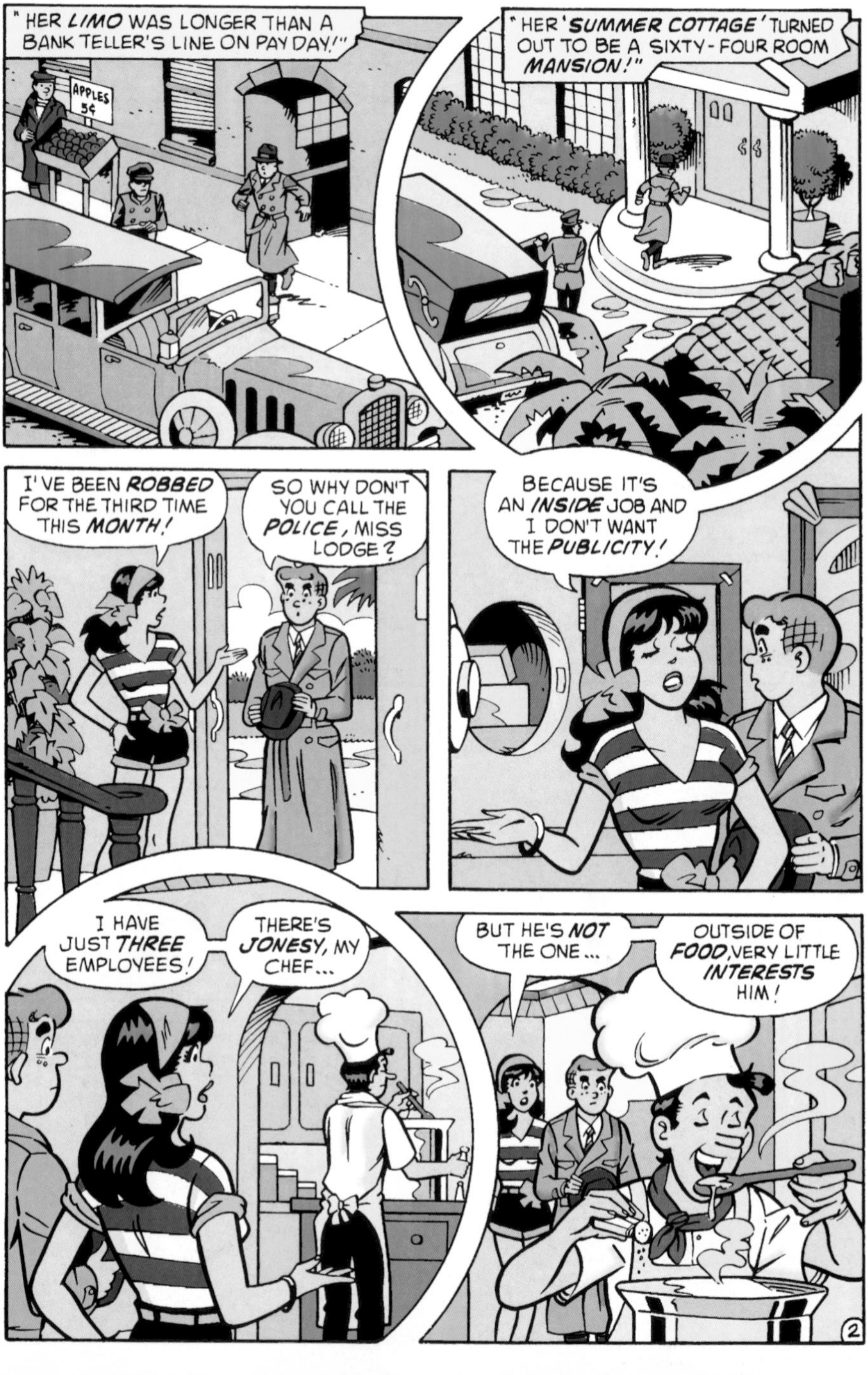
" HER LIMO WAS LONGER THAN A BANK TELLER'S LINE ON PAY DAY!"
APPLES 5¢
" HER 'SUMMER COTTAGE' TURNED OUT TO BE A SIXTY-FOUR ROOM MANSION!"
I'VE BEEN ROBBED FOR THE THIRD TIME THIS MONTH!
SO WHY DON'T YOU CALL THE POLICE, MISS LODGE?
BECAUSE IT'S AN INSIDE JOB AND I DON'T WANT THE PUBLICITY!
I HAVE JUST THREE EMPLOYEES!
THERE'S JONESY, MY CHEF...
BUT HE'S NOT THE ONE...
OUTSIDE OF FOOD, VERY LITTLE INTERESTS HIM!
2

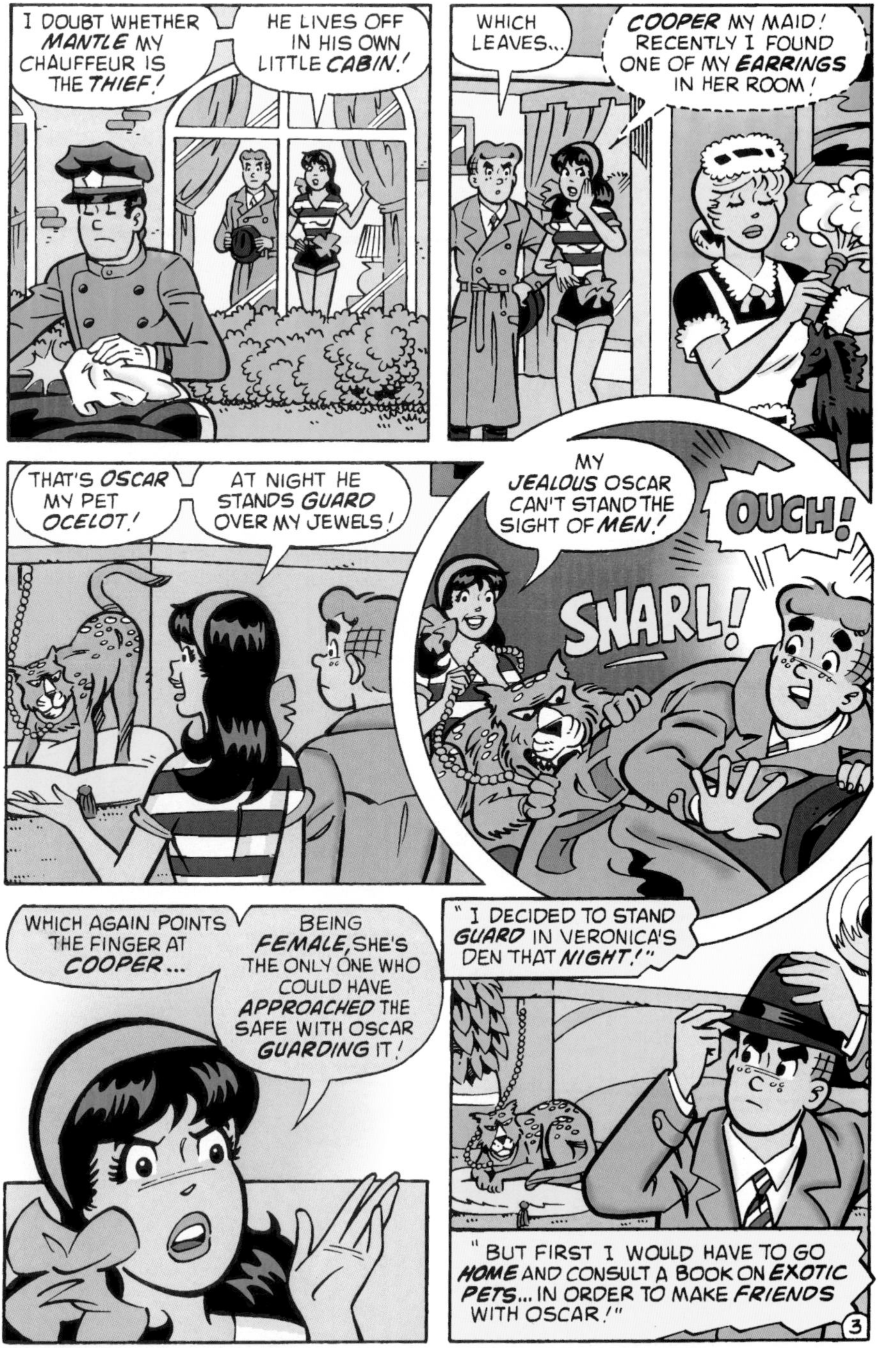
I DOUBT WHETHER MANTLE MY CHAUFFEUR IS THE THIEF!
HE LIVES OFF IN HIS OWN LITTLE CABIN!
WHICH LEAVES...
COOPER MY MAID! RECENTLY I FOUND ONE OF MY EARRINGS IN HER ROOM!
THAT'S OSCAR MY PET OCELOT!
AT NIGHT HE STANDS GUARD OVER MY JEWELS!
MY JEALOUS OSCAR CAN'T STAND THE SIGHT OF MEN!
OUCH!
SNARL!
WHICH AGAIN POINTS THE FINGER AT COOPER...
BEING FEMALE, SHE'S THE ONLY ONE WHO COULD HAVE APPROACHED THE SAFE WITH OSCAR GUARDING IT!
" I DECIDED TO STAND GUARD IN VERONICA'S DEN THAT NIGHT!"
" BUT FIRST I WOULD HAVE TO GO HOME AND CONSULT A BOOK ON EXOTIC PETS... IN ORDER TO MAKE FRIENDS WITH OSCAR!"
3

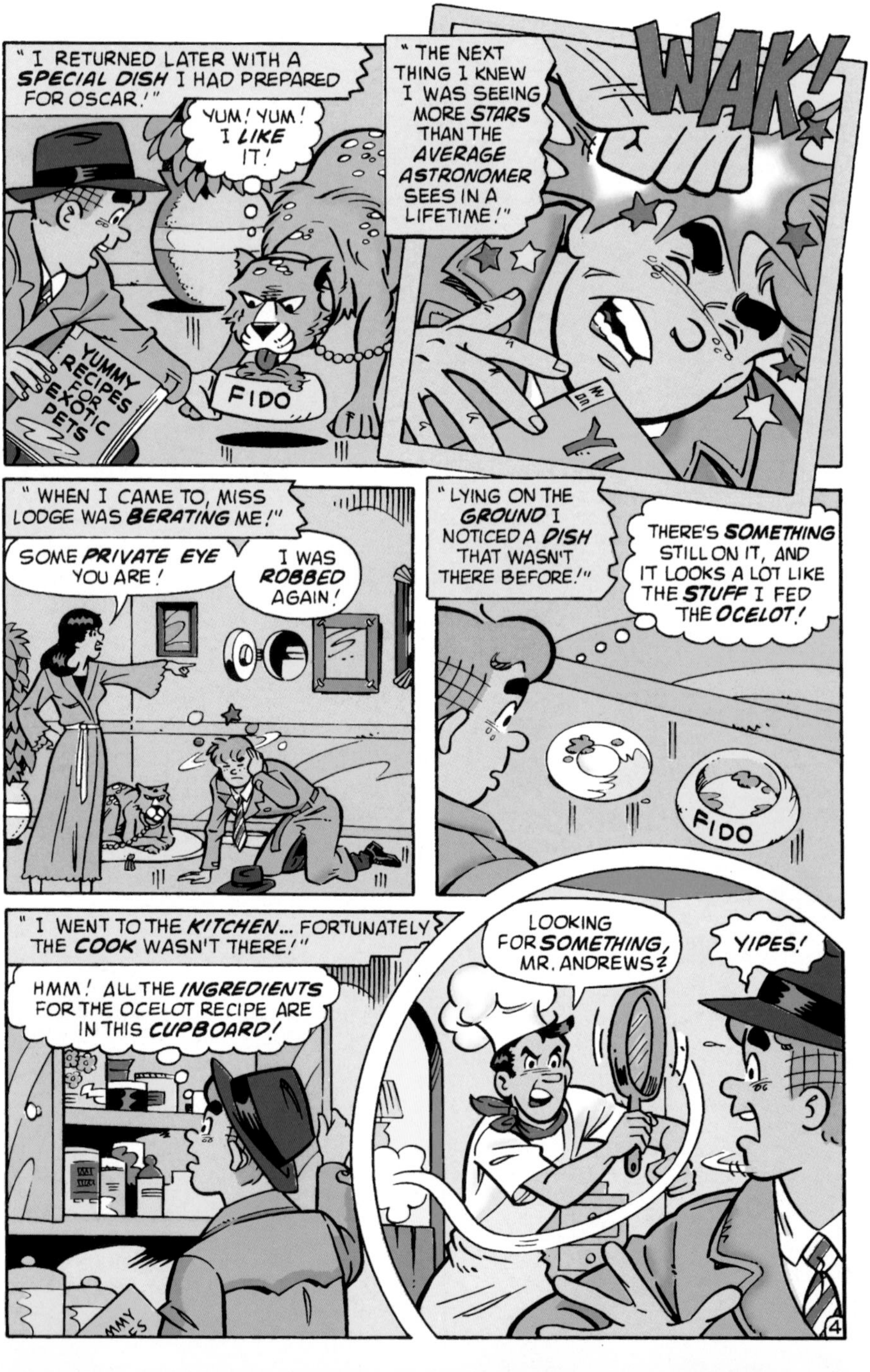
" I RETURNED LATER WITH A SPECIAL DISH I HAD PREPARED FOR OSCAR!"
YUM! YUM! I LIKE IT!
YUMMY RECIPES FOR EXOTIC PETS
FIDO
" THE NEXT THING I KNEW I WAS SEEING MORE STARS THAN THE AVERAGE ASTRONOMER SEES IN A LIFETIME!"
WAK!
" WHEN I CAME TO, MISS LODGE WAS BERATING ME!"
SOME PRIVATE EYE YOU ARE!
I WAS ROBBED AGAIN!
" LYING ON THE GROUND I NOTICED A DISH THAT WASN'T THERE BEFORE!"
THERE'S SOMETHING STILL ON IT, AND IT LOOKS A LOT LIKE THE STUFF I FED THE OCELOT!
FIDO
" I WENT TO THE KITCHEN... FORTUNATELY THE COOK WASN'T THERE!"
HMM! ALL THE INGREDIENTS FOR THE OCELOT RECIPE ARE IN THIS CUPBOARD!
LOOKING FOR SOMETHING, MR. ANDREWS?
YIPES!
4

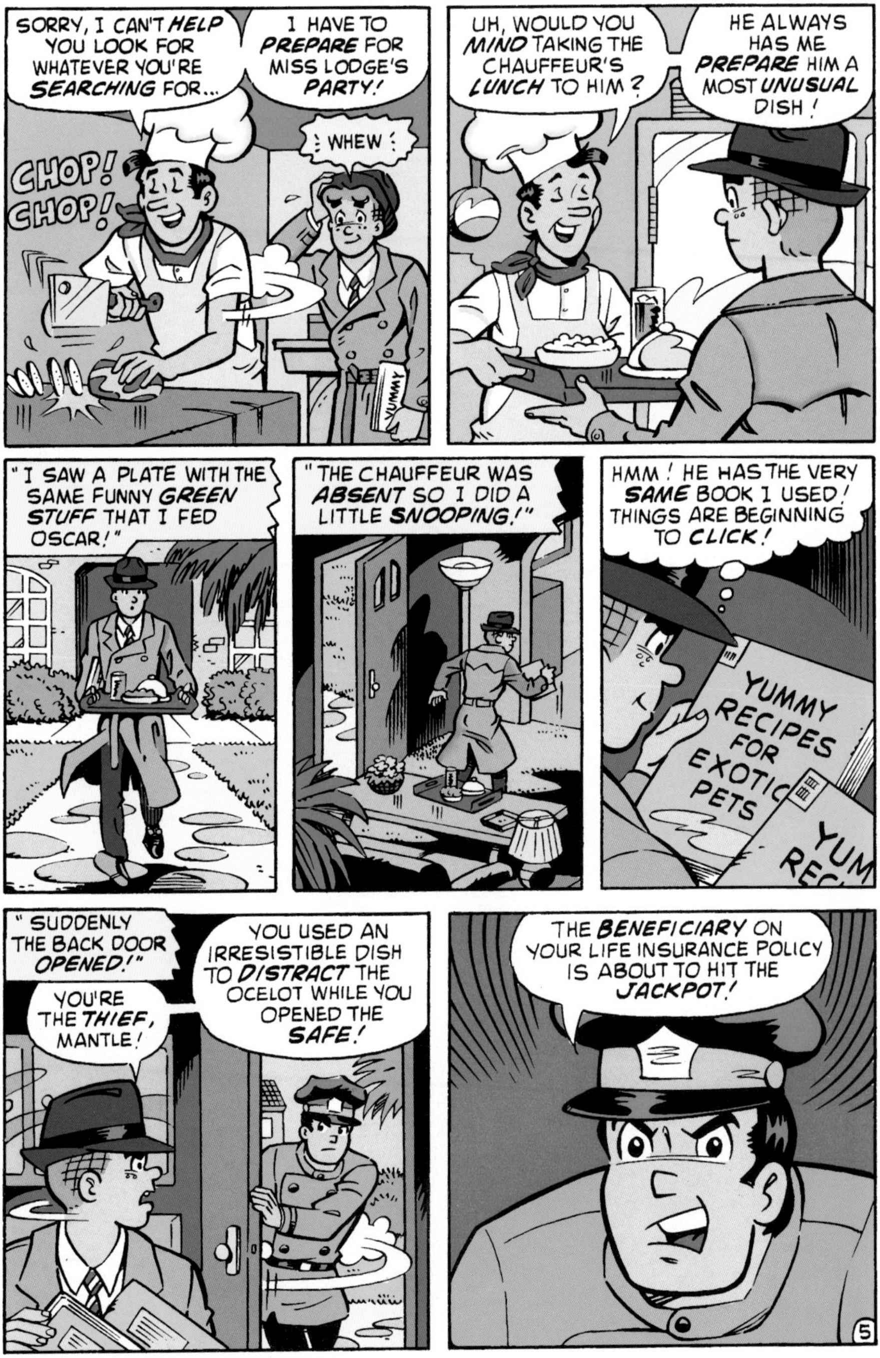
SORRY, I CAN'T HELP YOU LOOK FOR WHATEVER YOU'RE SEARCHING FOR...
I HAVE TO PREPARE FOR MISS LODGE'S PARTY!
CHOP! CHOP!
WHEW
YUMMY
UH, WOULD YOU MIND TAKING THE CHAUFFEUR'S LUNCH TO HIM?
HE ALWAYS HAS ME PREPARE HIM A MOST UNUSUAL DISH!
"I SAW A PLATE WITH THE SAME FUNNY GREEN STUFF THAT I FED OSCAR!"
"THE CHAUFFEUR WAS ABSENT SO I DID A LITTLE SNOOPING!"
HMM! HE HAS THE VERY SAME BOOK I USED! THINGS ARE BEGINNING TO CLICK!
YUMMY RECIPES FOR EXOTIC PETS
"SUDDENLY THE BACK DOOR OPENED!"
YOU'RE THE THIEF, MANTLE!
YOU USED AN IRRESISTIBLE DISH TO DISTRACT THE OCELOT WHILE YOU OPENED THE SAFE!
THE BENEFICIARY ON YOUR LIFE INSURANCE POLICY IS ABOUT TO HIT THE JACKPOT!
5

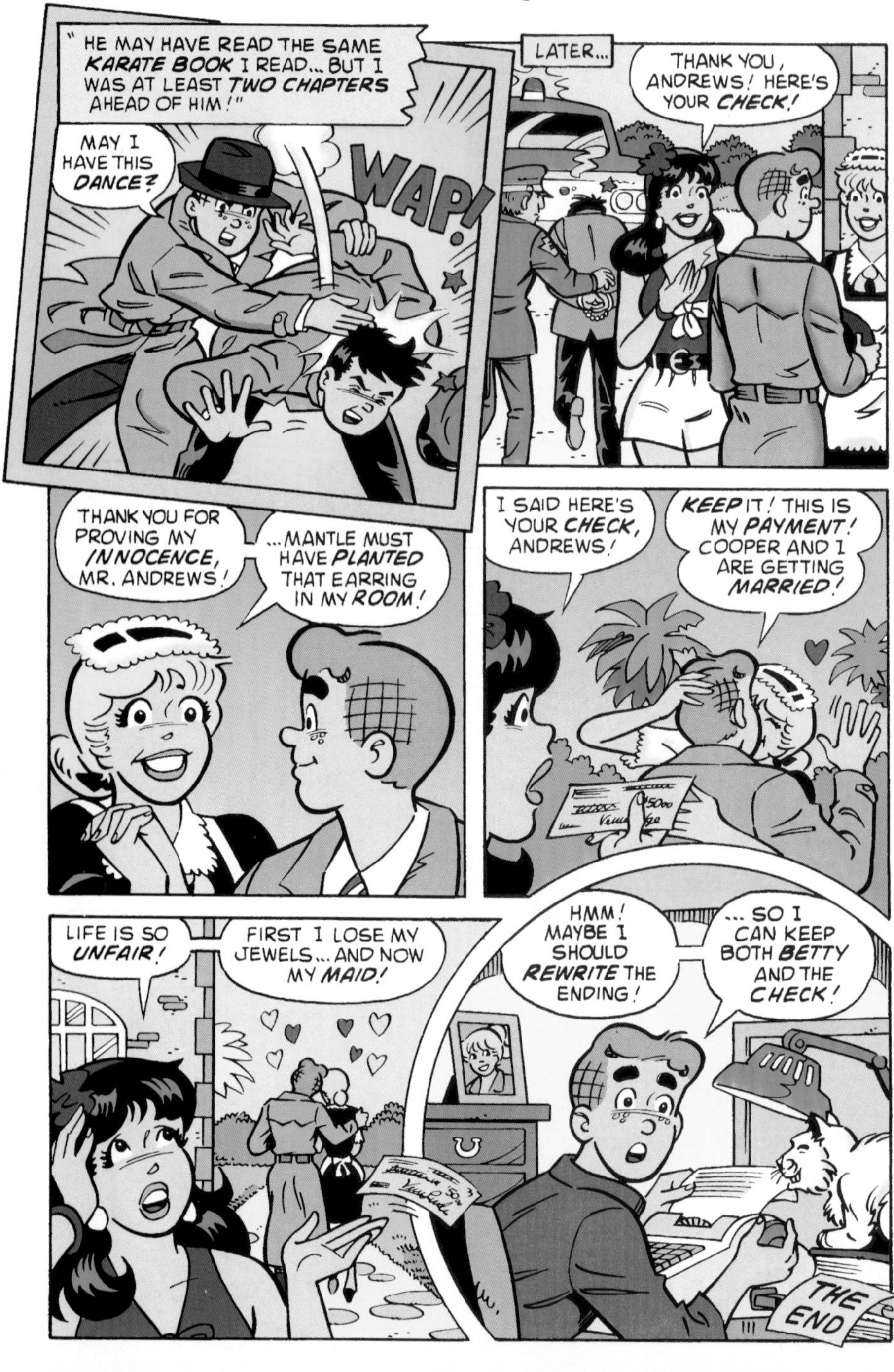
" HE MAY HAVE READ THE SAME KARATE BOOK I READ... BUT I WAS AT LEAST TWO CHAPTERS AHEAD OF HIM!"
MAY I HAVE THIS DANCE?
WAP!
LATER...
THANK YOU, ANDREWS! HERE'S YOUR CHECK!
THANK YOU FOR PROVING MY INNOCENCE, MR. ANDREWS!
...MANTLE MUST HAVE PLANTED THAT EARRING IN MY ROOM!
I SAID HERE'S YOUR CHECK, ANDREWS!
KEEP IT! THIS IS MY PAYMENT! COOPER AND I ARE GETTING MARRIED!
LIFE IS SO UNFAIR!
FIRST I LOSE MY JEWELS... AND NOW MY MAID!
HMM! MAYBE I SHOULD REWRITE THE ENDING!
... SO I CAN KEEP BOTH BETTY AND THE CHECK!
THE END

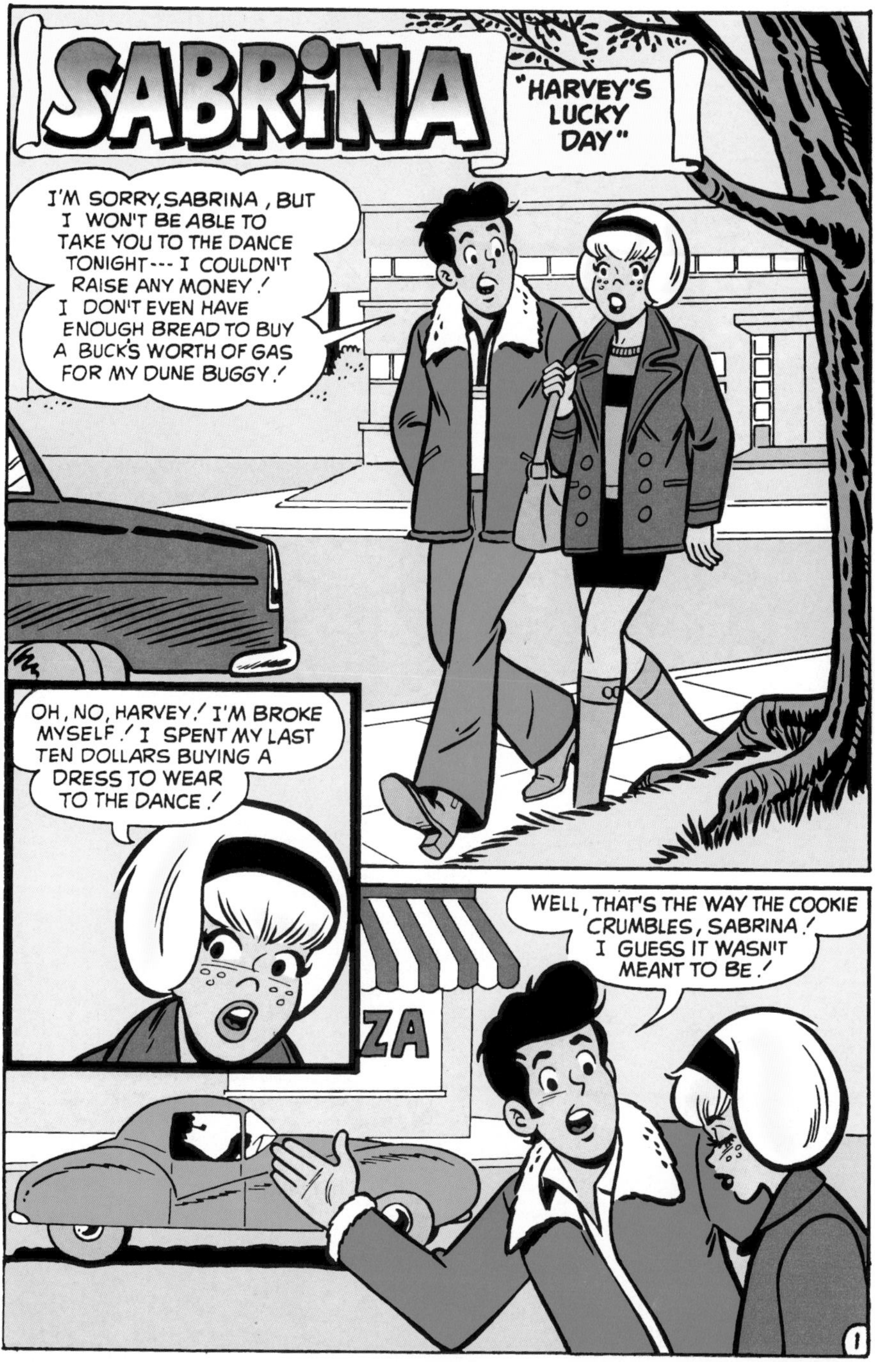
SABRINA
"HARVEY'S LUCKY DAY"
I'M SORRY, SABRINA, BUT I WON'T BE ABLE TO TAKE YOU TO THE DANCE TONIGHT--- I COULDN'T RAISE ANY MONEY! I DON'T EVEN HAVE ENOUGH BREAD TO BUY A BUCK'S WORTH OF GAS FOR MY DUNE BUGGY!
OH, NO, HARVEY! I'M BROKE MYSELF! I SPENT MY LAST TEN DOLLARS BUYING A DRESS TO WEAR TO THE DANCE!
ZA
WELL, THAT'S THE WAY THE COOKIE CRUMBLES, SABRINA! I GUESS IT WASN'T MEANT TO BE!
1

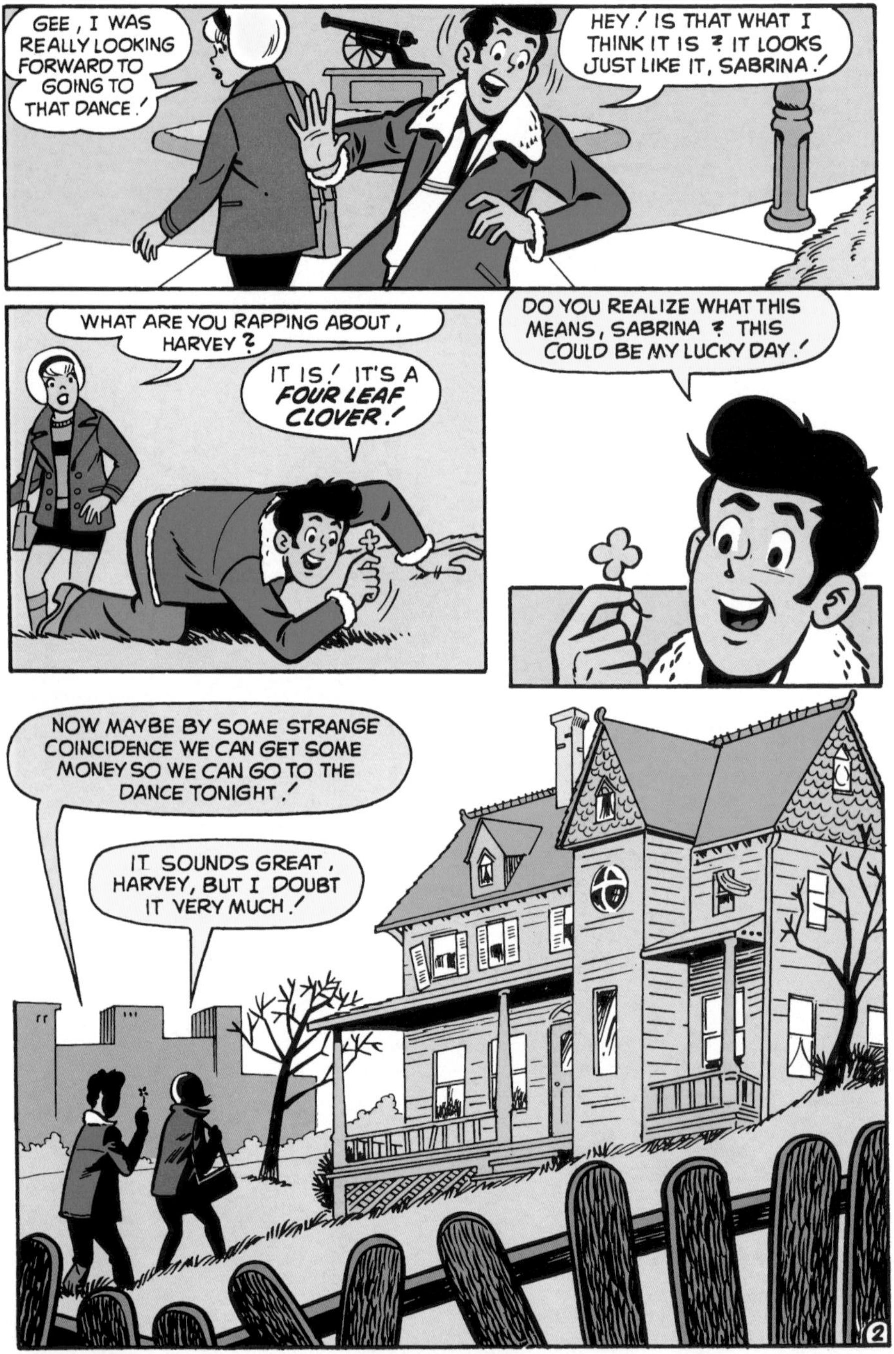
GEE, I WAS REALLY LOOKING FORWARD TO GOING TO THAT DANCE!
HEY! IS THAT WHAT I THINK IT IS? IT LOOKS JUST LIKE IT, SABRINA!
WHAT ARE YOU RAPPING ABOUT, HARVEY?
IT IS! IT'S A FOUR LEAF CLOVER!
DO YOU REALIZE WHAT THIS MEANS, SABRINA? THIS COULD BE MY LUCKY DAY!
NOW MAYBE BY SOME STRANGE COINCIDENCE WE CAN GET SOME MONEY SO WE CAN GO TO THE DANCE TONIGHT!
IT SOUNDS GREAT, HARVEY, BUT I DOUBT IT VERY MUCH!
2

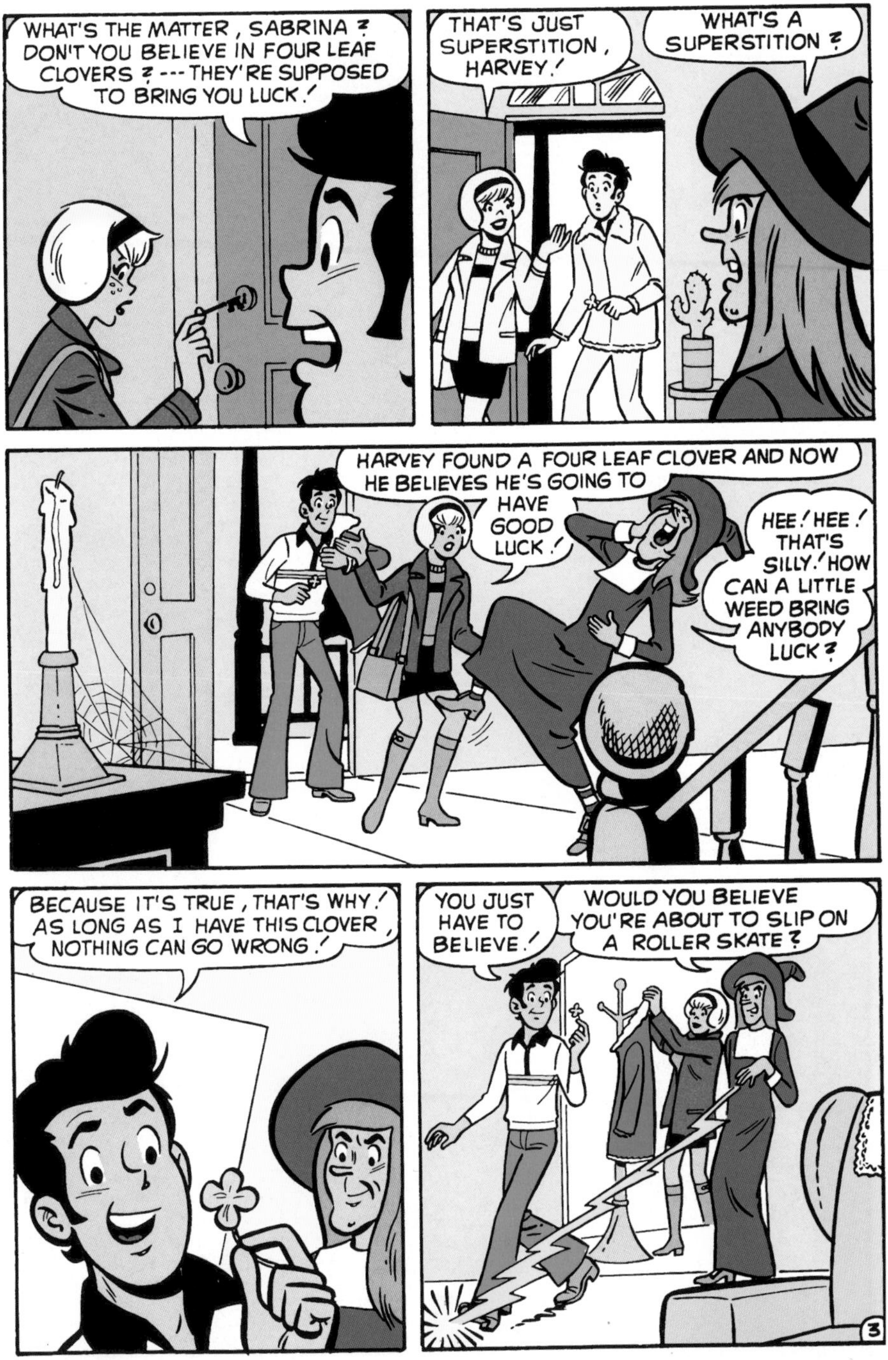
WHAT'S THE MATTER, SABRINA? DON'T YOU BELIEVE IN FOUR LEAF CLOVERS? --- THEY'RE SUPPOSED TO BRING YOU LUCK!
THAT'S JUST SUPERSTITION, HARVEY!
WHAT'S A SUPERSTITION?
HARVEY FOUND A FOUR LEAF CLOVER AND NOW HE BELIEVES HE'S GOING TO HAVE GOOD LUCK!
HEE! HEE! THAT'S SILLY! HOW CAN A LITTLE WEED BRING ANYBODY LUCK?
BECAUSE IT'S TRUE, THAT'S WHY! AS LONG AS I HAVE THIS CLOVER, NOTHING CAN GO WRONG!
YOU JUST HAVE TO BELIEVE!
WOULD YOU BELIEVE YOU'RE ABOUT TO SLIP ON A ROLLER SKATE?
3

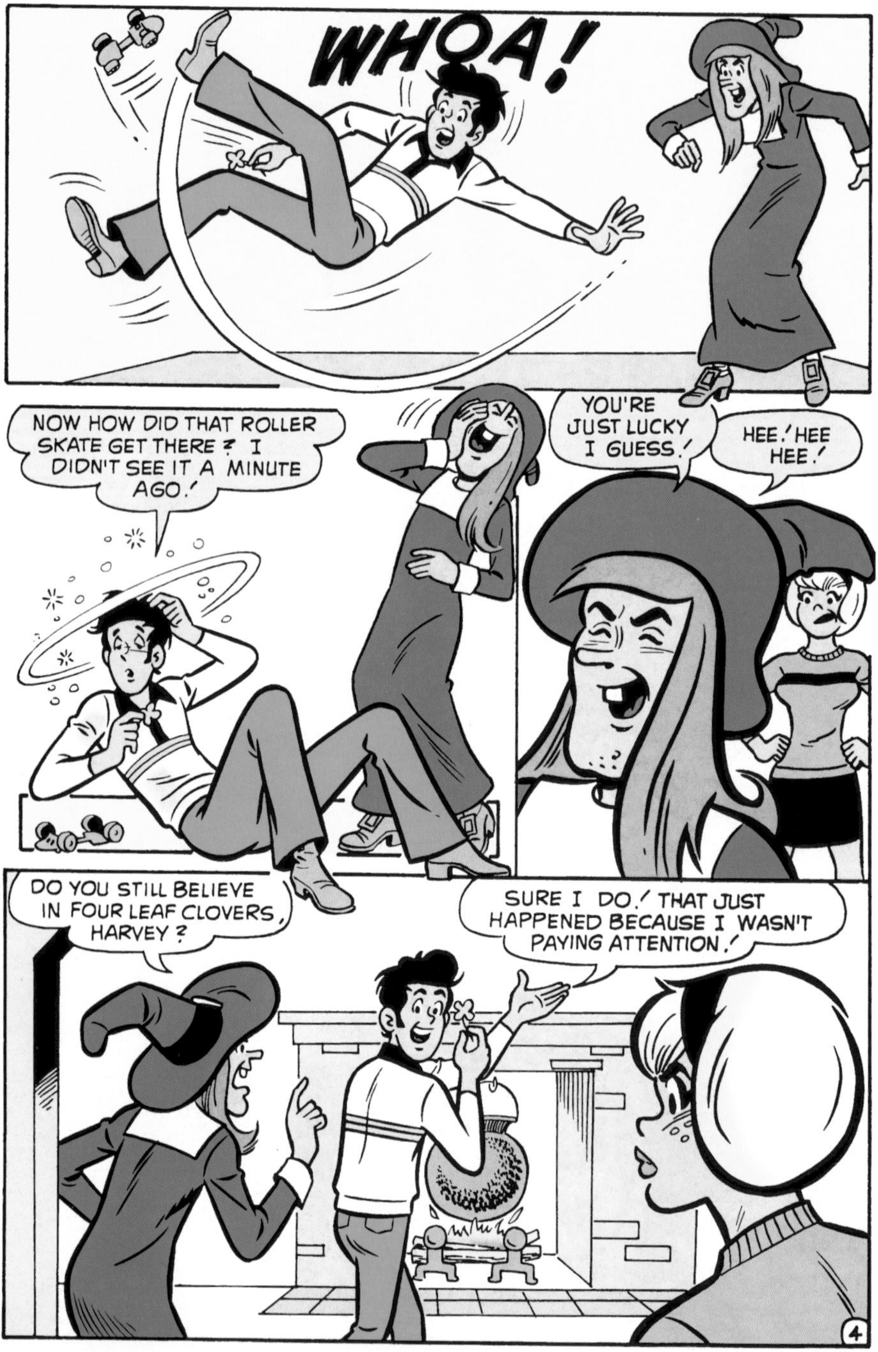
WHOA!
NOW HOW DID THAT ROLLER SKATE GET THERE? I DIDN'T SEE IT A MINUTE AGO!
YOU'RE JUST LUCKY I GUESS!
HEE! HEE HEE!
DO YOU STILL BELIEVE IN FOUR LEAF CLOVERS, HARVEY?
SURE I DO! THAT JUST HAPPENED BECAUSE I WASN'T PAYING ATTENTION!
4

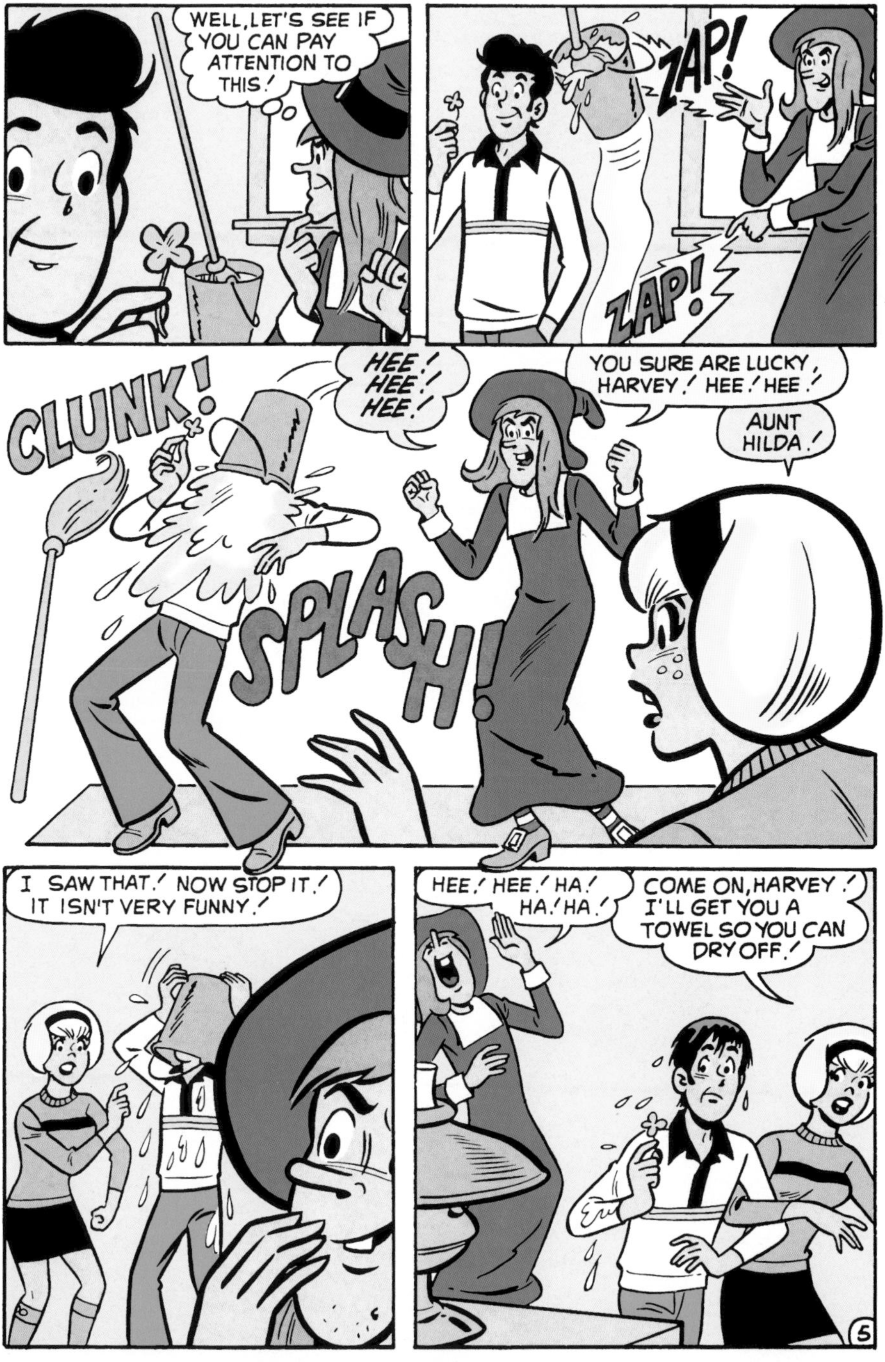
WELL, LET'S SEE IF YOU CAN PAY ATTENTION TO THIS!
ZAP!
ZAP!
CLUNK!
HEE! HEE! HEE!
YOU SURE ARE LUCKY, HARVEY! HEE! HEE!
AUNT HILDA!
SPLASH!
I SAW THAT! NOW STOP IT! IT ISN'T VERY FUNNY!
HEE! HEE! HA! HA! HA!
COME ON, HARVEY! I'LL GET YOU A TOWEL SO YOU CAN DRY OFF!
5

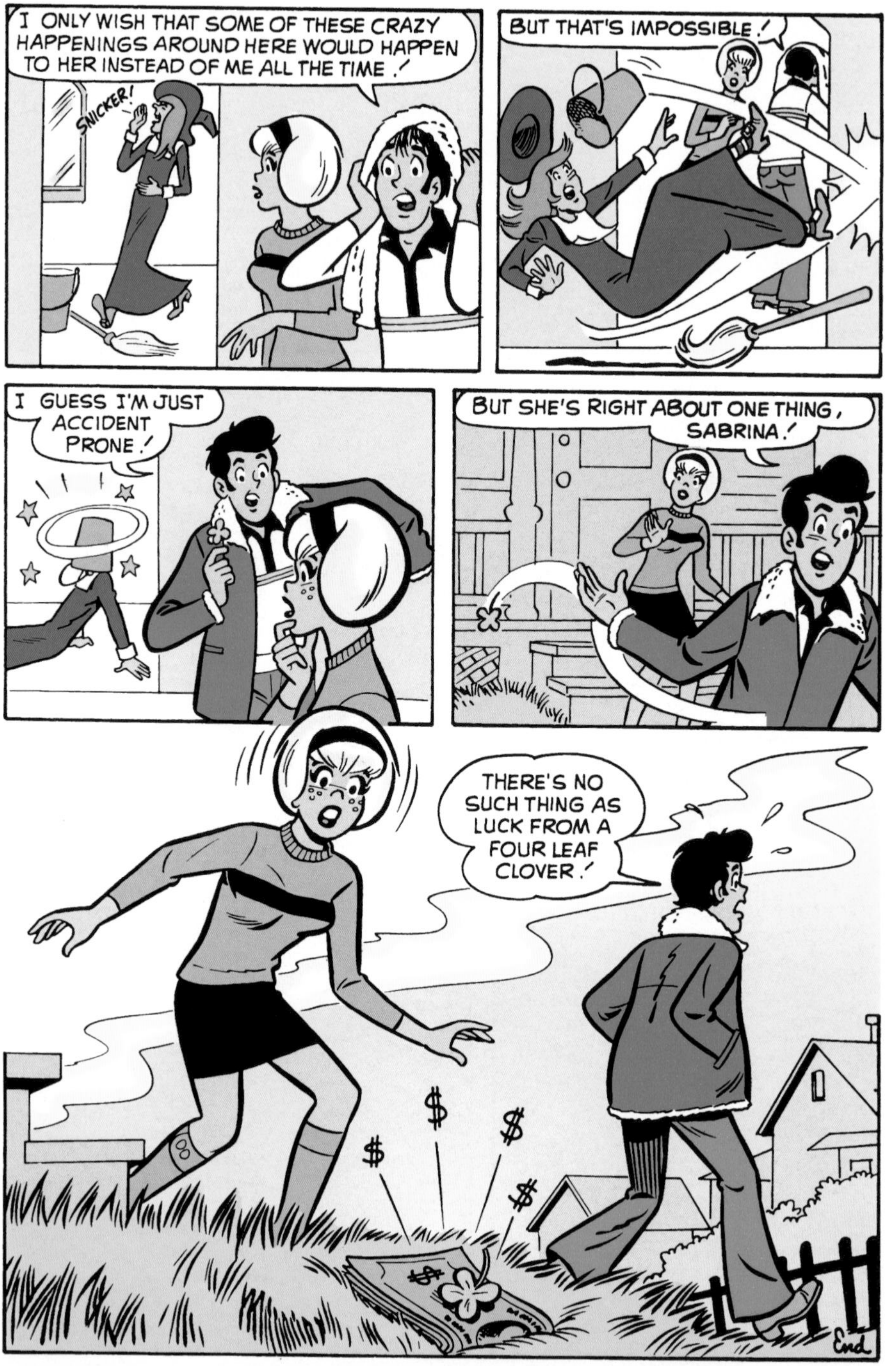
I ONLY WISH THAT SOME OF THESE CRAZY HAPPENINGS AROUND HERE WOULD HAPPEN TO HER INSTEAD OF ME ALL THE TIME!
SNICKER!
BUT THAT'S IMPOSSIBLE!
I GUESS I'M JUST ACCIDENT PRONE!
BUT SHE'S RIGHT ABOUT ONE THING, SABRINA!
THERE'S NO SUCH THING AS LUCK FROM A FOUR LEAF CLOVER!
$
$
$
$
End

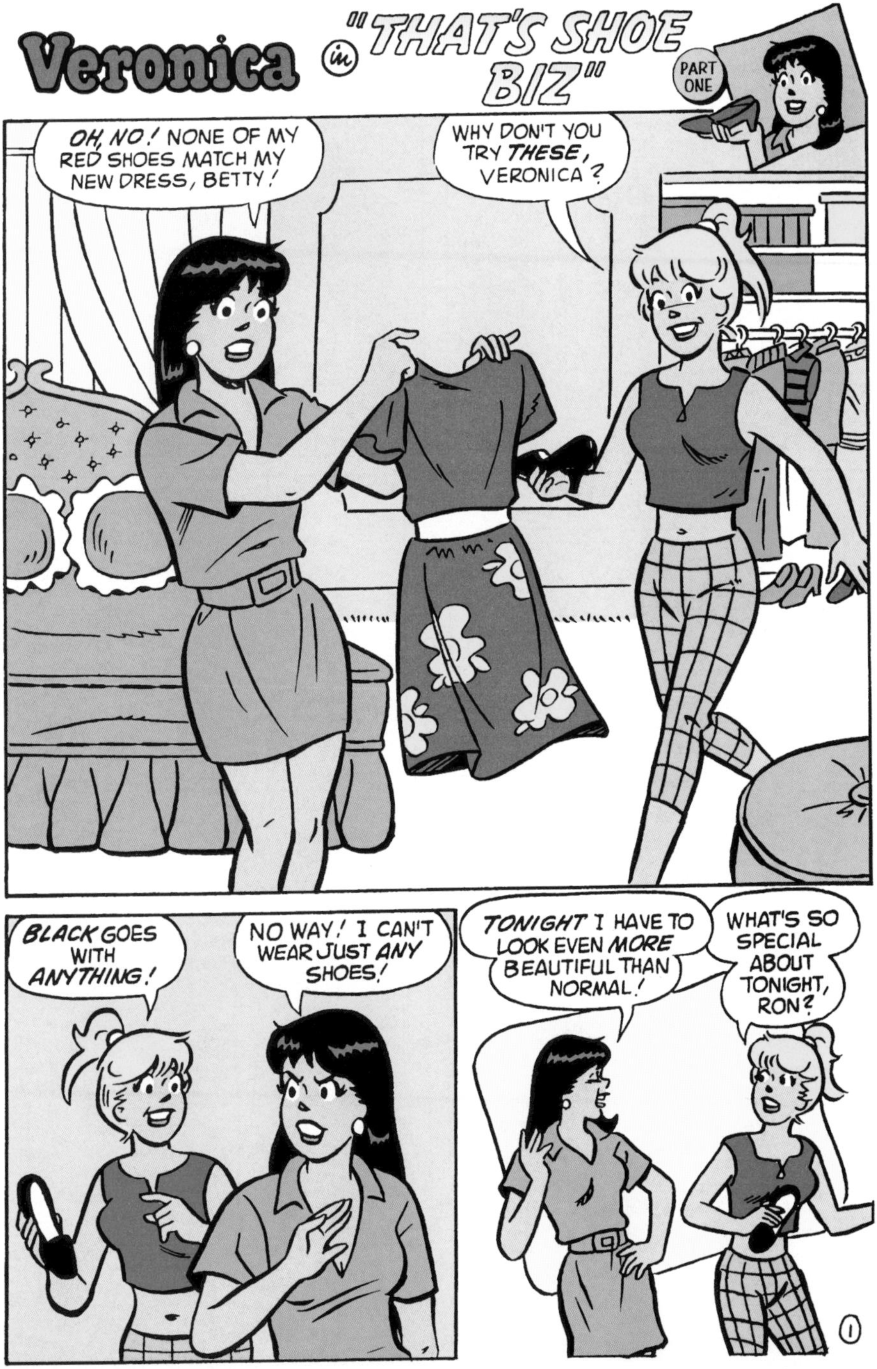
Veronica in "THAT'S SHOE BIZ"
PART ONE
OH, NO! NONE OF MY RED SHOES MATCH MY NEW DRESS, BETTY!
WHY DON'T YOU TRY THESE, VERONICA?
BLACK GOES WITH ANYTHING!
NO WAY! I CAN'T WEAR JUST ANY SHOES!
TONIGHT I HAVE TO LOOK EVEN MORE BEAUTIFUL THAN NORMAL!
WHAT'S SO SPECIAL ABOUT TONIGHT, RON?
1

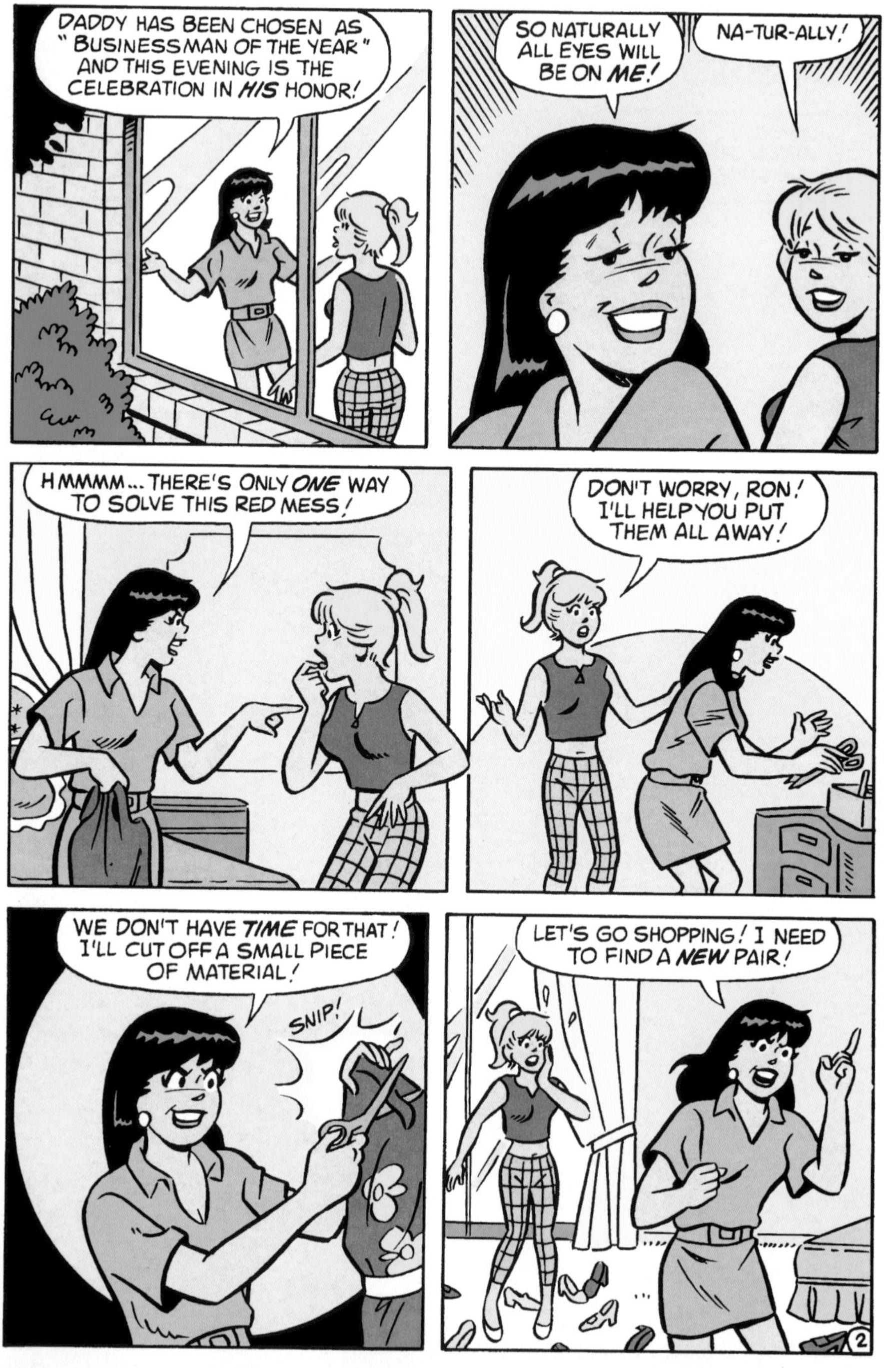
DADDY HAS BEEN CHOSEN AS "BUSINESSMAN OF THE YEAR" AND THIS EVENING IS THE CELEBRATION IN HIS HONOR!
SO NATURALLY ALL EYES WILL BE ON ME!
NA-TUR-ALLY!
HMMMM... THERE'S ONLY ONE WAY TO SOLVE THIS RED MESS!
DON'T WORRY, RON! I'LL HELP YOU PUT THEM ALL AWAY!
WE DON'T HAVE TIME FOR THAT! I'LL CUT OFF A SMALL PIECE OF MATERIAL!
SNIP!
LET'S GO SHOPPING! I NEED TO FIND A NEW PAIR!
2

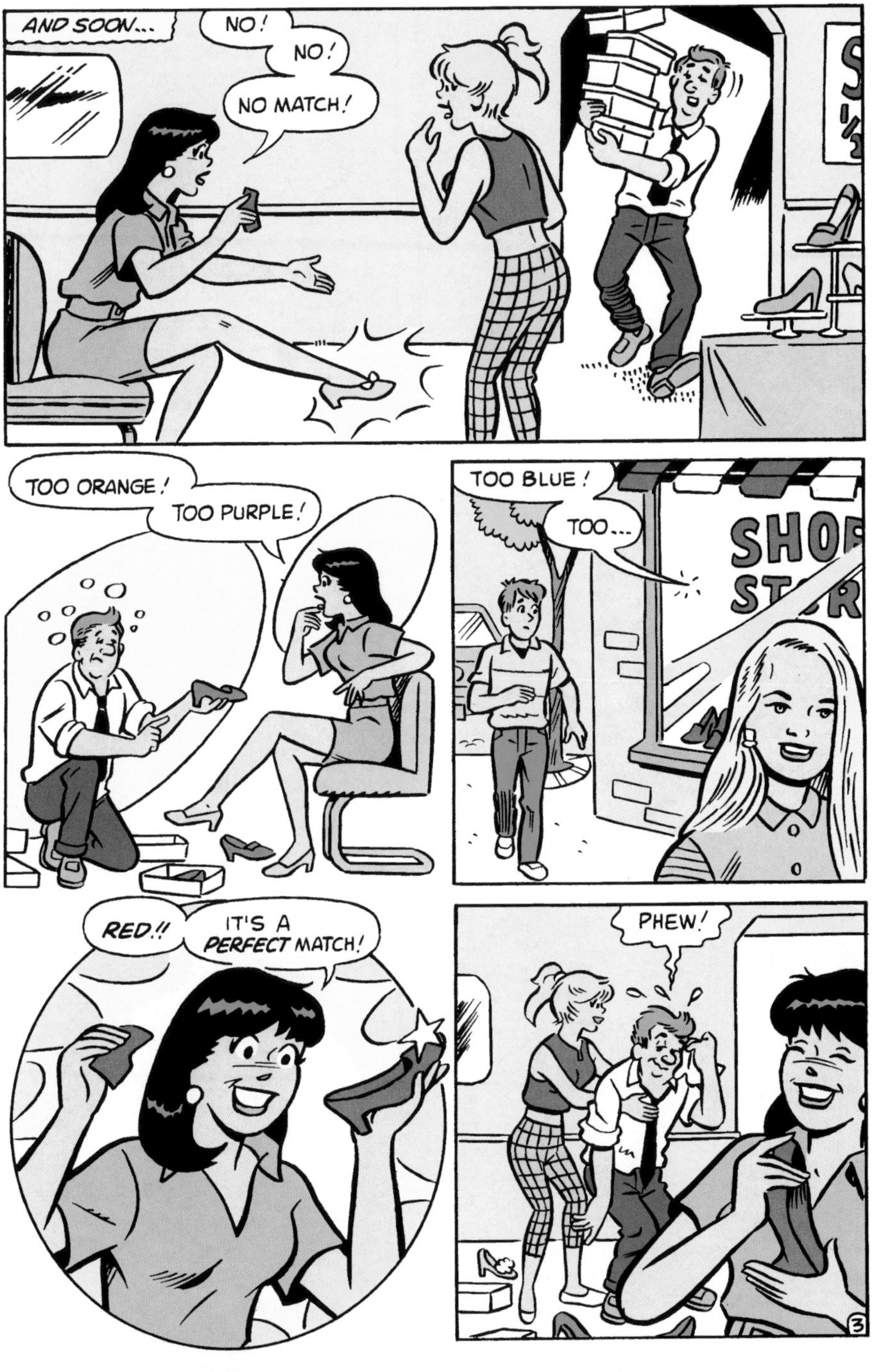
AND SOON...
NO!
NO!
NO MATCH!
TOO ORANGE!
TOO PURPLE!
TOO BLUE!
TOO...
SHO
STO
RED!!
IT'S A PERFECT MATCH!
PHEW!
3

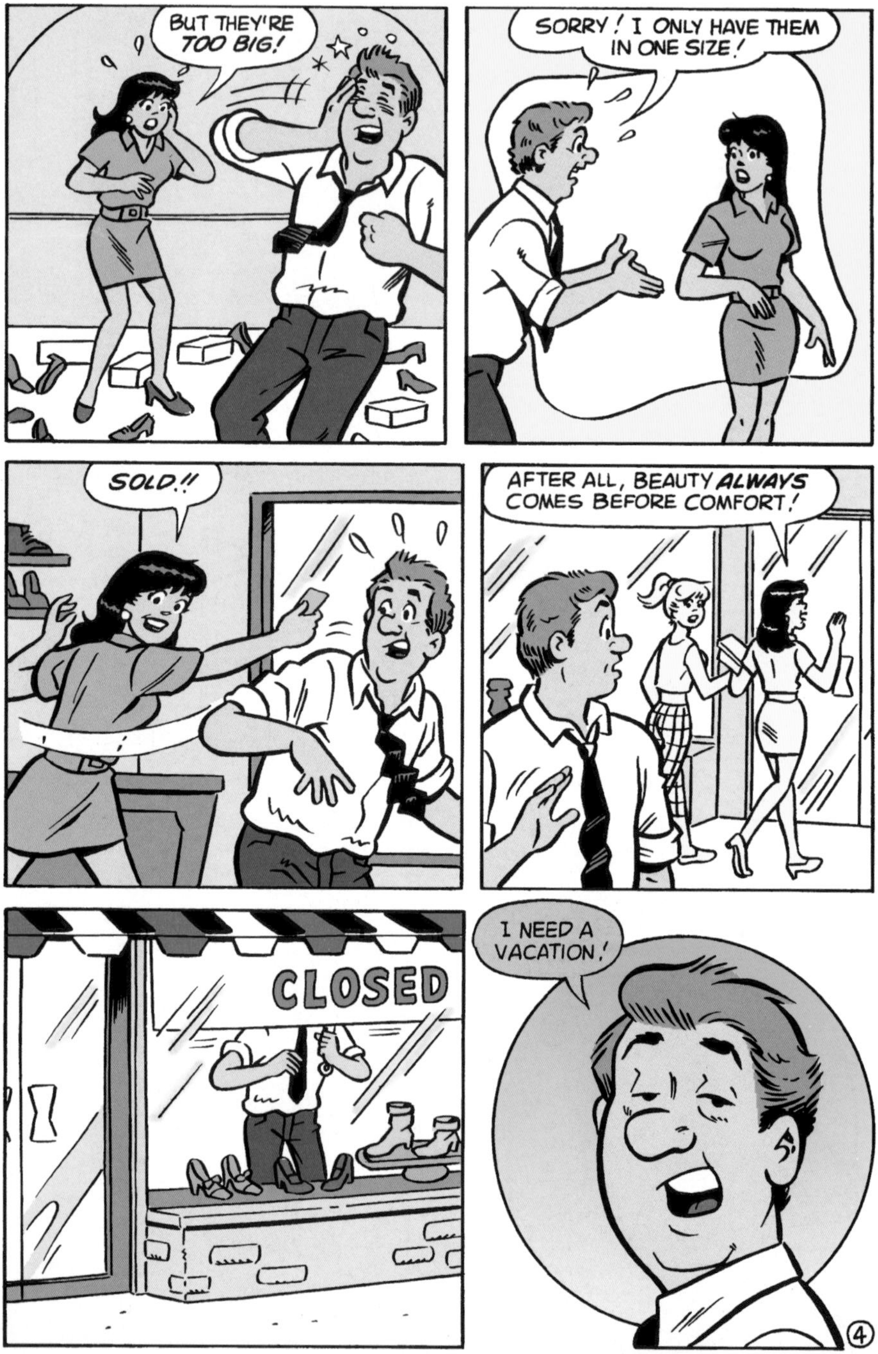
BUT THEY'RE *TOO BIG!*
SORRY! I ONLY HAVE THEM IN ONE SIZE!
SOLD!!
AFTER ALL, BEAUTY ***ALWAYS*** COMES BEFORE COMFORT!
CLOSED
I NEED A VACATION!
4

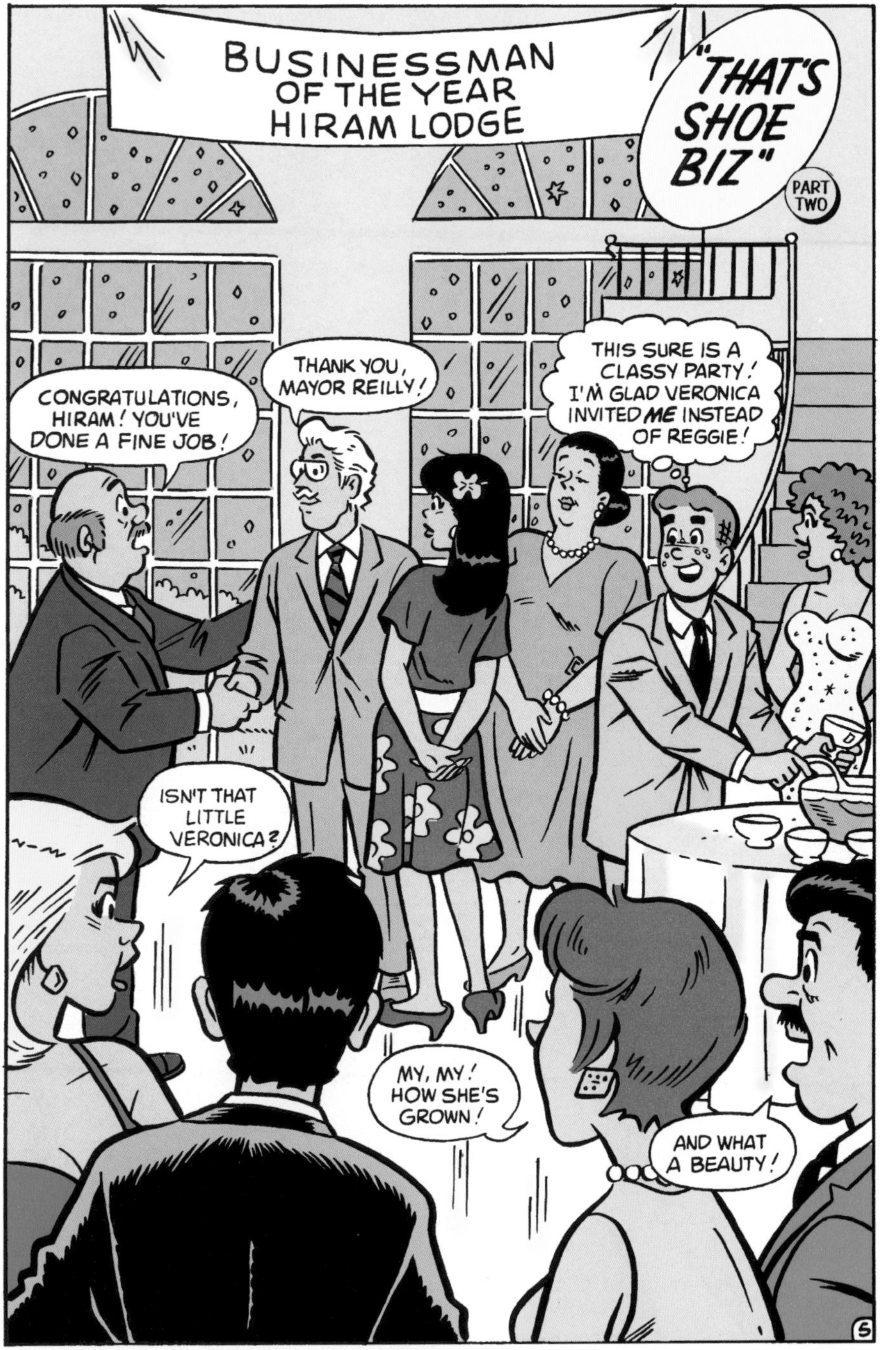
BUSINESSMAN OF THE YEAR HIRAM LODGE
"THAT'S SHOE BIZ"
PART TWO
CONGRATULATIONS, HIRAM! YOU'VE DONE A FINE JOB!
THANK YOU, MAYOR REILLY!
THIS SURE IS A CLASSY PARTY! I'M GLAD VERONICA INVITED ME INSTEAD OF REGGIE!
ISN'T THAT LITTLE VERONICA?
MY, MY! HOW SHE'S GROWN!
AND WHAT A BEAUTY!
5

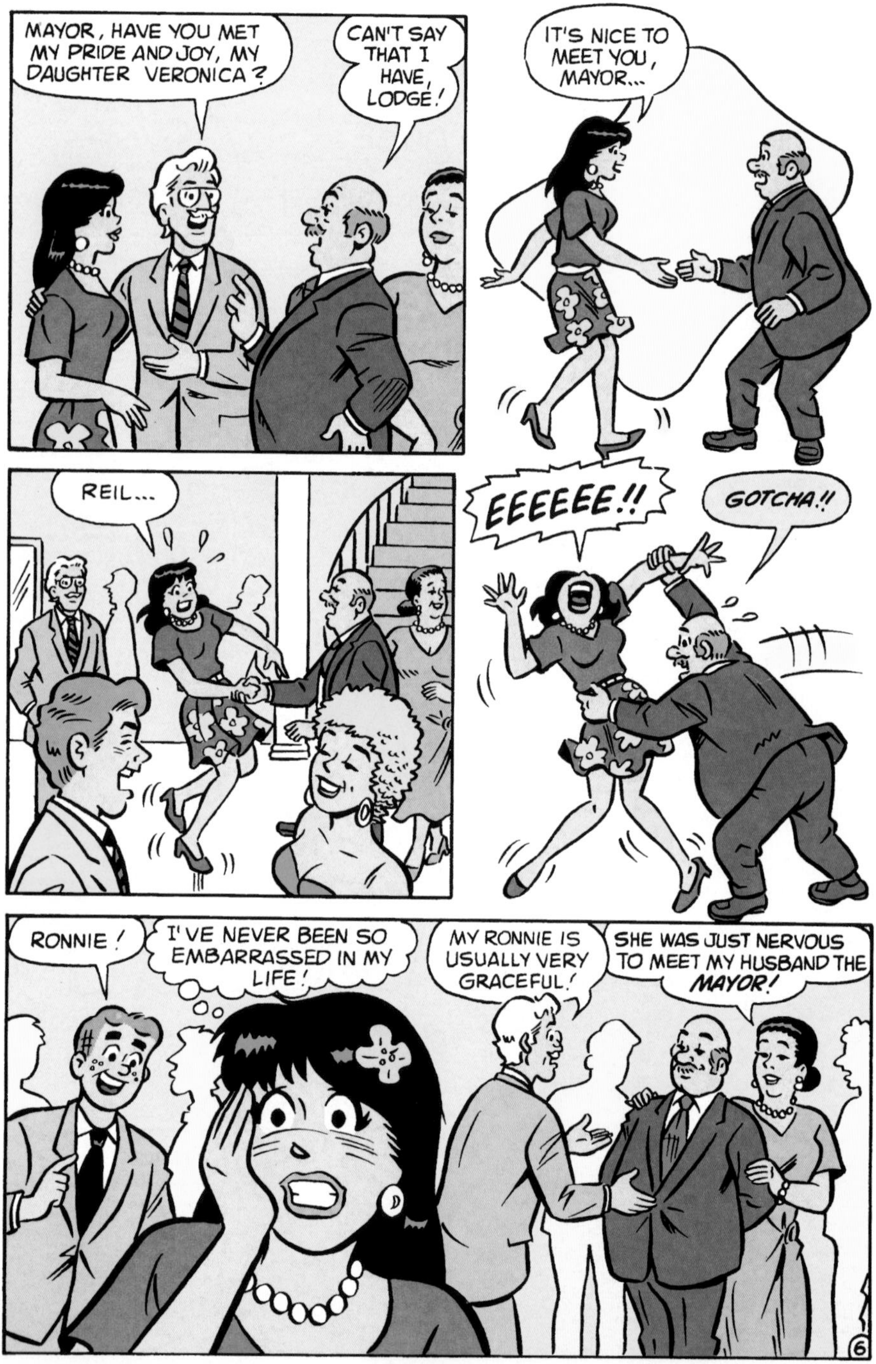
MAYOR, HAVE YOU MET MY PRIDE AND JOY, MY DAUGHTER VERONICA?
CAN'T SAY THAT I HAVE, LODGE!
IT'S NICE TO MEET YOU, MAYOR...
REIL...
EEEEEE!!
GOTCHA!!
RONNIE!
I'VE NEVER BEEN SO EMBARRASSED IN MY LIFE!
MY RONNIE IS USUALLY VERY GRACEFUL!
SHE WAS JUST NERVOUS TO MEET MY HUSBAND THE MAYOR!
6

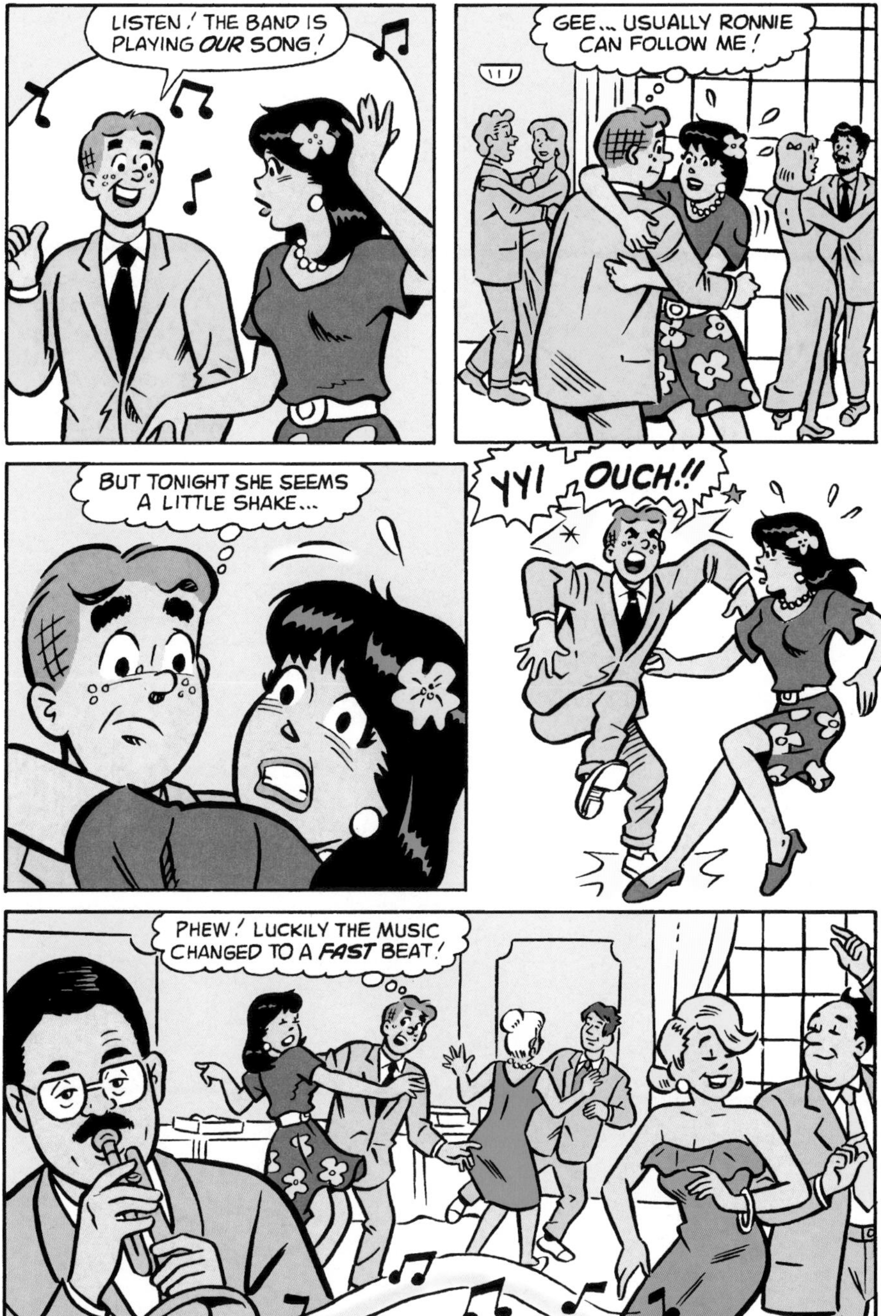
LISTEN! THE BAND IS PLAYING OUR SONG!
GEE... USUALLY RONNIE CAN FOLLOW ME!
BUT TONIGHT SHE SEEMS A LITTLE SHAKE...
YYI
OUCH!!
PHEW! LUCKILY THE MUSIC CHANGED TO A FAST BEAT!
7

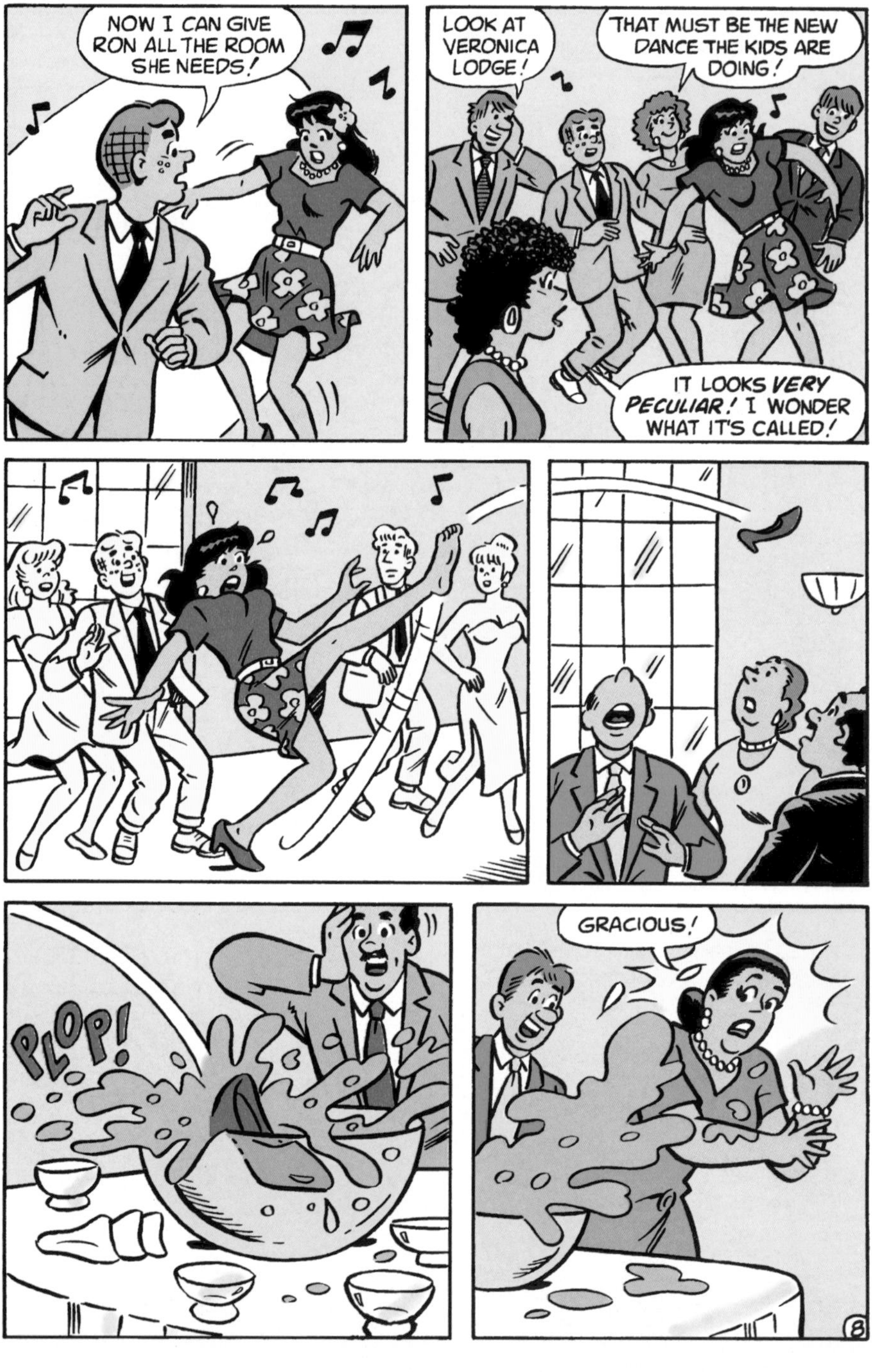
NOW I CAN GIVE RON ALL THE ROOM SHE NEEDS!
LOOK AT VERONICA LODGE!
THAT MUST BE THE NEW DANCE THE KIDS ARE DOING!
IT LOOKS **VERY PECULIAR!** I WONDER WHAT IT'S CALLED!
PLOP!
GRACIOUS!
8

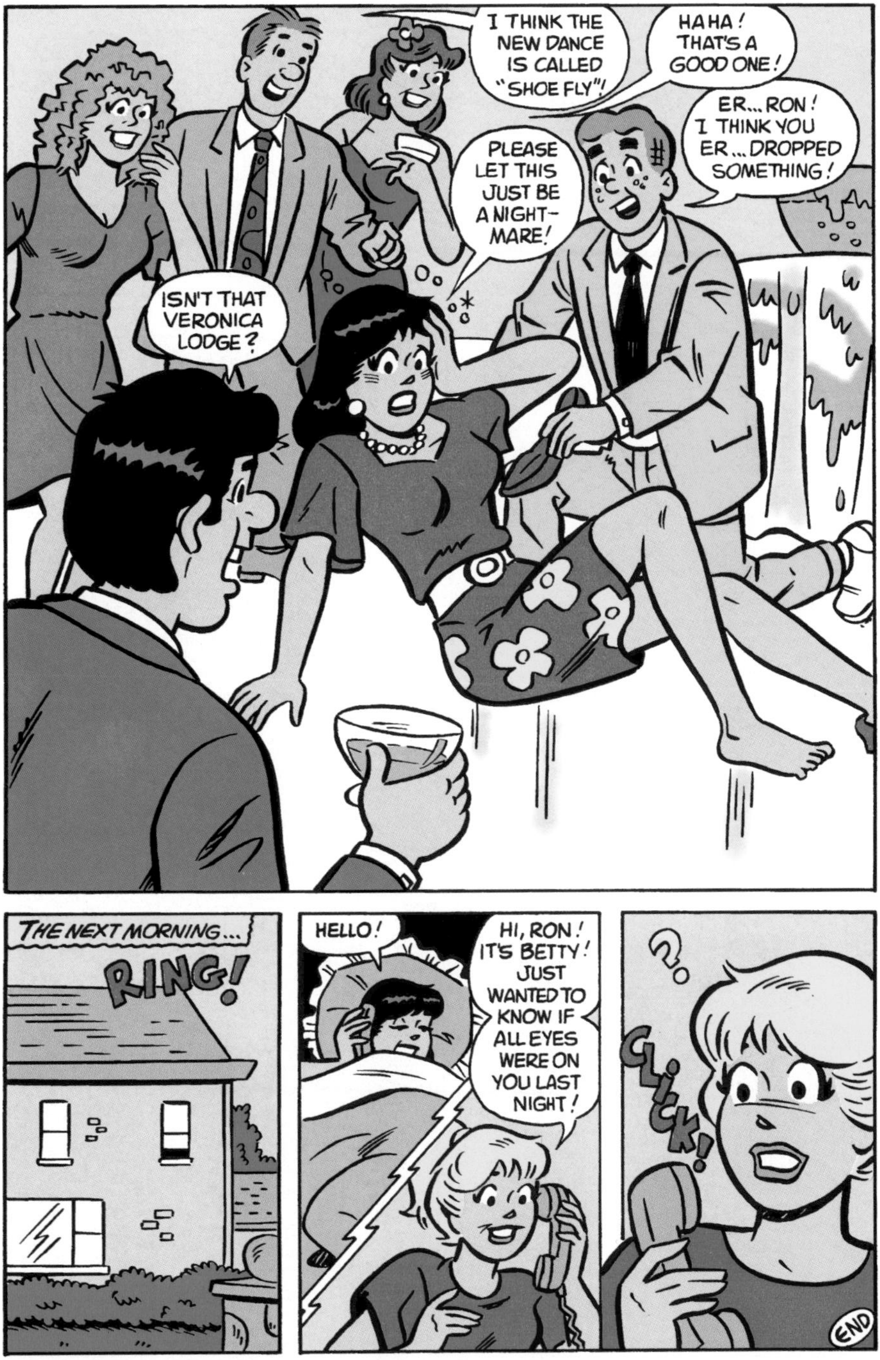
I THINK THE NEW DANCE IS CALLED "SHOE FLY"!
HA HA! THAT'S A GOOD ONE!
ER... RON! I THINK YOU ER... DROPPED SOMETHING!
PLEASE LET THIS JUST BE A NIGHT-MARE!
ISN'T THAT VERONICA LODGE?
THE NEXT MORNING...
RING!
HELLO!
HI, RON! IT'S BETTY! JUST WANTED TO KNOW IF ALL EYES WERE ON YOU LAST NIGHT!
?
CLICK!
END

Sabrina in "Good Neighbor Sam"

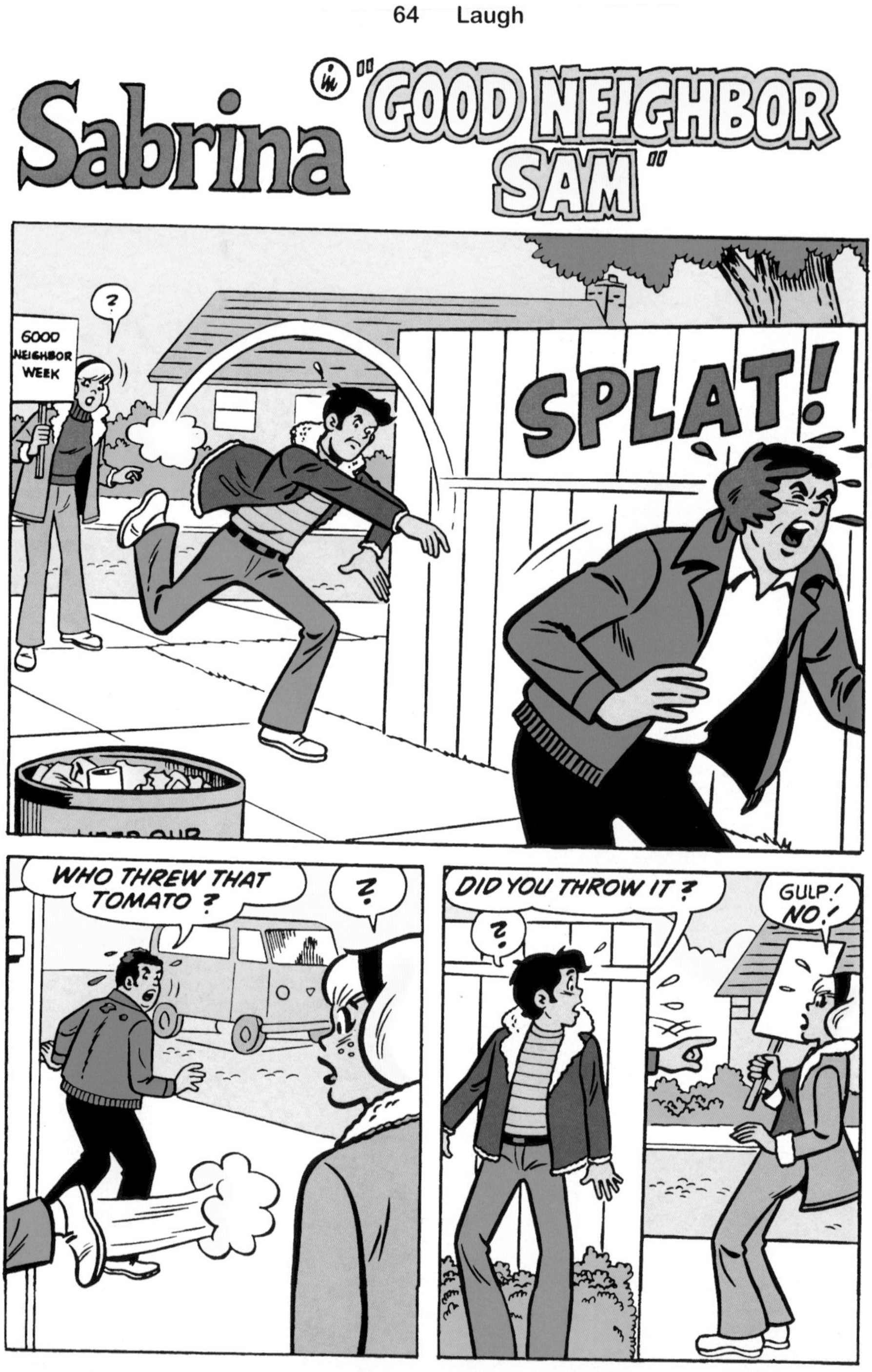
?
GOOD NEIGHBOR WEEK
SPLAT!
WHO THREW THAT TOMATO ?
?
DID YOU THROW IT ?
?
GULP! NO!

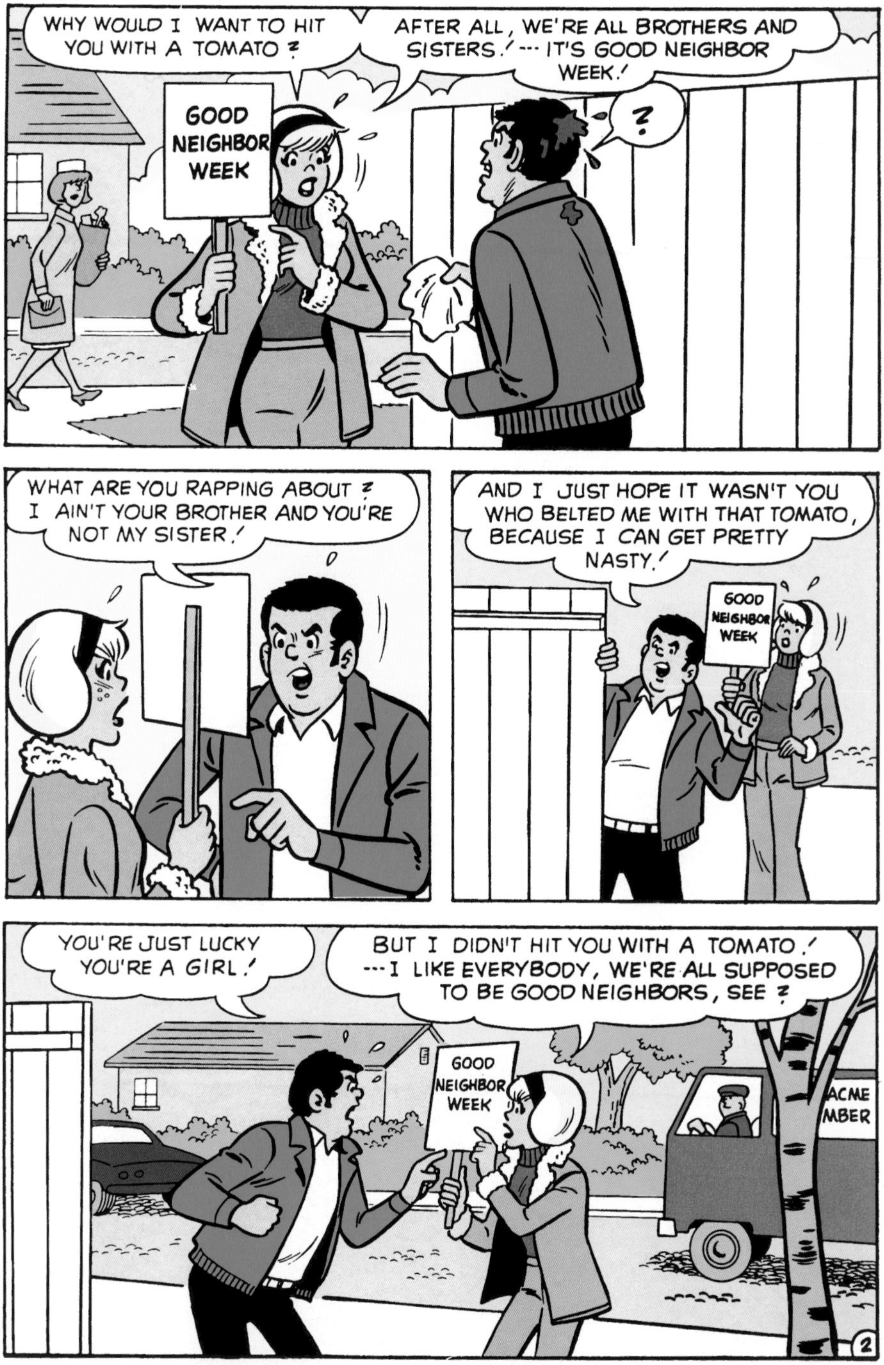
WHY WOULD I WANT TO HIT YOU WITH A TOMATO ?
AFTER ALL, WE'RE ALL BROTHERS AND SISTERS.! --- IT'S GOOD NEIGHBOR WEEK.!
GOOD NEIGHBOR WEEK
?
WHAT ARE YOU RAPPING ABOUT ? I AIN'T YOUR BROTHER AND YOU'RE NOT MY SISTER.!
AND I JUST HOPE IT WASN'T YOU WHO BELTED ME WITH THAT TOMATO, BECAUSE I CAN GET PRETTY NASTY.!
GOOD NEIGHBOR WEEK
YOU'RE JUST LUCKY YOU'RE A GIRL.!
BUT I DIDN'T HIT YOU WITH A TOMATO.! --- I LIKE EVERYBODY, WE'RE ALL SUPPOSED TO BE GOOD NEIGHBORS, SEE ?
GOOD NEIGHBOR WEEK
ACME
MBER
2

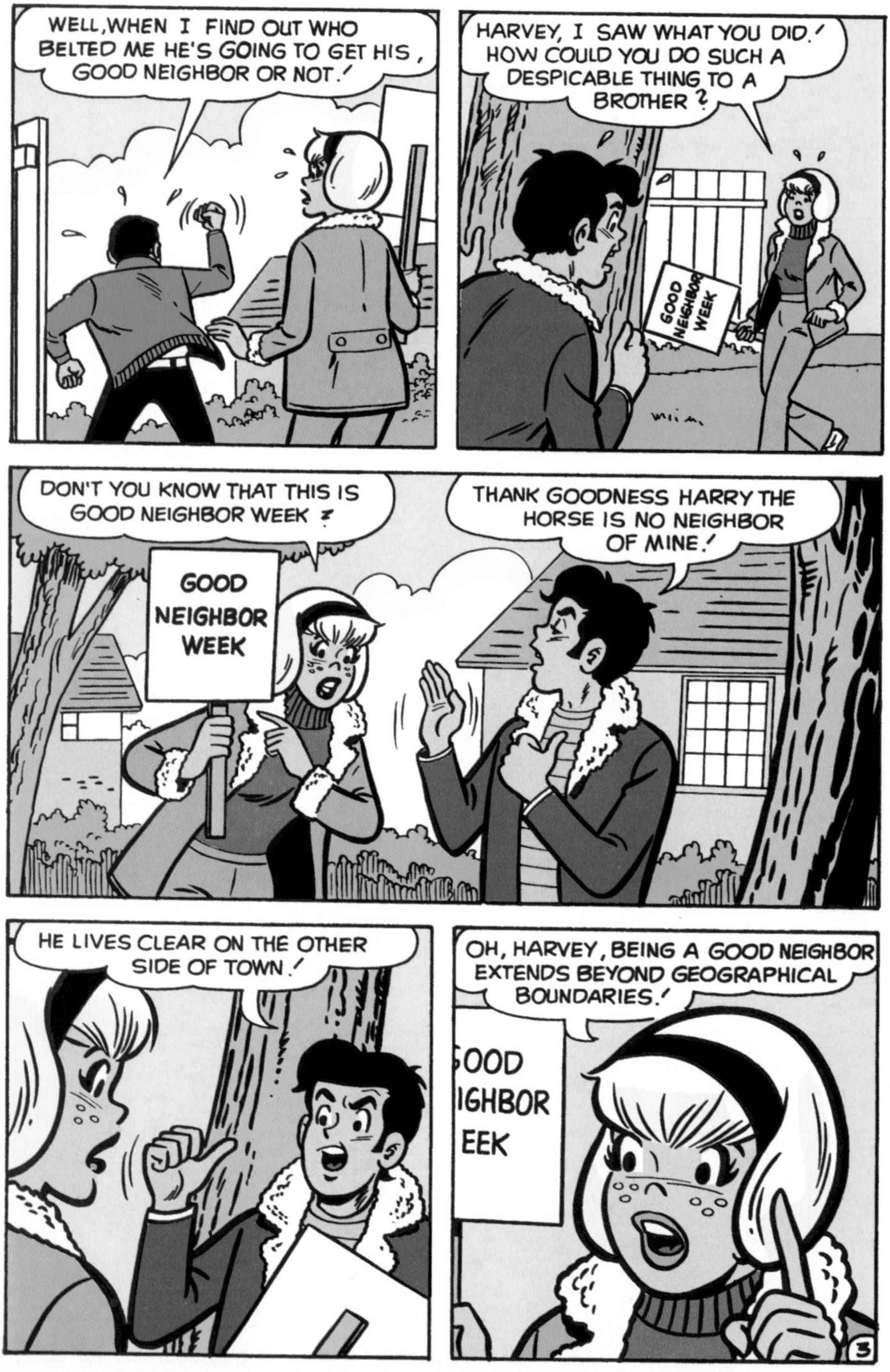
WELL, WHEN I FIND OUT WHO BELTED ME HE'S GOING TO GET HIS, GOOD NEIGHBOR OR NOT!
HARVEY, I SAW WHAT YOU DID! HOW COULD YOU DO SUCH A DESPICABLE THING TO A BROTHER?
GOOD NEIGHBOR WEEK
DON'T YOU KNOW THAT THIS IS GOOD NEIGHBOR WEEK?
GOOD NEIGHBOR WEEK
THANK GOODNESS HARRY THE HORSE IS NO NEIGHBOR OF MINE!
HE LIVES CLEAR ON THE OTHER SIDE OF TOWN!
OH, HARVEY, BEING A GOOD NEIGHBOR EXTENDS BEYOND GEOGRAPHICAL BOUNDARIES!
3

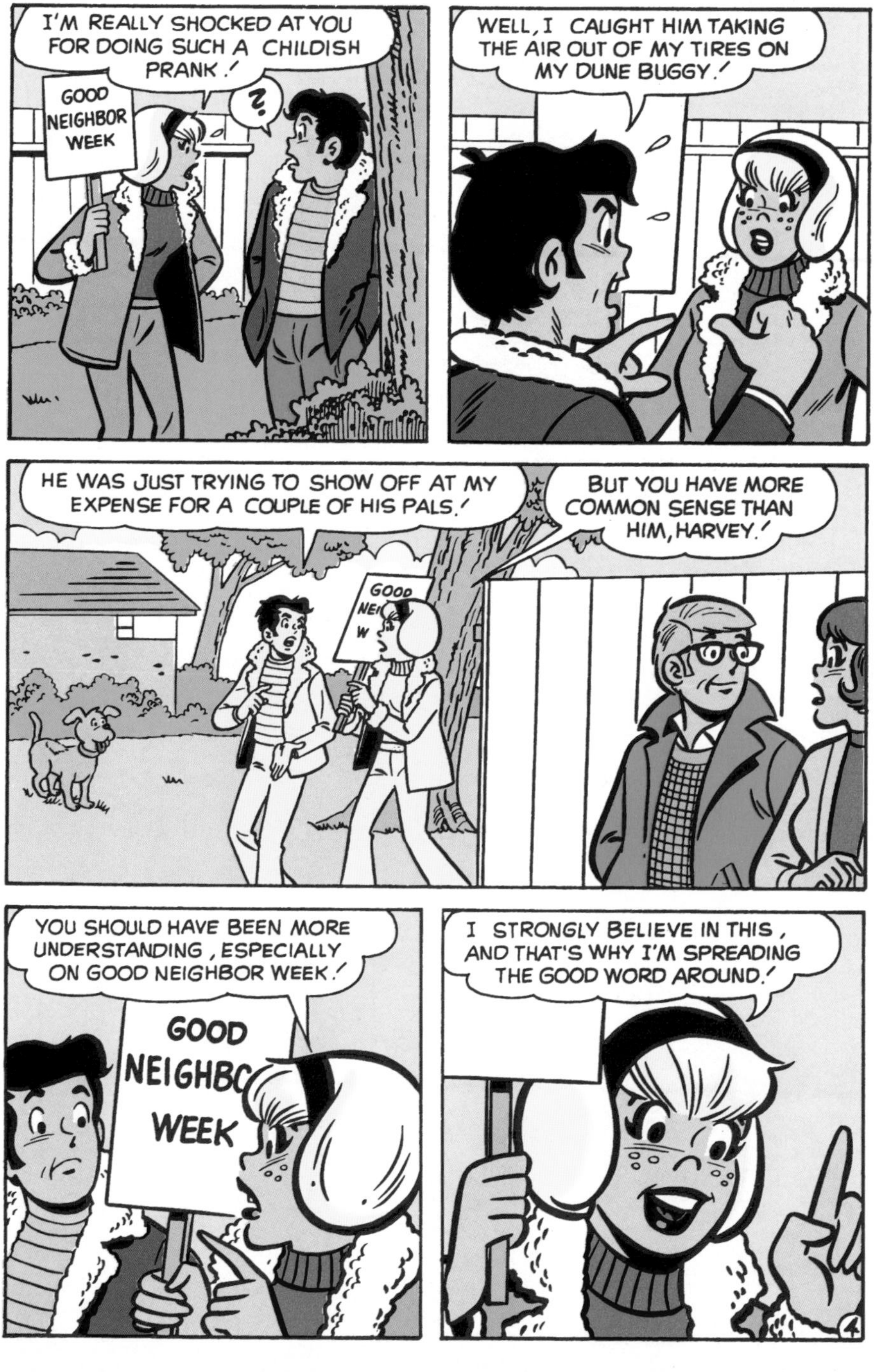
I'M REALLY SHOCKED AT YOU FOR DOING SUCH A CHILDISH PRANK!
GOOD NEIGHBOR WEEK
?
WELL, I CAUGHT HIM TAKING THE AIR OUT OF MY TIRES ON MY DUNE BUGGY!
HE WAS JUST TRYING TO SHOW OFF AT MY EXPENSE FOR A COUPLE OF HIS PALS!
BUT YOU HAVE MORE COMMON SENSE THAN HIM, HARVEY!
YOU SHOULD HAVE BEEN MORE UNDERSTANDING, ESPECIALLY ON GOOD NEIGHBOR WEEK!
GOOD NEIGHBC WEEK
I STRONGLY BELIEVE IN THIS, AND THAT'S WHY I'M SPREADING THE GOOD WORD AROUND!
4

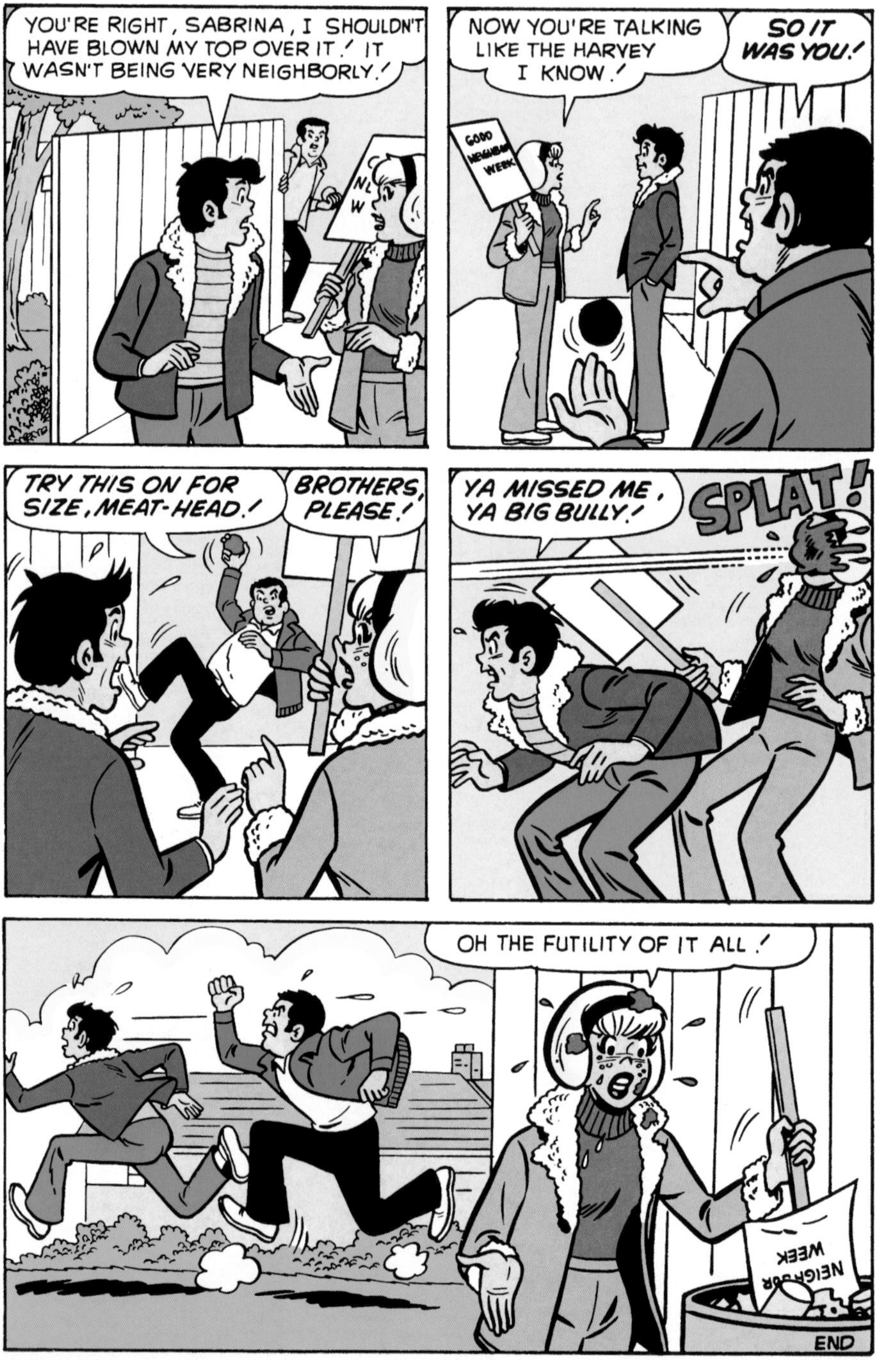
YOU'RE RIGHT, SABRINA, I SHOULDN'T HAVE BLOWN MY TOP OVER IT! IT WASN'T BEING VERY NEIGHBORLY!
NLW
NOW YOU'RE TALKING LIKE THE HARVEY I KNOW!
SO IT WAS YOU!
GOOD NEIGHBOR WEEK
TRY THIS ON FOR SIZE, MEAT-HEAD!
BROTHERS, PLEASE!
YA MISSED ME, YA BIG BULLY!
SPLAT!
OH THE FUTILITY OF IT ALL!
NEIGHBOR WEEK
END

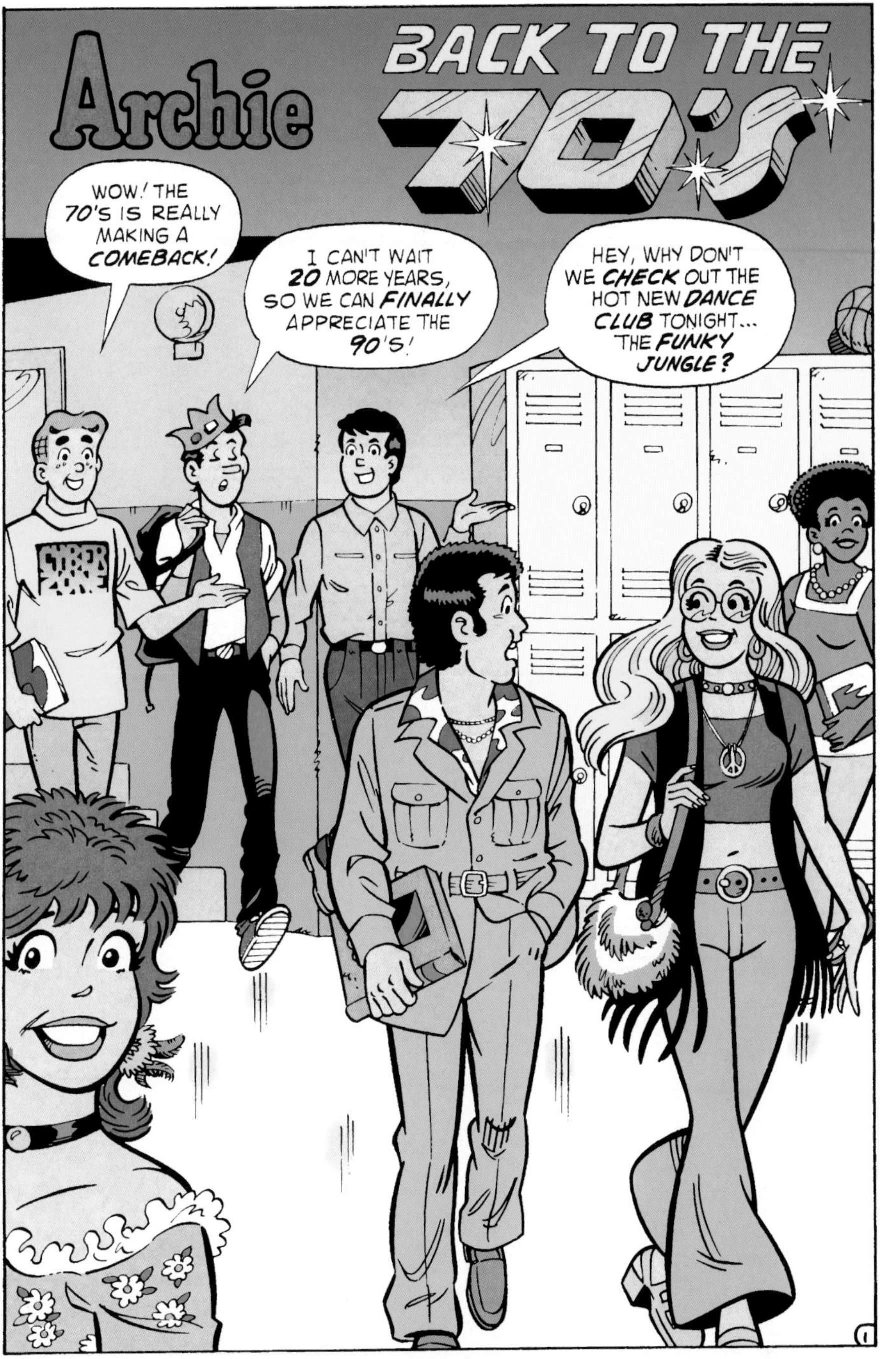
Archie
BACK TO THE 70'S
WOW! THE 70'S IS REALLY MAKING A COMEBACK!
I CAN'T WAIT 20 MORE YEARS, SO WE CAN FINALLY APPRECIATE THE 90'S!
HEY, WHY DON'T WE CHECK OUT THE HOT NEW DANCE CLUB TONIGHT... THE FUNKY JUNGLE?
1

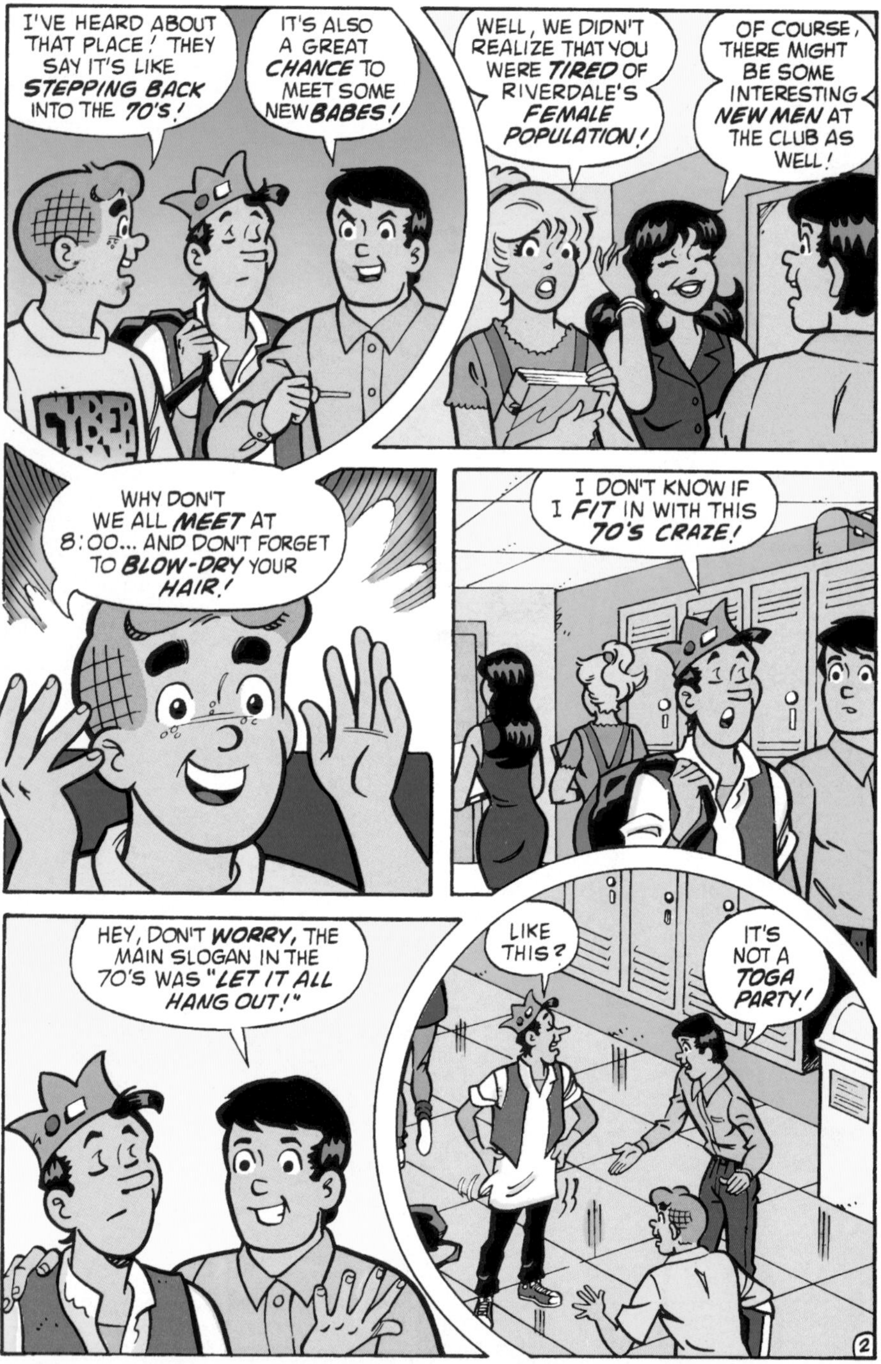
I'VE HEARD ABOUT THAT PLACE! THEY SAY IT'S LIKE STEPPING BACK INTO THE 70'S!
IT'S ALSO A GREAT CHANCE TO MEET SOME NEW BABES!
WELL, WE DIDN'T REALIZE THAT YOU WERE TIRED OF RIVERDALE'S FEMALE POPULATION!
OF COURSE, THERE MIGHT BE SOME INTERESTING NEW MEN AT THE CLUB AS WELL!
WHY DON'T WE ALL MEET AT 8:00... AND DON'T FORGET TO BLOW-DRY YOUR HAIR!
I DON'T KNOW IF I FIT IN WITH THIS 70'S CRAZE!
HEY, DON'T WORRY, THE MAIN SLOGAN IN THE 70'S WAS "LET IT ALL HANG OUT!"
LIKE THIS?
IT'S NOT A TOGA PARTY!
2

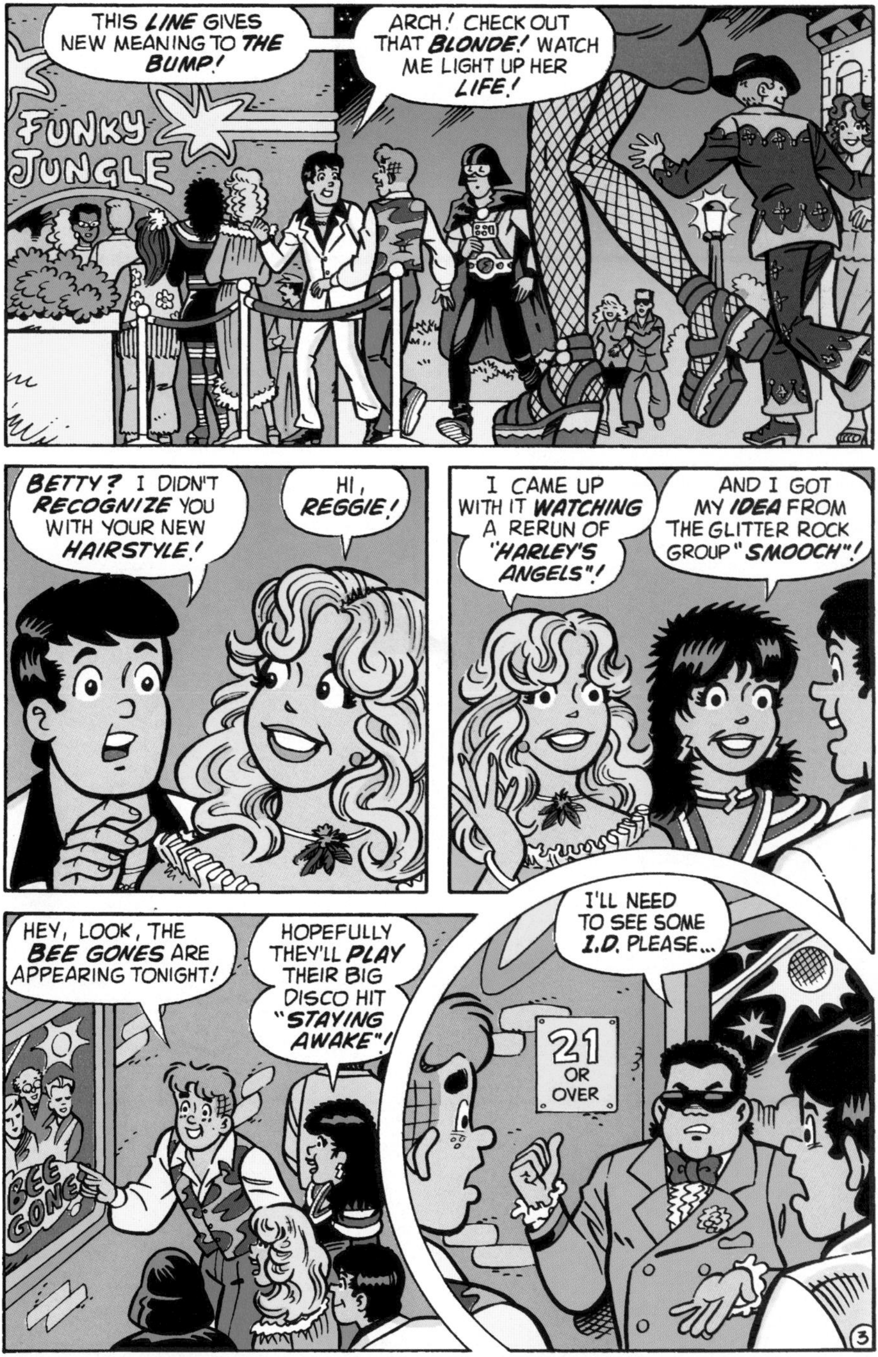
THIS LINE GIVES NEW MEANING TO THE BUMP!
ARCH! CHECK OUT THAT BLONDE! WATCH ME LIGHT UP HER LIFE!
FUNKY JUNGLE
BETTY? I DIDN'T RECOGNIZE YOU WITH YOUR NEW HAIRSTYLE!
HI, REGGIE!
I CAME UP WITH IT WATCHING A RERUN OF "HARLEY'S ANGELS"!
AND I GOT MY IDEA FROM THE GLITTER ROCK GROUP "SMOOCH"!
HEY, LOOK, THE BEE GONES ARE APPEARING TONIGHT!
HOPEFULLY THEY'LL PLAY THEIR BIG DISCO HIT "STAYING AWAKE"!
BEE GONES
I'LL NEED TO SEE SOME I.D. PLEASE...
21 OR OVER
3

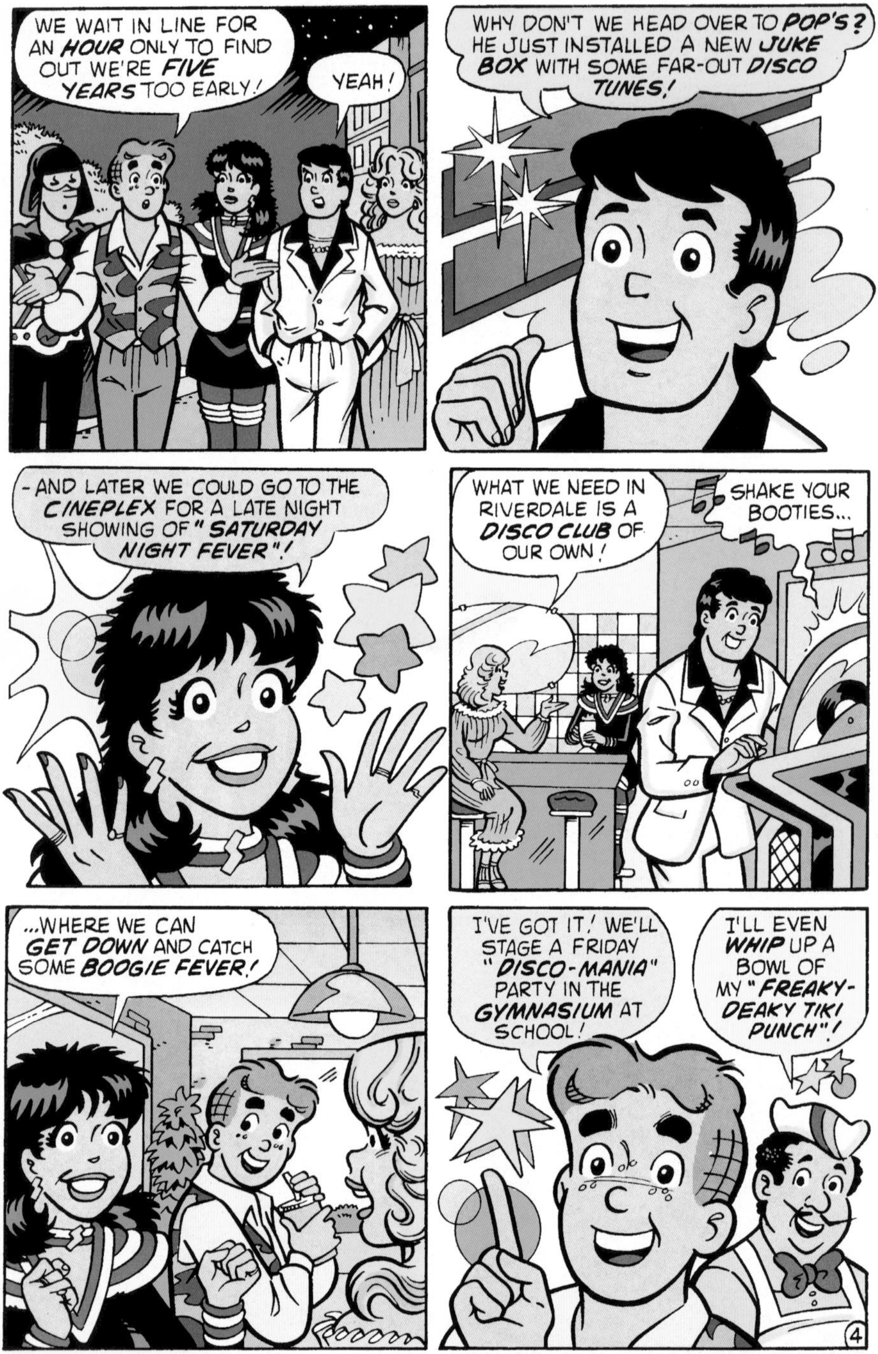
WE WAIT IN LINE FOR AN HOUR ONLY TO FIND OUT WE'RE FIVE YEARS TOO EARLY!
YEAH!
WHY DON'T WE HEAD OVER TO POP'S? HE JUST INSTALLED A NEW JUKE BOX WITH SOME FAR-OUT DISCO TUNES!
-AND LATER WE COULD GO TO THE CINEPLEX FOR A LATE NIGHT SHOWING OF "SATURDAY NIGHT FEVER"!
WHAT WE NEED IN RIVERDALE IS A DISCO CLUB OF OUR OWN!
SHAKE YOUR BOOTIES...
...WHERE WE CAN GET DOWN AND CATCH SOME BOOGIE FEVER!
I'VE GOT IT! WE'LL STAGE A FRIDAY "DISCO-MANIA" PARTY IN THE GYMNASIUM AT SCHOOL!
I'LL EVEN WHIP UP A BOWL OF MY "FREAKY-DEAKY TIKI PUNCH"!
4

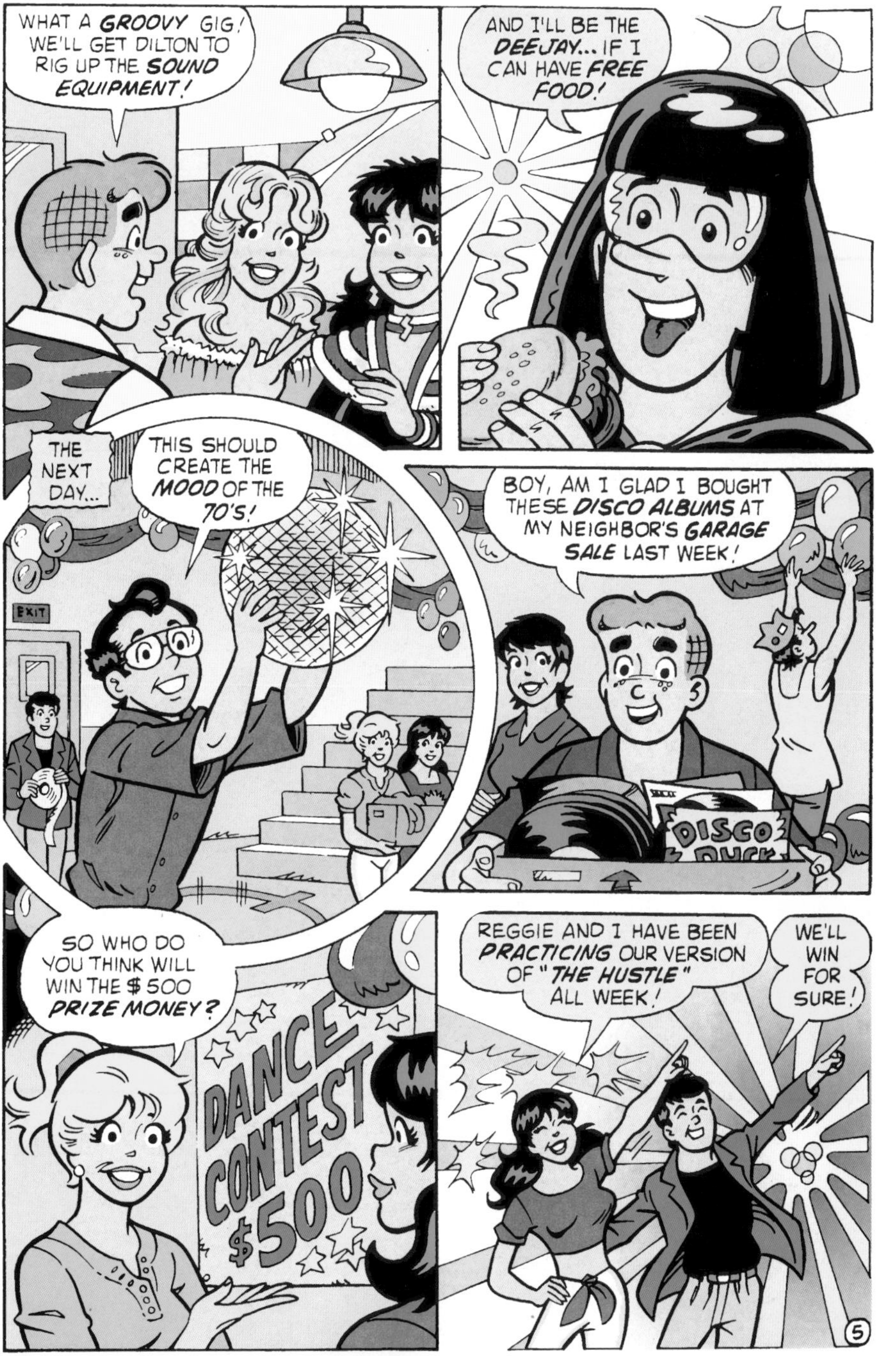
WHAT A GROOVY GIG! WE'LL GET DILTON TO RIG UP THE SOUND EQUIPMENT!
AND I'LL BE THE DEEJAY... IF I CAN HAVE FREE FOOD!
THE NEXT DAY...
THIS SHOULD CREATE THE MOOD OF THE 70'S!
EXIT
BOY, AM I GLAD I BOUGHT THESE DISCO ALBUMS AT MY NEIGHBOR'S GARAGE SALE LAST WEEK!
DISCO
SO WHO DO YOU THINK WILL WIN THE $500 PRIZE MONEY?
DANCE CONTEST $500
REGGIE AND I HAVE BEEN PRACTICING OUR VERSION OF "THE HUSTLE" ALL WEEK!
WE'LL WIN FOR SURE!
5

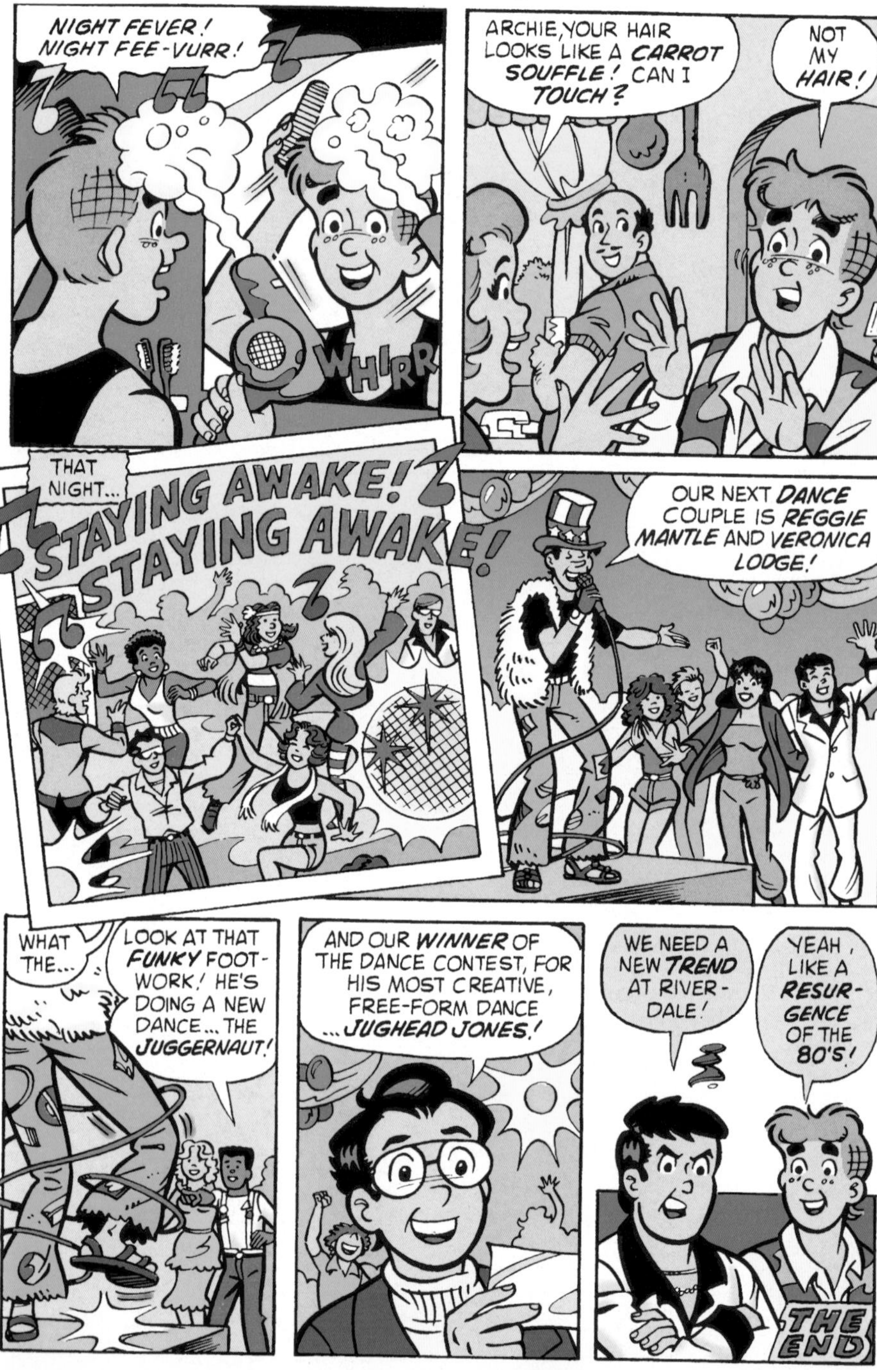
NIGHT FEVER! NIGHT FEE-VURR!
WHIRR
ARCHIE, YOUR HAIR LOOKS LIKE A CARROT SOUFFLE! CAN I TOUCH?
NOT MY HAIR!
THAT NIGHT...
STAYING AWAKE! STAYING AWAKE!
OUR NEXT DANCE COUPLE IS REGGIE MANTLE AND VERONICA LODGE!
WHAT THE...
LOOK AT THAT FUNKY FOOT-WORK! HE'S DOING A NEW DANCE... THE JUGGERNAUT!
AND OUR WINNER OF THE DANCE CONTEST, FOR HIS MOST CREATIVE, FREE-FORM DANCE ...JUGHEAD JONES!
WE NEED A NEW TREND AT RIVER-DALE!
YEAH, LIKE A RESURGENCE OF THE 80'S!
THE END

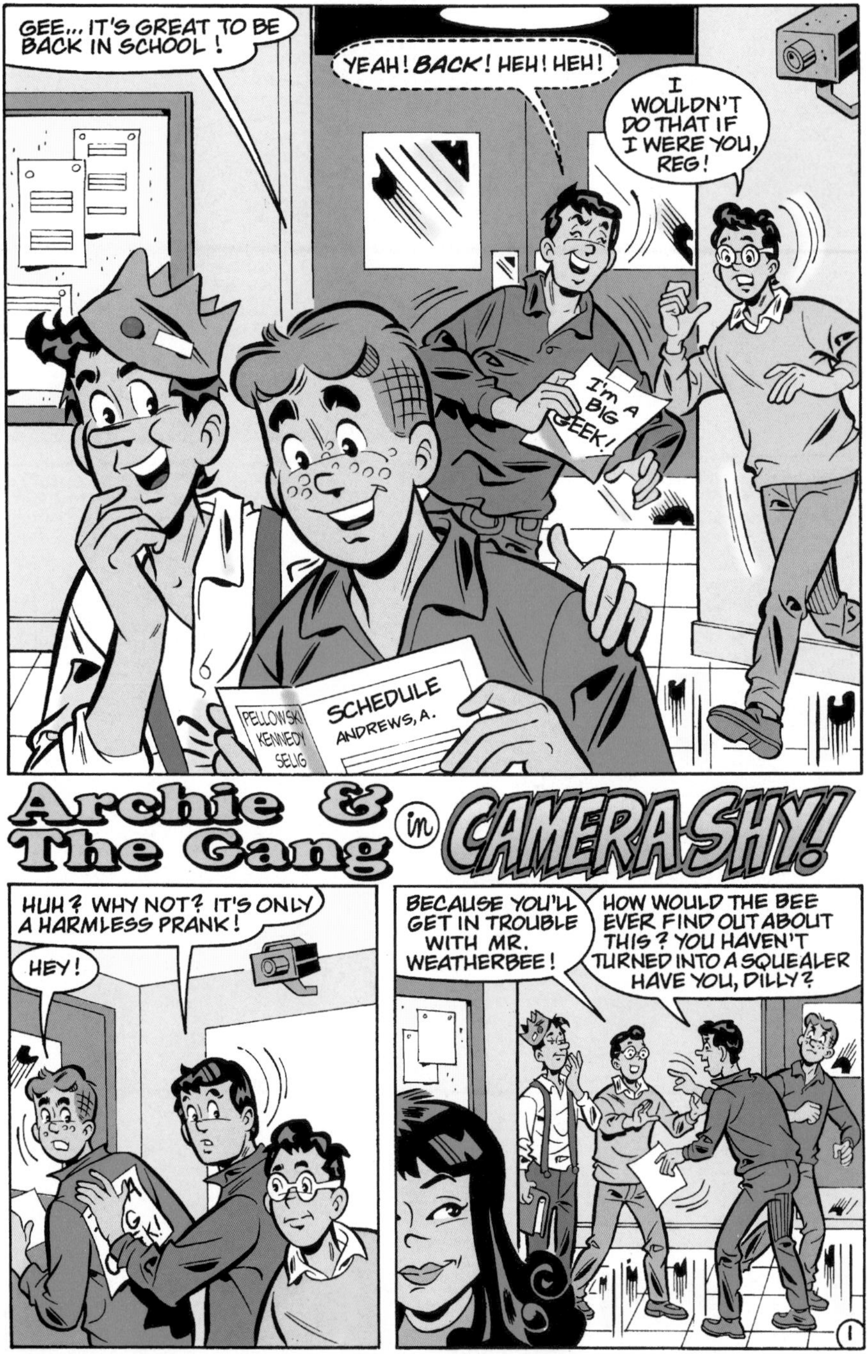
GEE... IT'S GREAT TO BE BACK IN SCHOOL!
YEAH! BACK! HEH! HEH!
I WOULDN'T DO THAT IF I WERE YOU, REG!
I'm A BIG GEEK!
SCHEDULE
ANDREWS, A.
PELLOWSKI
KENNEDY
SELIG
Archie & The Gang in CAMERA SHY!
HUH? WHY NOT? IT'S ONLY A HARMLESS PRANK!
HEY!
BECAUSE YOU'LL GET IN TROUBLE WITH MR. WEATHERBEE!
HOW WOULD THE BEE EVER FIND OUT ABOUT THIS? YOU HAVEN'T TURNED INTO A SQUEALER HAVE YOU, DILLY?
1

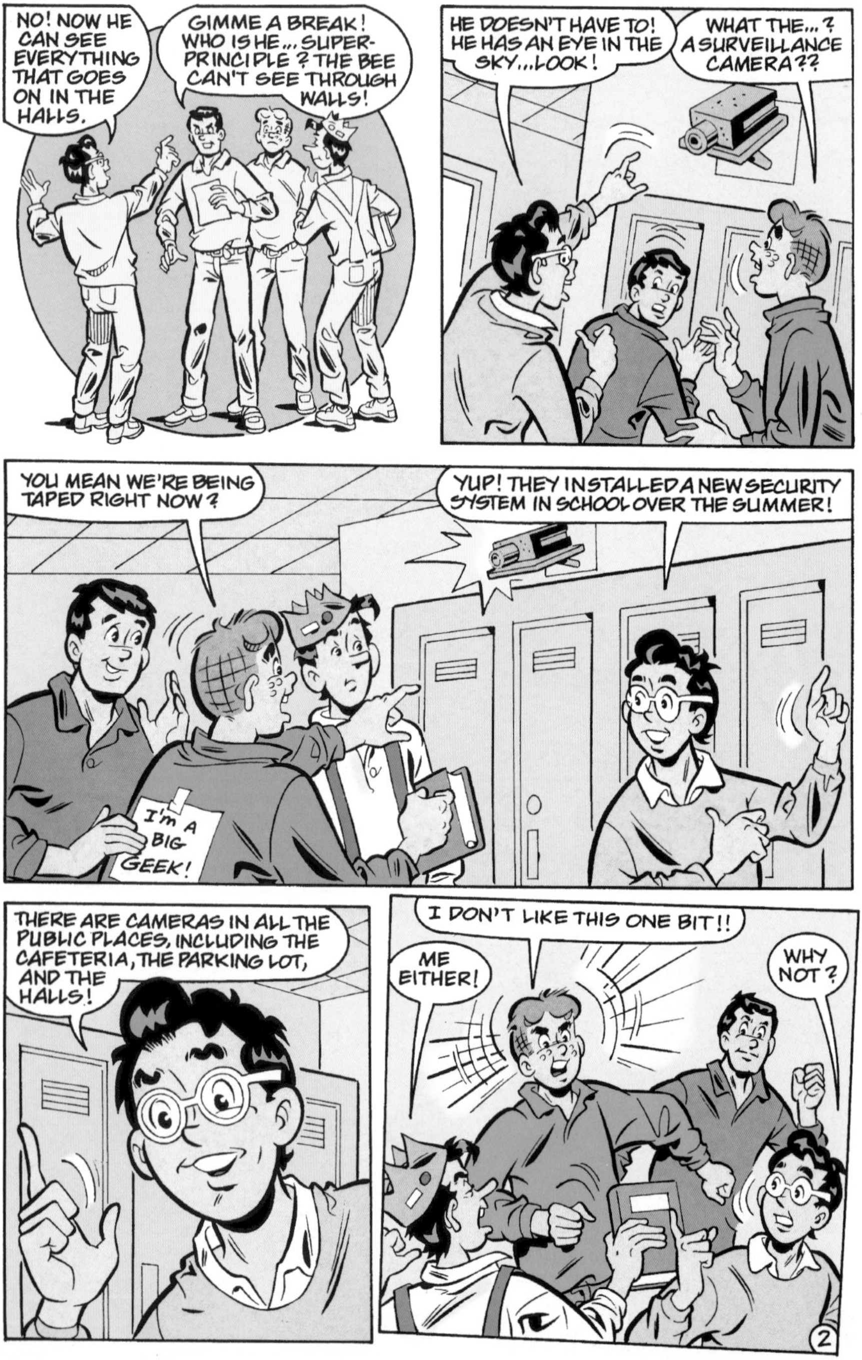
NO! NOW HE CAN SEE EVERYTHING THAT GOES ON IN THE HALLS.
GIMME A BREAK! WHO IS HE... SUPER-PRINCIPLE? THE BEE CAN'T SEE THROUGH WALLS!
HE DOESN'T HAVE TO! HE HAS AN EYE IN THE SKY...LOOK!
WHAT THE...? A SURVEILLANCE CAMERA??
YOU MEAN WE'RE BEING TAPED RIGHT NOW?
YUP! THEY INSTALLED A NEW SECURITY SYSTEM IN SCHOOL OVER THE SUMMER!
I'm A BIG GEEK!
THERE ARE CAMERAS IN ALL THE PUBLIC PLACES, INCLUDING THE CAFETERIA, THE PARKING LOT, AND THE HALLS!
I DON'T LIKE THIS ONE BIT!!
ME EITHER!
WHY NOT?
2

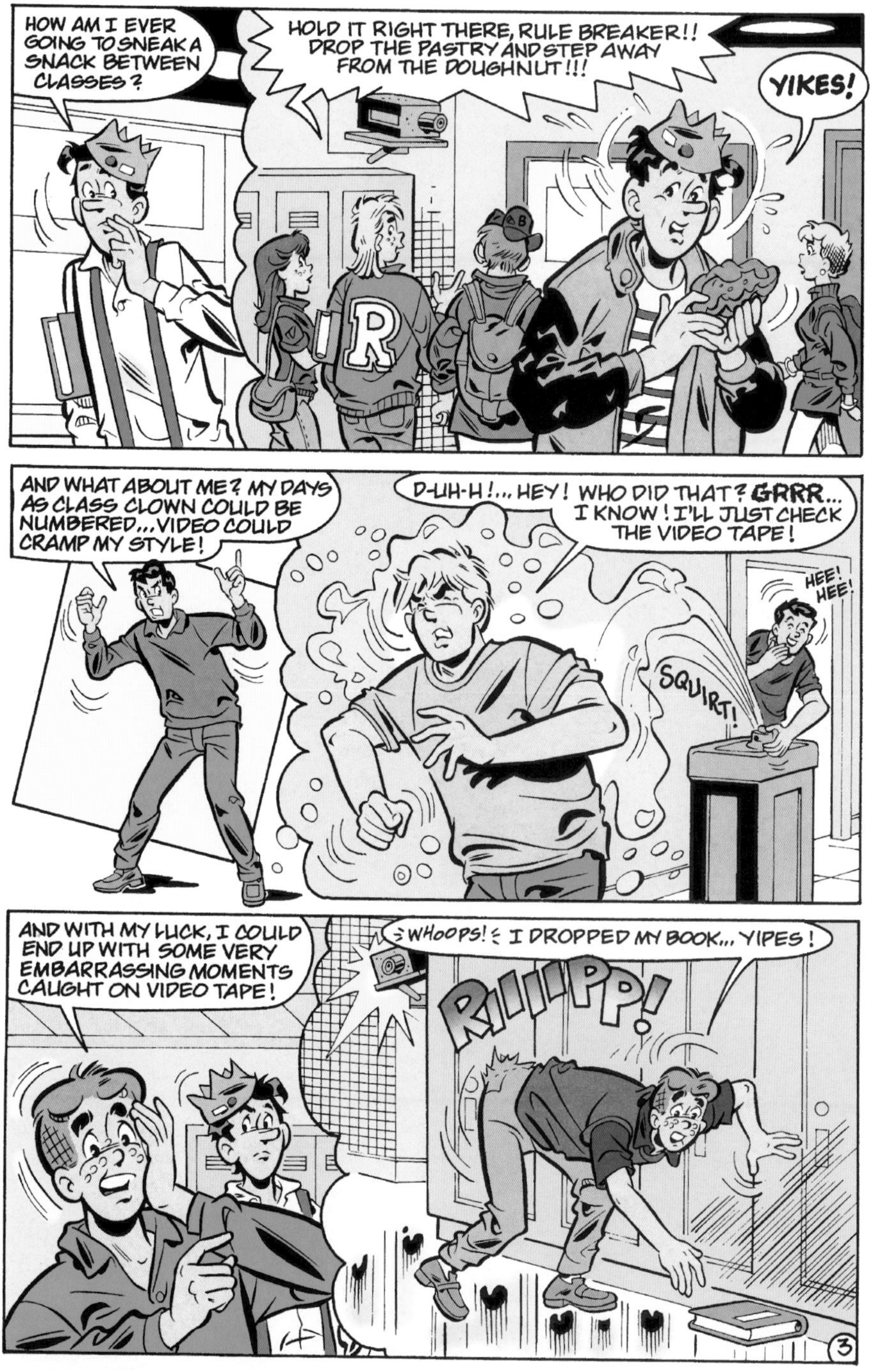
HOW AM I EVER GOING TO SNEAK A SNACK BETWEEN CLASSES?
HOLD IT RIGHT THERE, RULE BREAKER!! DROP THE PASTRY AND STEP AWAY FROM THE DOUGHNUT!!!
YIKES!
AND WHAT ABOUT ME? MY DAYS AS CLASS CLOWN COULD BE NUMBERED... VIDEO COULD CRAMP MY STYLE!
D-UH-H!... HEY! WHO DID THAT? GRRR... I KNOW! I'LL JUST CHECK THE VIDEO TAPE!
HEE! HEE!
SQUIRT!
AND WITH MY LUCK, I COULD END UP WITH SOME VERY EMBARRASSING MOMENTS CAUGHT ON VIDEO TAPE!
WHOOPS! I DROPPED MY BOOK... YIPES!
RIIIIPP!
3

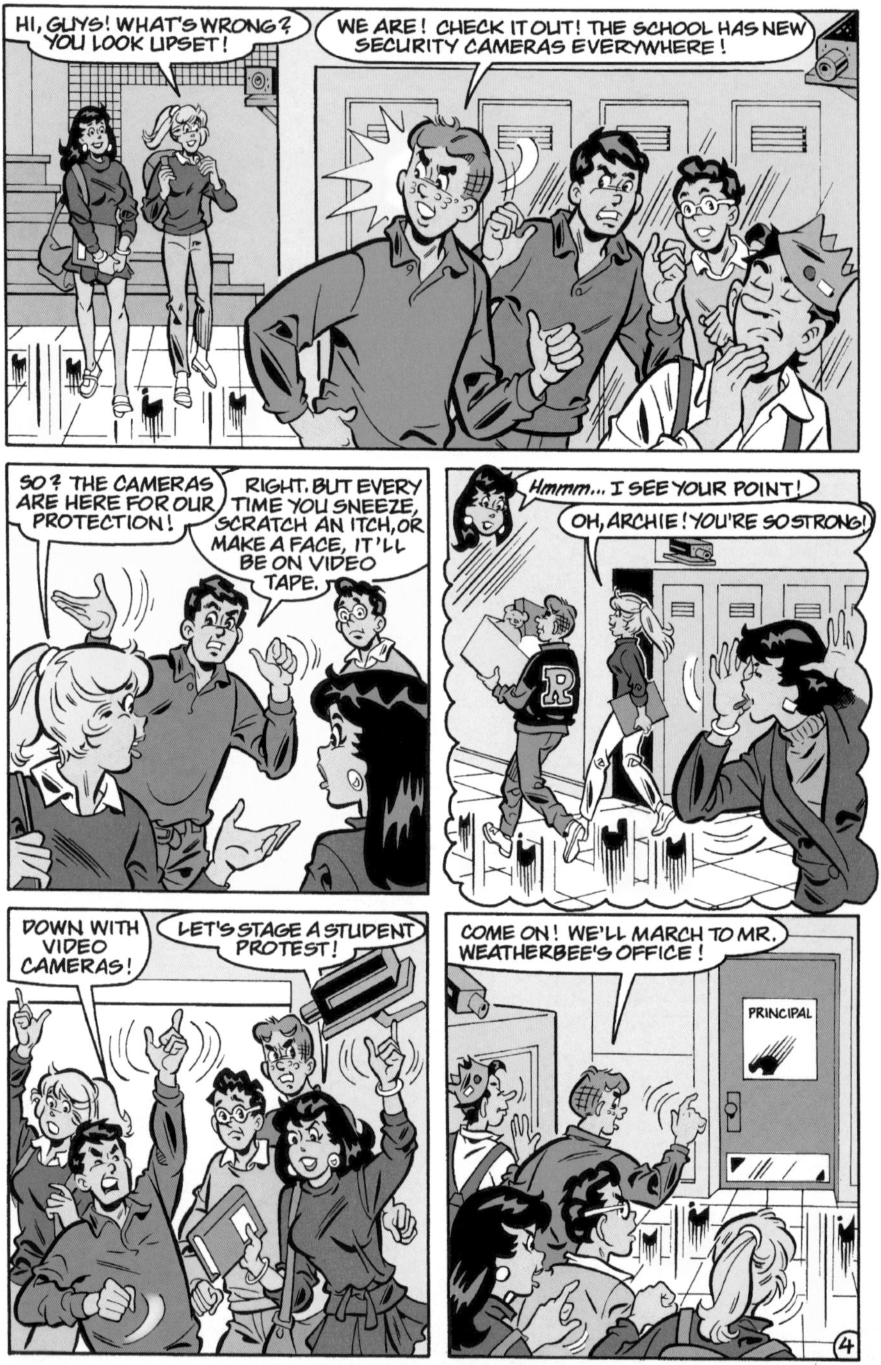
HI, GUYS! WHAT'S WRONG? YOU LOOK UPSET!
WE ARE! CHECK IT OUT! THE SCHOOL HAS NEW SECURITY CAMERAS EVERYWHERE!
SO? THE CAMERAS ARE HERE FOR OUR PROTECTION!
RIGHT. BUT EVERY TIME YOU SNEEZE, SCRATCH AN ITCH, OR MAKE A FACE, IT'LL BE ON VIDEO TAPE.
Hmmm... I SEE YOUR POINT!
OH, ARCHIE! YOU'RE SO STRONG!
DOWN WITH VIDEO CAMERAS!
LET'S STAGE A STUDENT PROTEST!
COME ON! WE'LL MARCH TO MR. WEATHERBEE'S OFFICE!
PRINCIPAL
4

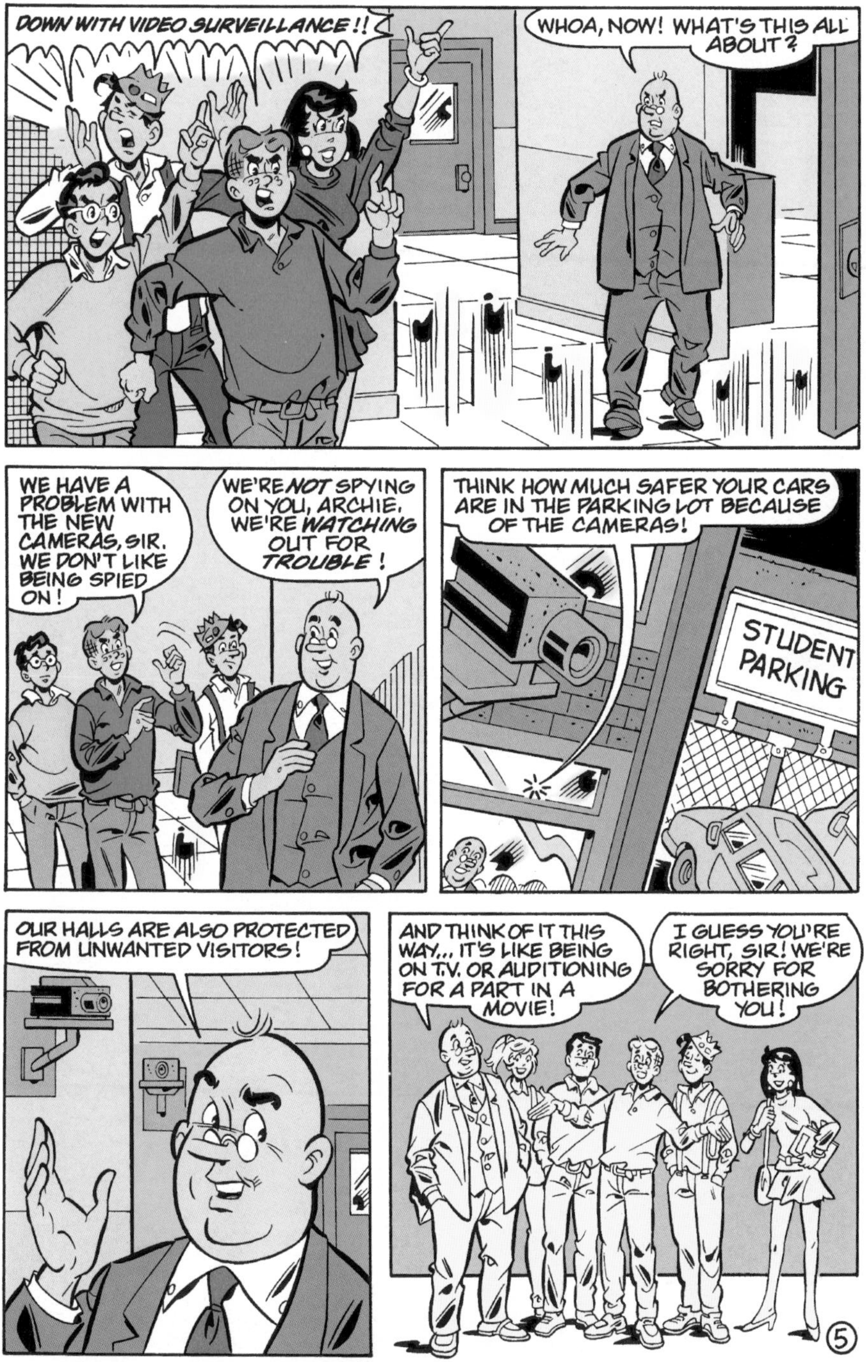
DOWN WITH VIDEO SURVEILLANCE!!
WHOA, NOW! WHAT'S THIS ALL ABOUT?
WE HAVE A PROBLEM WITH THE NEW CAMERAS, SIR. WE DON'T LIKE BEING SPIED ON!
WE'RE NOT SPYING ON YOU, ARCHIE. WE'RE WATCHING OUT FOR TROUBLE!
THINK HOW MUCH SAFER YOUR CARS ARE IN THE PARKING LOT BECAUSE OF THE CAMERAS!
STUDENT PARKING
OUR HALLS ARE ALSO PROTECTED FROM UNWANTED VISITORS!
AND THINK OF IT THIS WAY... IT'S LIKE BEING ON T.V. OR AUDITIONING FOR A PART IN A MOVIE!
I GUESS YOU'RE RIGHT, SIR! WE'RE SORRY FOR BOTHERING YOU!
5

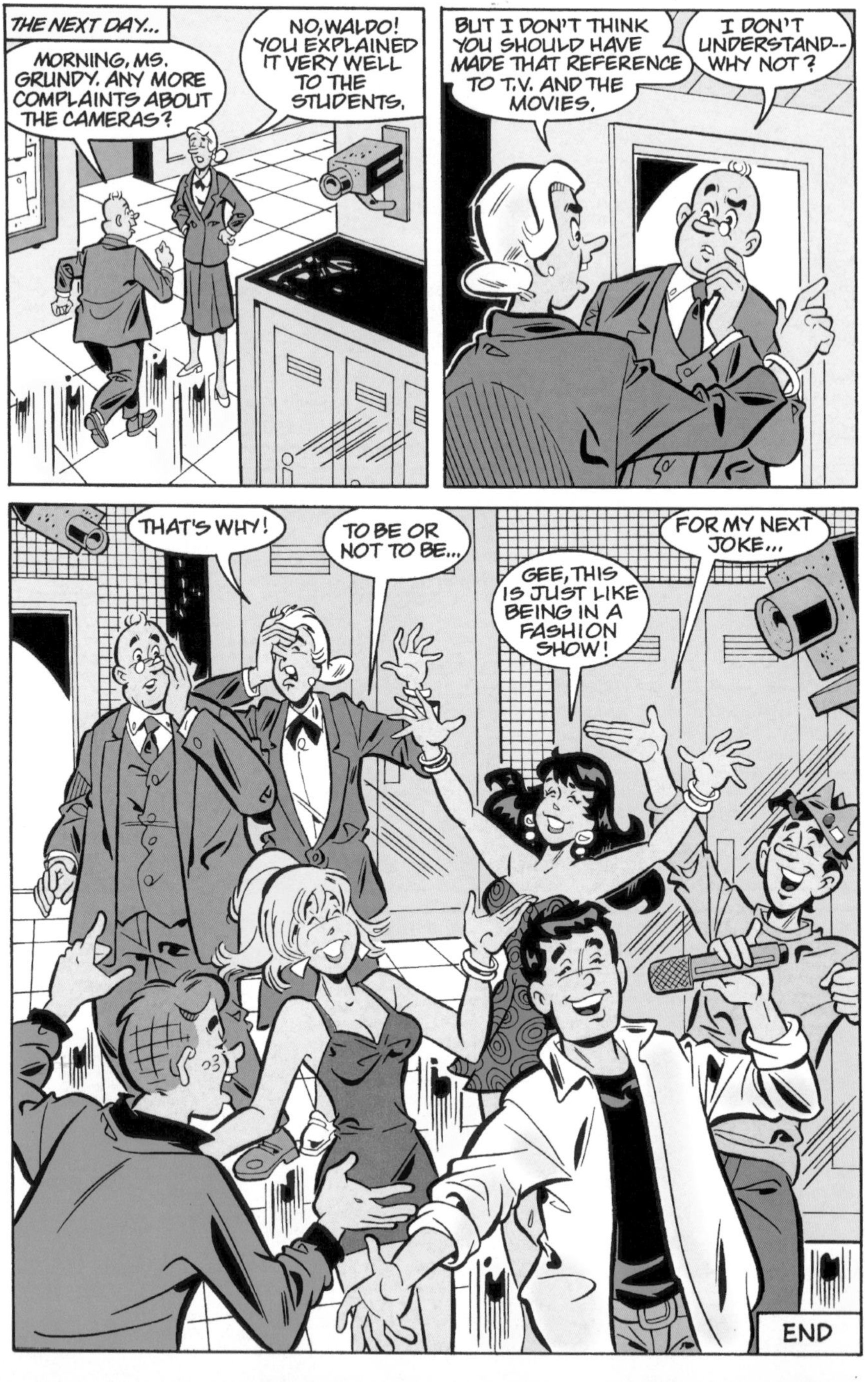
THE NEXT DAY...
MORNING, MS. GRUNDY. ANY MORE COMPLAINTS ABOUT THE CAMERAS?
NO, WALDO! YOU EXPLAINED IT VERY WELL TO THE STUDENTS.
BUT I DON'T THINK YOU SHOULD HAVE MADE THAT REFERENCE TO T.V. AND THE MOVIES.
I DON'T UNDERSTAND-- WHY NOT?
THAT'S WHY!
TO BE OR NOT TO BE...
GEE, THIS IS JUST LIKE BEING IN A FASHION SHOW!
FOR MY NEXT JOKE...
END